THIS TIME AROUND

A NOVEL

KIMBERLY PACKARD

abalos
publishing

Book cover designed by okay creations.
Edited by C.A. Szarek
The text in this book is set in Baskerville.
Library of Congress Cataloging-in-Publication Data
Available Upon Request

ISBN-13 Print: 979-8-9904395-0-4

ISBN-13 Ebook: 979-8-9904395-1-1

AWARD WINNING AUTHOR

KIMBERLY PACKARD

For Colby
My Every Time Around

CHAPTER 1

There is a special place in Heaven for women who juggle it all. Successful career. Loving, harmonious marriage. Well-adjusted children who don't require an armada of pills to make it through the day. And, never forgetting a PTA meeting or snack duty.

It's my goal in life to make it to this heavenly retreat. I can almost see it now. Quiet and serene as a spa. Hushed music. Always-flowing champagne. The softest bathrobe. Bookshelves filled with an eternity's worth of romance novels.

However, I won't be lounging on a chair, having my feet rubbed by a handsome, muscled masseuse who is also an incredible listener. Nope. I'll be outside looking in. Left off the guest list of an exclusive club, standing there waiting while my friends party, holding all their coats.

"Josie, are you even listening to me?"

The sardonic tone of my fifteen-year-old daughter, Aubrey, told me I'd zoned out at a crucial moment.

It's still jarring to hear her use my first name. Obviously, a phase, but I can't help but imagine the dressing down my mom would've given me if I'd done that.

"Yeah, you were saying…" I don't even finish my verbal tap-dance.

There it is again, a brief moment where we could speak the same language, but it passes and now my daughter's back to the world of communicating in modern hieroglyphics, likes, and atrocious spelling.

Are my kids' lives better or worse with a device permanently attached?

In some ways, they're smarter. Anything they want to know is a quick Google search away. In other ways, they're giving up valuable life skills, like conversing with their parents.

I hide my worry in a long sip of coffee. Then again, Mom constantly worried about drugs, devil worshippers, and hidden messages in the music I listened to. Aside from a few tries of pot in college and that Pagan wedding I attended, I'd made it into adulthood fairly sane and with my soul intact.

While Aubrey's thumbs fly across her phone at unnatural speed, I scroll through my tablet. Meetings, meetings, and more meetings. How is it that the more my company, Mamacita, grows, the busier I get?

New employees mean new product offerings, which leads to new distribution channels then back again to more employees.

It's a never-ending cycle. While I'm thankful for the success, each win takes me farther from the beginnings of my company, tinkering with oils and fragrances for an all-natural home in my kitchen with a newborn Aubrey sleeping nearby.

"Don't forget, your dad's picking you and Ben up from school." I scroll past appointments on the shared calendar we keep for the kids. There it is, in a magenta meeting notice: *Peter getting kids, Spring Break ski trip.*

Aubrey drops her phone on the kitchen counter with an exasperated sigh. "That's exactly what I thought. You *weren't* listening. I *said,* Ben and I don't want to go."

I set down my toast. "What? You guys love Vail."

The phone doesn't stay out of her hands for long. "It's not where we're going, it's who's coming." Her eyes are glued to her screen while she speaks.

Ah, the new girlfriend.

If I couldn't win at my marriage, I can definitely win at my divorce.

By winning, I mean to make everyone's lives as seamless as possible. As if nothing changes, we're all one big happy family.

Even if Peter's new girlfriend is young enough to be our daughter, and he moved into a contemporary condo in a downtown Austin high-rise that barely had space for his upstart health and wellness company, much less his children.

That didn't matter one bit, because I'm going to win so frickin' hard Peter will feel like a giant loser for letting me go.

"Kirsten is…nice." The pause is pregnant enough to be nearly full-term with twins.

Aubrey arches an eyebrow, and one side of her pretty mouth pulls into a proves-her-point smile.

My breath catches. It's these moments when I feel like I'm looking back in time at my dad. Where my hair is more reddish-blond, Aubrey got the full force of the red hair gene from Dad, but with enough of Peter's dark brown to come out in the perfect auburn color. Rather than pass along my blue-green eyes, genetics gifted Aubrey with my dad's deep, playful blue hue.

The same blue eyes that never met her grandfather.

I often daydream about my dad and my daughter. They'd be thick as thieves, that's for sure. At least, I hope they would. Hope that his only granddaughter would pull him back into my life after I so horribly shoved him out of it.

That's the thing about cutting people off. Sometimes the universe has the last laugh and cuts them off permanently.

Like Dad.

Like Daniel Palmer. The boy I loved in high school.

It's a harsh lesson, but life was never advertised as being easy.

"Anyway," I say, clearing the emotion clogging my throat. "It's non-negotiable. You guys have to go."

"Because some lawyer said so?"

Damn. Kids today are too good at divorce.

"No, because your parents said so." I lift my coffee cup to my lips, smiling into it. "Plus, I'm going to have a huge orgy this weekend, and I can't do it with minors in the house."

Aubrey appropriately rolls her eyes. "If Dad can have a bendy twenty-three-year-old girlfriend, why can't you have a boy toy?"

"Because he's a few years ahead of me in the mid-life crisis phase of life." I lean on my elbows. The classic we're-gonna-have-a-talk pose. "Aubrey, trust me on this one. There will be a day when you wished you'd put up with Kirsten, and whoever comes after her. And, after her…"

She tugs on a strand of my hair.

I do the same on Aubrey's beautiful red locks.

A secret gesture we'd started when Aubrey could still barely speak. A way to show my shy little girl who just wanted to hide behind her mom that everything would be okay.

What I wouldn't give to go back in time. To hold Aubrey in my arms one more time. A perfect baby who wanted nothing but her mom. I was so busy simply keeping her alive that I didn't spend enough time just reveling in this tiny human Peter and I made.

That was the thing we'd succeeded at. Making two perfect children, individuals yet pieces of each of us. It's hard to call our marriage a failure when we look at it that way.

Ben stumbles into the kitchen. His dark-blond hair rumpled; eyes half-open behind his glasses. Without a word, my twelve-year-old pulls a coffee mug from the tree and fills it to the top with black coffee.

"Since when do you let Ben drink coffee?" Aubrey says with an accusatory huff.

"Since never." I turn in my barstool. "Ahem, rough night?"

He tumbles into the stool next to his sister, one hand holding his head up while the other brings the cup to his lips. "I got like two hours of sleep."

Is he having nightmares again?

There was a spell when he had dreams so terrifying, instead of consulting a child psychologist I'd thought about calling an exorcist.

"I had to rewrite the algorithm. I realized it had a fatal flaw that would have made the whole app crash," Ben says before I can vocalize my concerns.

Where Aubrey came out as a baby and grew into her ornery

teenage self, Ben came out as a little adult. The way my cervix felt after he was born, he even came with a laptop in hand.

"All right you two, get dressed and bring your bags down. I'll drop them off at your dad's on my way to the office."

Ben levels a serious stare. "Are you sure you're going to be okay without us? You'll be here all by yourself. What if someone tries to break in and strangle you?"

Aubrey snorts. "That could happen with us here. Do you think you're the man of the house now?"

My kids continue their bickering up the stairs.

I grab my coffee cup and stare out the back window at the sun rising over Austin. We bought this house in the hills of west Austin after Peter's tech company was bought out. Even after all these years, the scenery of the hills, the green of newborn leaves, and the sun sparkling off Lake Travis in the distance, never fails to steal my breath.

I won't lie, when Peter said I could keep the house and he'd move downtown I was happier about that than sad to see our marriage dissolve.

It's in these quiet moments that my mind drifts to the past. To summer nights with a chorus of cicadas. To a handsome boy with sun-bleached hair and golden-green eyes that sparkled like the sun off the lake. To first loves. A future as wide and open as the Texas sky.

It's in these moments I find myself wondering what life would be like if I hadn't panicked and shunned Daniel's advances. Afraid to lose his friendship, and that I'd somehow screw up an actual relationship and be left with nothing.

Maybe that's what makes teenage love so special. The unrequited-ness of it. The newness of every touch, every kiss, every murmur. Like babies learning to walk, teenage love is full of falls and stumbles.

It's also full of regrets that turn into scar tissue and linger long after the feel of a stolen kiss fades from the lips.

CHAPTER 2

The traffic into downtown Austin the Friday before spring break is schizophrenic. The typical slowdowns move at warp speed, then I crawl through areas where I'd usually gun it.

It didn't matter. I barely register the brake lights in front of me. Instead, my thoughts swirl around the boy who'd lived behind me throughout high school.

It's not the first time my mind drifts on a current of nostalgia. There've been plenty of nights when I'd pour another glass of wine and spend hours scouring social media, Google search results and, during a night of too many vodka-cranberries, obituaries for any mention of *my* Daniel Palmer. The results are always the same.

Nada.

The music cuts off and my best friend's name flashes on my screen.

"Hey, Em."

Heavy breathing answers me.

"Oh God, please don't tell me you accidentally called me during sex. *Again.*"

"Happened *one* time." Emily is breathless, but the voice of a coach booms in the background. "I'm just finishing a Peloton ride. Are you free of dependents for the week?"

My best friend since childhood never married, and the most she'd managed to keep alive was Ben's betta fish while we were on a two-week vacation. At least, I always assumed it was the same fish. Somehow it wouldn't surprise me if Emily bought a replacement.

"Almost, about to drop off their bags at Peter's and head into the office."

"So, what's the plan? A week of partying like we're teenagers? Living at the spa and getting every treatment available? Lots of meaningless sex?"

A sea of red brake lights flare in front of me. I hitch my left elbow on the door, cupping my head. "Mmm...I was thinking of catching up on Netflix, maybe eating meals that don't have vegetables. Drinking a bottle of wine a night and waking up the next morning to see what I drunk-bought. You know, the way a mid-life divorcee likes to party."

Emily's blender growls through the car speakers. "Okay, but don't go too crazy on the carbs. A month until the reunion and our metabolisms called it quits a while back."

I sigh. "Another thing lost on the youth; a fast metabolism." I look behind me, hoping to flirt my way into changing lanes. Several cars drive by, their drivers staring sullenly straight. "Speaking of the reunion—Oh come *on*! I have my blinker on."

Flirting for a lane change, also lost on the youth.

"Nope, you're not going to back out again." Emily's voice is hard.

"I need an appendectomy."

"Sounds like a personal problem."

Would Aubrey find her person, the one she'd know her entire life that would both cheer her up and call her bullshit?

The person who knows her better than she knows herself. A priceless friendship that's more vital than air.

"Anyway, as I was saying. You've seen the guest list, right?" I ask.

My friend waits several beats before answering. "You want to know if Daniel will be there." It wasn't a question. Didn't need to be.

There'd been more than a few nights I'd called Em drunk and despondent because I couldn't find any trace of him.

"Last time I looked he wasn't on the list," her voice softens. "But that doesn't mean he still won't make it. You just need to have faith."

"I've been sitting here having faith someone will let me into the next lane, and that's not working out for me," I say on an annoyed sigh.

"This is a crazy idea, but why don't you hire a PI and see if someone can find him."

"And risk a restraining order?" A car finally lets me over, and I make my way to the exit. "Anyway, that's a terrible use of money."

"Any worse than your ex's ridiculous sports car he can't drive on Austin streets because of the potholes?"

"He's such a cliché, isn't he?" I pull into the valet at Peter's downtown high-rise. "I'll call you later."

I heave the kids' bags out of the car and up to the thirtieth floor. Flashes of the Texas State Capitol flicker between the steel beams of the glass elevator. The nascent leaves of the springtime bloom cushion the dome in a sea of green. The blue sky stretches overhead like a baby waking up. Clear and bright, refreshed and ready to take on the day.

Kirsten answers my quick knock. My almost ex-husband's "female friend" opens the door.

Apparently, she's very offended by the term girlfriend. Maybe it's because she'd only been old enough to drink for a couple of years.

"Hi, Mrs. Gardner. Happy Friday!"

I hate it when she calls me that. It's like she thinks I'm Peter's mother or something.

Wait, does she?

"Hey Kirsten, is Peter here? Dropping off the kids' stuff and making sure he's all set."

"Sure, I'll get him." The girl turns and sashays out of the foyer. Insanely long legs, freakishly long, thin arms.

Did the human race evolve somewhere between when Kirsten and I were born?

My own limbs feel stubby.

I let myself in and go over to the picture windows. The morning traffic below reminds me of Ben's toy cars, rolling through a make-believe town. Off to make-believe jobs, at make-believe companies. With perfect make-believe families waiting back home at the end of the day.

All I wanted from life was for my kids to have a normal family. To have parents who love each other as much as we love them. Divorce was an inevitable destination for Peter and me, but it sucks still the same.

"Hey, Josie." My estranged husband's voice is warm and kind.

It's always warm and kind, even when he told me he loved me but didn't feel *in love* with me anymore.

It's unfair that he's more handsome at the end of our marriage than at the beginning. When we'd met in our mid-twenties, he was a pudgy geek with some coding skills and a business degree. Now, he's trim and fit, having sold the company he started for enough money that we could live comfortably, the kids can go to any college they want, and invest in both my growing company and his own burgeoning business. A health and wellness app for men over fifty. His target audience, the kind who want to stay fit enough to attract a girlfriend half his age.

Female friend.

I roll Aubrey and Ben's suitcases toward him, delivering everything the kids will need for the next week.

Peter leans in for a hug. Even though the marriage is over, there's something about clinging to the man who'd made love to me, held my hair back during morning sickness, and smothered me in kisses after our babies were born that makes me feel like I'd walked into a house I'd sold, yet it still feels like home.

"You look good," I say. It's not a lie. His hair has settled into the gray, making his steel blue eyes even more captivating. The gingham blue shirt is untucked, sleeves haphazardly rolled, and the medium-wash jeans sit perfectly on his hips.

Dammit, why is Kirsten getting the best of him?

"So do you."

Do I?

I glance down at my outfit. Dark skinny jeans with a loose top to hide a softening middle. Luckily the teal color drew more attention to my eyes than my muffin top.

"Thanks. Well, this should have everything. Ben's backup inhaler is in the inside pocket." I immediately go into mom-mode. "Try to limit his screen time. I know you guys will be on the slopes most days, but he'll fight it. Same with Aubrey, you'll have to pry that phone out of her hands, but it'll be good for her. Plus, we don't need her breaking a leg because she tried to shoot a video while flying down the slopes."

He snorts. "Hashtag embarrassing."

I laugh. He always makes me laugh. Even when we were breaking up, we somehow kept it light.

"Why don't you stay for a cup of coffee?" Peter asks.

"Thanks, but I have to get into the office. Million things to do." I try to make my voice light. This is just a bag drop. If I could've left their luggage with the concierge, I would've, but I wanted to look in his eyes and make sure he'd bring my children home in the same condition.

My chest tightens with the thought of all the to-do's gathering dust on my list.

Peter drops his friendly façade, his forehead wrinkling. "Sit with me, Josie. Let's talk."

Concern tumbles in my stomach like sneakers in a dryer. This was the same face he'd made when he took our marriage away.

What else is he going to take from me?

"Is everything okay?" I mutter.

He crosses into the kitchen, sliding a manila envelope off the counter, offering it to me. "You can have your attorney read through it, but I wanted you to hear it from me."

I stare at the envelope as if it's rigged to explode. Something deep inside me knows I'm in the *before*.

Before I open it and read the document.

Before I know what Peter is going to do to me.

Before I have my heart ripped to shreds.

Again.

"What is it?"

"Look, we said we'd tackle the divorce this summer, but I wanted to go ahead and get the papers drawn up. What, with Kirsten..." His gaze drifts down the hall where the twenty-something had disappeared. "Anyway, with the custody arrangement, just hear me out. I'm thinking the kids can stay here with me during the week and see you on the weekends."

Like the old Graviton ride of my youth, the floor drops out from under me. Disbelief pins me to the spot, my hand halfway opening the envelope, stomach flying into my throat.

"What? Are you nuts?" My shriek echoes around the sparse apartment. There's no way in Hell he's bringing my kids here to live. "I'm a good mother. I'm a great mother. You have no grounds to do this."

"You *are* a great mother. That's not what this is about."

I finally convince my limbs to move. I cross my arms, crumpling the half-opened envelope. "Oh? Well, then, enlighten me."

Peter blows out a sigh and runs his hands through his hair. "You did so much while I built my career. You stayed home with them, fed them, changed God knows how many diapers. I'm doing this so you can do the same for your career, not because you did anything wrong. You had your time. Let me have mine."

A laugh bubbles up, hot, acrid, like magma from deep inside the earth. From deep inside my soul. "Oh, so I get to deal with sleepless nights and shitty diapers while you get to hang out and play video games. No, Peter, you don't get to do this. You don't get to swoop in and do all the fun stuff. Not this time. You're not taking my kids from me."

"They're my kids too, Josie." His jaw muscle flinches, as if he's holding back more heated words.

"Well, you should've thought that through before you decided you weren't in love with me anymore." I shove the crumpled envelope into my bag, scrambling to find my car keys before remembering the valet has them. "Anyway, my attorney *will* be reaching out to your attorney."

Peter grabs my wrist as I push past him, his thumb stroking the inside lightly.

It'd always been his way of calming me down.

I hate that he still uses this.

Hate it even more that it still works.

"Josie, look, maybe I said it all wrong then, but—" He swallows hard. The pain etched across his face is deep, as if it'd been there so long that it's part of his features. "You were always *the one*. For me. I just never felt like I was the one for you. I think I woke up one day and didn't have enough love to hold us together."

CHAPTER 3

I manage to hold it together until I'm back in the safety of my car. I pull out of the building's valet and drive around the corner, parking in a metered spot.

The sobs erupt like Vesuvius, and instead of spewing ash, spittle coats my steering wheel, dash, and windshield.

I cry for my ruined relationship with Peter. He was right. There was always a chasm between them, and while we'd somehow strung across a bridge, after nearly twenty years of marriage, it'd worn thin.

The rope fraying, planks missing. Finally, it was too dangerous for either of us to cross it. Peter just happened to be the one to say it.

I cry for my children. After my parents' divorce, I wanted nothing more than for this to be as painless as possible. For them to feel like their lives aren't going to be any different.

And, I cry for myself. For the truth that Peter flung at me. There's nothing harder than when the truth pierces one's heart. Truth is an arrow that is sharper than any other, able to breeze through the armor of lies I'd built up.

I never told him about Daniel, the boy I loved in high school, who I still manage to love today. I didn't need to say it; the ghost of unrequited love always lingered between us.

A knock at the window startles me. "Ma'am, are you okay?" A police officer stands on the other side. His aviator sunglasses reflect how I feel.

A hot damn mess.

I roll down my window, wiping the mascara from under my eyes. "Thank you, Officer, I just, uh, got some terrible news. Figured it was safer to pull over. Give me just a minute. I'll be fine."

"Is there someone you can call?"

"Yeah, my attorney. As soon as I've said all the bad words in my head."

He nods. "Well, if you're going to sit here much longer you might want to pay the meter."

Great, I can't even have a temper tantrum without pissing someone off.

I take another deep gulp of air, punch my attorney's number, and pull back into the flow of traffic.

It doesn't even ring before the recorded message fills the speakers. "This is Jeri Nader, family attorney. I'm either in court or in a meeting. Please leave a message."

The sobs strike again at the sound of the beep. "Jeri, he's trying to take them from me. Our kids. My kids. He wants primary custody and for me to have them on the weekends. What the fuck? We have to stop him. Call me as soon as you get this." I hit the end button on my screen and direct the phone's virtual assistant to text Jeri a 9-1-1 message.

I try Em next.

"Hi, this is Emily Murray. I'm with a client right now and can't—"

I don't even wait until the message finishes before ending the call. What good is having a best friend who's a therapist if she sees clients at the exact moment my entire world crashes down?

I pull into my parking spot at my building just north of downtown housing my third baby. Mamacita. A converted office-warehouse freshened up with white paint over the bricks, oversized, gridded windows, and an ivy creeping up one side. Large planters filled with tropical flowers adorn the front.

I open the heavy glass door, my chunky heels clomping on the concrete floor as I hurry to my office. Through the glass wall, I watch the warehouse workers loading boxes of my all-natural baby cleaning products into trucks. Mamacita was born partly out of boredom and partly out of that new-mother desire for no harm, negative vibes, or chemicals that were perfectly fine to clean my home before touching my children.

Yeah, didn't think about fathers trying to steal them away as something I needed to worry about.

Like kids growing up, bit by bit my business learned to crawl, then a few good accounts had it taking off at a run. Three years ago, Peter and I decided it was time to let my little business see what it could do as a mid-size business.

Now, we're poised for our most explosive growth yet. A regional grocery store chain was days away from closing a deal. If sales were strong there, it would only be a matter of time before national chains follow suit.

At least, I hope.

A warehouse full of products and a business loan the size of my house keeps me up most nights. With the closing of this deal, I'd clear away inventory and debt.

I slip into my office, hoping to gather a few calming breaths ahead of the weekly sales meeting. Before I grab my laptop out of the bag, my accounts director, Marla, pops into the office.

"Hey, got a minute?" Her usually pale complexion is waxy, as if she has the flu.

"Sure, you okay?"

She drops into the guest chair. "No, it's Bixby's." Marla holds her phone up. A news story stares back at me. *Grocery Chain Files Bankruptcy.*

Not the flu—really, *really* shitty news.

"I've been calling everyone I know since I saw this, but no one is answering. Either they're all gone already or they don't know what to tell me." Marla picks at her nails as she speaks. "I've already made some calls to contacts I have at other chains, but Friday before spring break, I'm just leaving a lot of voicemails."

I back into the table behind my desk, using it to keep me upright. This time, I'm not on the Graviton.

This time I'm on the Tilt-A-Whirl, insides getting twisted left, then spun right, the world around me blurring in a dizzying, undulating circle.

My gaze bounces around the room, trying to find something to hold on to. Various photos, pictures my kids drew. Awards for business achievement. Finally, it finds the anchor it's looking for.

A small frame hanging on the adjacent wall. The drawing isn't childish, but it's not professional either. It was drawn by a teenage hand. One that could either go on to perfect its talent, or move on to another vocation and stay relatively passable.

It's a charcoal drawing of me, although most people who see it now think it's Aubrey. The girl in the picture was caught in the waning moment of a laugh. Her eyes crinkled, full mouth pulled into a wide smile, the apples of her cheeks full and, even though it was done in tones of gray, I can almost see the rosiness in them. My hair is long and wild, like I'd spent the day swimming and sunning, hiking and forgetting to brush my locks.

The picture was drawn by someone who loved me.

Someone I'd loved.

Still love.

Looking at the picture calms me. The room slows its spinning. The ride of panic almost over.

"Okay," my voice comes out hollow and raspy. "All right, it's okay. You did a fabulous job nearly getting them to the finish line. Think of it this way, better to find out now than after the deal closes, where we'd have to go to court to get half of what they owe us. Keep following up with other leads. Let me know if there is any other news on Bixby's."

Marla takes a deep breath and nods before escaping my office.

I ease into my chair, expecting the ground to buck like an ornery horse. I grab my planner and start a list:

Call bank.

Call accountant.

Try not to panic.

Meet with the marketing department to see if we can do a warehouse sale on social media.

Try not to panic.

Pick up a case of wine to get through the weekend.

Try not to panic.

My phone rings.

I skip the pleasantries. "Jeri, he's trying to take the kids." Pleasantries are for when things are good. Things are definitely not good. Maybe the opposite of pleasantries should be the shitteries.

For when everything is in the shitter.

"He can't take them, can he? I haven't done anything wrong. I kept them alive. And, not just alive, but with all their limbs, and no juvenile records. There're worse mothers out there who get to keep their kids, right?"

"Calm down, Josie." My attorney's voice is echoey, as if she stood in marbled hallway. "It may not be as bad as you think. Sometimes spouses say things in the heat of an argument."

"It wasn't an argument." My legs develop a case of restless leg syndrome. I pace the office, hoping movement will alleviate the thudding headache. "I dropped off their bags so they can spend spring break with him, and he handed me the paperwork. Said it's nothing I did, some bullshit claim about letting me focus on my career." A career that now smells as bad as an unfortunate concoction that boiled over in my kitchen.

Jeri pauses a beat before speaking again. "Look, this recess is almost over. I'll be honest, there's a judge in family courts that tends to side with dads, especially if the mom works. His attorney could be angling to get us before that judge."

Judge. That means a hearing. Us sitting at opposite tables. This is contrary to what we'd talked about.

My pacing turns into circles. The room spins. A pain spikes in my chest. Is it the pain of having the man I'd loved for so many years betray me, or the pain that just when I start to have some footing over my new normal I find myself tripping over a wrinkle in the carpet of life.

Jeri continues to speak, but her voice is far away, like we're being pulled apart—correction, like *I'm* being pulled apart.

I stop pacing, yet the room twists and spins, up and down, like I'd hopped on another ride at the fair, the one that I rode with glee when I was young but would never let my kids on. The Hammer. Spinning. Throwing me about. Flinging me against the safety belt of my life. It's only a matter of time before that belt breaks.

Then what?

I drop to my knees. My lungs call it quits. They won't push out the air, or draw in a fresh breath. I'm a fish, drowning in my office. Ringing pierces my ears. Long, loud, absorbing all sound. I rub my temples, hoping to dislodge whatever is stuck in my head. In my heart.

It's a panic attack. That's all.

I slide to my butt. To find more steady ground to calm my erratic heart and traitorous lungs, but instead I land on my side. I try to push up, but my arms refuse to move.

The only body part that's compliant are my eyes. I move my gaze around my office, looking for my anchor to hold on to while this storm rages in my body.

In my heart.

The office flashes, warps. Like I'd gotten off the jarring ride and ran straight into the funhouse.

My gaze lands back on the picture, but instead of seeing the whole thing, I zero in on the girl's eyes. My eyes. Young, ready for the future.

I send silent warnings to the girl in the picture. *You can fall in love with your best friend. Don't push away the people who love you most. Don't stress about what you can't control.*

The picture grows and grows and grows, until I have no choice but to fall into my younger self.

CHAPTER 4

The roar of the lawnmower invades my sleep. I sink deeper under the covers. When did the landscaper switch days?

They come on Tuesdays, when I'm at work and not home to be subjected to the never-ending growl of the leaf blower or the angry churning of the mower.

I roll over, pulling the pillow over my splitting head.

Did I drink too much wine again? Who'd blame me after the day I had?

Peter's impossibly skinny, impossibly young new girlfriend. Almost losing my kids. Then my business. Good lord, did I get out over my skis betting on that new account or what?

The mower is now outside my window.

I fling myself on my back, still ensconced in the cocoon of sheets. My stomach heaves at the movement, like someone wringing out a dishrag.

I sit up, throwing the comforter off, ready to sprint to the bathroom, but my nausea is quickly forgotten.

Gone is my crisp white bedroom. The California king is now a full-sized bed. There is no chaise lounge opposite me. Instead, a light brown vanity covered in teenage clutter.

Not just any teenager clutter.

My teenage clutter.

"What the fuck?"

I *did* just have wine last night, right?

I lay back down, clenching my eyes shut, willing myself back to sleep. Instead, all I can think about is the day before. Everything from the morning is there.

Sadly, so is everything from dropping by Peter's and then the office.

The panic attack. I remember that. Maybe I'm still asleep. Someone must've given me something pretty good to help with the freakout.

All I have to do is drift back into the dream. Allow the meds to work their magic, and I'll wake up, refreshed and calm, ready to repair the FUBARed parts of my life.

"Josie! You were supposed to get up an hour ago. You're going to be late." My mom's voice rattles me out of slumber. Except it isn't Mom's voice from when I'd talked to her just days before, worn with age and weary with regret. This voice is crisp, youthful, unencumbered by heartbreak and grief.

I pop up.

Mom stands in the middle of my childhood bedroom. Hands on her hips, dressed in denim shorts that graze the top of her knees and a simple T-shirt, her dark blonde hair cut in the bob I'd made fun of her getting back in the nineties.

The nineties…

"What the fuck?" I repeat the curse.

Mom's jaw drops. "Josephine Elise Berry, *what* has gotten into you? You are not too old to wash your mouth out with soap, young lady. It's nearly ten; you have to be at the school by eleven for your appointment. You can't just sleep your Saturday away." While mom fusses, she opens my closet; foreign clothes stare back.

I lean over, catching my reflection in the vanity. My hair is longer, leaning more into the blonde side of strawberry blonde. The wrinkles I'd earned through worrying about my kids aren't there. Instead, a bronze tan kisses my face, bringing out the smattering of freckles across my nose.

My jaw drops, matching Mom's at my earlier curse. They gave me too many meds.

I'm overdosing.

That's the only explanation.

I pound my fist on my thigh. "Wake up, wake up." I pinch my right arm, then the left. "Wake up, dammit, wake up."

Panic swarms my body like stepping on a fire ant mound, stinging my stomach, my heart, invading my lungs.

Mom drops the white dress she'd pulled from the closet. One that I wouldn't have fit into since I was a teenager. She grips my shoulders. "Josie, what's gotten into you? Is it drugs?" My mother's hazel eyes are wide with worry. "Did you not learn anything from Mrs. Reagan?"

"I have to wake up, Mom. I have to wake up. I'm glad you're here, please don't get me wrong, but Aubrey and Ben need me, and Peter is trying to take them."

She kneels on the bed beside me, clutching me to her chest. "Breathe, honey, just breathe. Who's Aubrey and Ben? And this Peter guy? Are they new friends?"

New friends?

Surely even in my dream, Mom would know who her grandchildren and son-in-law are.

Wouldn't she?

I open my eyes and glance around the room. After I graduated, Mom sold this house and moved into a townhome along the coast.

There'd been so many times since then I'd dream I was back in the quaint two-story home that didn't know just how cool it was with the sunken living room and breakfast nook that looks out over a backyard dominated by a grand Live Oak.

One of my windows faces the next-door neighbor, the other, with a window seat built in, at our backyard, and more importantly, in line with Daniel's window behind us. I'd even gone so far as to drive by the house a few times over the year, watching a couple of young hipsters and their kids play on the front lawn.

Maybe that's what this is. After a day that spun out of control like a carnival ride with lost nuts and bolts, and the mother of all panic attacks, I was put under with some strong drugs, and my mind went straight back to the place where it felt the safest. My parents' home.

I can almost hear Emily. *Embrace it. Your broken ego needs this. To revert back to simpler times. Luxuriate in this feeling. Carry it with you.*

I pull back from Mom. "I'm okay, sorry, just a weird dream."

She smiles that closed-lip don't-believe-your-bullshit smile. "Get moving, Josie. You don't want to be late for your senior pictures. I know you think senior pictures are lame but do it for your dad and me."

My breath catches at the mention of my father. I've reached the point in my life where he's been gone for more years than I had him in my life. In quiet moments, I flip through old photo albums to keep his face firmly planted in my mind. To undo the teenage damage I did so many years ago.

"Is Dad here?" my voice is don't-wake-the-baby quiet.

My mother hides a steadying breath in a cocked eyebrow. "He's at the office. Said he'll be home sometime this afternoon."

With a final stroke of my hair, she pushes off my bed and leaves me alone with only the tangy floral notes of her Charlie's perfume.

"These *are* some really good drugs," I mumble.

I wander around the bedroom, soaking in the faux realism that surrounds me. The desk adjacent to my bed. A binder decorated with my teenage handwriting, my name looping with thick green and gold markers. Tabs inside marked with the names of my senior classes. World History. AP Calculus. Physics. Yearbook. AP English IV. My bonus period, spent working in the library. Which is code for "senior knock-off period."

I move over to my bookshelf. The little stereo system I'd saved up a summer of babysitting gigs to buy sits in the middle surrounded by CDs. R.E.M. Sonic Youth. U2. Madonna. Beastie Boys. Nirvana. Dolly Parton. Loretta Lynn. Pearl Jam. Guns n Roses. Everything an angsty teenager needs in the early nineties. The rest of the shelves are filled with a combination of books I had to read but secretly enjoyed, and various volumes of V.C. Andrews and Sweet Valley High.

I venture into my bathroom. Makeup strewn across the counter, three different types of hairspray, hair dryer half hanging off the counter. Photos of Em, Sofia, and me frame the edges of the mirror. I pluck one. It was Halloween our freshmen year, we'd gone as triplets, which was hilarious because the three of us couldn't have looked more different.

Emily was even more of a pixie with long brunette hair and bright blue eyes. Sofia, the Latina beauty with her dark curly hair and soulful brown eyes. Me, the strawberry blonde with a mouthful of braces and zits dotting my forehead.

I look in the mirror and jump.

Really, what drugs *am* I on?

The reflection staring back definitely isn't the forty-something version I scrutinize every evening but is the seventeen-year-old I'd almost forgotten. Braces gone, teeth are shiny and white, not the fake white to erase the effects of coffee and red wine, but the white of youth. My face had cleared up, both of the zits and the wrinkles I'd stared at just the day before.

I lift my pajama top. Small breasts, unburdened by nursing two kids, sit atop a perfectly smooth stomach. "I have a six-pack? I don't ever want to wake up."

Mom said it was senior picture day. I might as well play along with the dream.

But…

A memory strikes like a spitwad to the back of the head. I open a drawer. There in the back is an unfulfilled dare. A box of hot pink hair dye that Emily made me buy. I'd planned to do it the first day of summer but had chickened out. Em had forgotten it, and I thought I'd skated that one.

I glance back at a reflection as foreign as a friend I hadn't seen in more than twenty years, someone I would have walked by at the mall, only to realize later that I knew her once.

A girl who wasn't afraid to cause a few waves. Would jump overboard and not worry about what the ocean held.

Anyway, it was just a dream, after all.

CHAPTER 5

With my clothes draped over my arm, I sneak past my parents' bedroom. Even if this were nothing more than a drug-induced dream, I wasn't about to piss off my dream-mom for having hot pink hair for my senior pictures.

Then again, maybe dream-mom would be cool with it. Might even let me go to the mall next and get my nose pierced. Maybe even a tattoo. Because this is my dream, and I can go crazy if I want to.

What harm can it do?

It's incredible how the mind remembers things. The smell of the inside of my hand-me-down Subaru; the coconut-y sweetness of sunscreen mixed in with a spilled Diet Coke in the back seat and the stench of running shoes. Sweet, acidic and stinky. Basically, everything that makes up a teenage girl.

The drive to the school was automatic. As if I'd done it every day for the past three years, not like it was the first time in nearly thirty. I pull around to the gym at the back of the building. Nondescript beige brick made interesting with the painted depiction of a panther prowling toward the front door, as if to frighten off the opposing team. Our sports record proved it didn't.

I've barely gotten out of my car when Em's scream slices through the otherwise quiet morning. "You did it!" She flings her body into me. "I thought you chicken-shitted out, but you freaking did it!" Her big blue eyes widen as she touches a strand of my bright pink locks. "You're my hero."

It was strange, seeing my best friend as I'd forgotten her. She was still as petite as ever, with eyes that seemed almost too big for her small face, and long dark hair that overwhelmed her body. Midway through college, she'd go through a nasty breakup and shave her head. That prompted her to become a therapist, and when her hair grew out, she realized the pixie cut suited her lifestyle and body way better.

"Holy crap."

My eyes welled at the voice behind me. Sofia Diaz. She, Emily, and I were a threesome of best friends. We were the embodiment of a scale. Emily's loud brassiness on one end, Sofia's shy sweetness on the other. I sat right in the middle.

Utterly inseparable until something fractured Sofia from us.

Over the years, Sofia had crept into my brain, and I'd find myself missing her soft voice and kind spirit. It was strange how she left us. It wasn't a major blowout, no shouting or tears. She just quietly slipped away from us.

What was worse?

A split with the loud gnashing of earth being ripped apart, or a friendship that fades like a spent bloom.

"Sof." I hug her tighter than a seventeen-year-old who had probably seen her the day before should. What the hell, it's just a dream.

"Josie, your mom is going to freak," Sofia says. "How did you get out of the house?"

I smirk. "It's amazing what one is capable of while humming the *Mission Impossible* theme."

"All right, girls." Em threads her arms through ours. "Let's get these God-forsaken senior pictures over with."

We'd intentionally booked our appointments back-to-back, wanting to make sure we captured a group shot. Emily went first. Changing into the black faux-fur-lined top that would be the girls' standard to the boys' tuxes. She looks so fresh-faced, innocent. Nothing like the hardened, afraid-to-fall-in-love-again woman.

After the official yearbook photo, I help her change into one of her other outfits for the more casual shots. I'm zipping up the light blue dress when I try an experiment.

"I called you yesterday to tell you about the latest shit Peter pulled."

Emily glances over her shoulder. "What d'you mean? We were by the pool all day yesterday. When did you call? Who's Peter? Did you have a summer fling while Daniel was gone and forget to tell us?"

I step back and gnaw on a cuticle. This dream is holding together way better than any other I'd had. Dreams are like bubbles. As long as they float along unbothered, they exist, but the moment reality pokes its finger at it, it pops.

Why hasn't this dream popped?

"Oh, no, sorry, I'm just babbling. I'll tell you later."

Emily finishes her shots while Sofia and I change.

"This is just weird, right?" Sofia says, adding a layer of mascara to her already insanely long lashes. "I should be excited, but I'm really… sad."

I was too, but not for the reasons she's aware of. "Sof, you'll tell me if I ever do something bad, right? Like something to piss you off."

She meets my eyes in the bathroom mirror. At first, they're wide, like a kid getting caught in a lie, then she recovers.

Has it already started? Have the strings of our friendship frayed away while I was an ignorant, selfish teenager?

"Of course, Jo. Always."

Emily bursts through the door like the force of nature she is. "Josie Posey, you're up."

I hurry out of the bathroom, my feet moving on their own to carry me into the darkened gym. The big fluorescent lights would be hell on pictures, so the gym is dark with black pipe and drape sectioning off the makeshift studio.

There's an eeriness about being there on a Saturday morning, like seeing a supermodel without her makeup doing something mundane like picking up dog poop.

The photographer tries not to stare at my hair, but she's failing miserably. Even if this weren't a dream, it was suburban Austin in 1993.

The slogan "Keep Austin Weird" is still several years off, meaning it's already weird. So, seeing a teenage girl with hot pink hair shouldn't be that—well, weird.

"Josie Berry," the photographer says. "Am I going to get an angry call when your parents get the proofs?"

"Nope."

Because this is all a dream and I'll wake up by then.

The photos happen as photos do. Impossible body posture that only looks good on film. Smiles held for so long that they turn into grimaces. Flashbulbs that leave their mark every time I blink.

Once we're each done with our individuals, Sofia, Emily, and I pose for our group shots. Group hugs, arms wrapped around each other. Holding tight to our sisterhood like our young lives depend on it.

When the photographer announces she has enough to work with, essentially dismissing us, I don't want to let go. Even if it is a dream, standing there with my two best friends feels as real as the air in my lungs, the sun on my face, the ground beneath my feet.

Both girls have to run to their summer jobs and sprint out the door, leaving me to pack up my clothes and makeup alone. My mind has done an incredible job reconstructing the girls' locker room. The white cinderblock, green mashed-down carpet. Gray bathroom stalls with dingy white tile. I can barely call up the inside of my first adult apartment, but this, this is so…tangible.

I trace my fingers along the wall next to the bathroom sink. The cool tile juxtaposed against the rough grout. Could I feel things in my other dreams?

I lean forward and study my face, looking for the hint of crow's feet or the fault line wrinkle across my forehead.

"Hi, Josie."

I jump back, banging my knee into the underside of the sink. Apparently, this dream has a wide cast of characters.

Ruby Bell drops her makeup bag next to mine. Her shoulders hunch forward, forcing her stringy blonde hair to hide her face. We were in the same class in second grade and best friends, until we weren't. But why? That's less solid. It's there, hovering between us like a bad smell, wrinkling our noses, making it uncomfortable.

"Hey, Ruby. Did you have a good summer?"

She shrugs. "Worked. You?"

What did I do that summer?

That's right, beer cart girl at the country club. "Same. Well, good luck with the photos. I gotta run." I load up my clothes on the hangers, smoothing them out, something I've asked Aubrey to do a million times and that she'd ignored a million times.

The foyer of the gym was filling up. A group of tiny, wide-eyed freshmen huddle in a tight circle, united by their shared fear of what the next year might bring as the smallest fish in a big lake. In just a couple of years, my sweet, nerdy little Ben will be one of those scared freshmen.

And, Aubrey. She's just finishing her freshman year, but she has as much in common with these kids as a hummingbird does a penguin. Sure, both were birds, but where my generation waddled in an orderly fashion, hers flits about wherever their phones and social media take them.

Were Ben and Aubrey off racing down the slopes of Vail?

My son would do a run or two to appease his dad and then find a coffeeshop with decent wi-fi. And Aubrey. Hopefully, she'll put her phone down long enough to be present.

I watch as an upperclassman gives his spiel about freshmen rules. "During home games, you guys have to sit at the bottom of the bleachers, for both football and basketball. Don't even dare to go to the top, seniors only, and you might get thrown off the top."

A gasp escapes my lips before I can stop it. "Don't bully them!"

Heads whip in my direction, and the upperclassman scowls at me. "Hippie freak," he mumbles under his breath and herds them out of the foyer and away from the incoming senior who doesn't follow protocol. In my dreams, at least.

I'm halfway to my car when I stumble to a stop.

Leaning against the driver-side door is the very person I'd spent most of my adult life cyberstalking.

Daniel Palmer.

His family moved into the house behind mine midway through our freshman year. The first six months I watched him, falling in love, working up the courage to finally speak to him. As soon as school let out that year, he was gone. Turns out, he spent his summers helping out at his grandfather's ranch up in the Panhandle.

When he returned before the start of our sophomore year, I looked out the window one day to find a large sheet of sketch paper taped to his window. It was a drawing of us, him leaning out his window and me out mine.

That's all it took to break the ice.

Our friendship was unlike the one with Emily and Sofia. It was built on long conversations on everything from religion, to the meaning of life, from aliens to baseball. In the short time that Daniel was in my life, there wasn't a topic we didn't cover.

Wait. That's a lie.

There was.

It would come at the end of our senior year when he tried to kiss me and I freaked out. Freaking out because something I wanted so badly was finally happening and I was afraid I'd ruin it. We'd never talked about how we were falling in love and how scared shitless we felt by it.

"Hey, Jo, you got some gum in your hair," he calls out.

Once again, my dream mind is working miracles. Daniel is as I remember him. Tall, lean from a summer of working a ranch. Dressed in faded jeans, Doc Martens, a white T-shirt, and a worn flannel shirt open with the sleeves rolled up, showing off the work tan. His hair is long, grazing his chin, streaks of sun-bleached blond mingle with the brown.

I try to draw in a deep breath, but my lungs rebel. Am I experiencing respiratory failure in real life?

Like dyeing my hair, I could walk right up to him, grab the back of his head, and pull his mouth down to mine.

However, no matter how ballsy I was earlier, seeing him turns me into a bashful, self-conscious teen.

I pick up my pace, hoping to smell the sunshine on his skin once more before I wake up. "Yeah? Where?"

"Everywhere." His eyes are a golden-green in the bright Texas sun. "Patty let you out of the house like that?"

"The real question is, will Patty let me back *into* the house." I lean against my car beside him.

Our shoulders are inches from touching, but the butterflies in my stomach act like there's contact.

"Anyway, Katy Perry did it first. My kids will think I'm pretty badass."

His brow furrows. "Katy who? Berry, you might be the only senior to dye her hair to make her future kids think she's cool. Ever the planner. Speaking of plans, going out to the lake tonight for the end-of-summer bonfire?"

Ah, the senior kegger. I had gone, but I can't recall much about it. Except for the aftermath. Waking up at Em's, feeling like my head was stuck in an automatic door that kept opening and closing on it. Again and again and again.

"Wouldn't miss it." Because if I'm stuck in a dream, where the hell else do I have to be? "You going?"

"Yep, see you there."

Daniel pushes off the side of my car.

Before he steps away, I lean up and plant a kiss on his cheek. Warm, smooth but a hint of a bristle from stubble. Most importantly, solid. Way too solid for a dream.

His lips parts slightly, either by surprise or to move the kiss to our mouths. Daniel draws in a sharp breath. He looks down at me through half-closed eyes. "What's that for?" His voice is low and raspy.

"I missed you. That's all. See you tonight." I watch him walk across the parking lot and into the gym before digging out my keys, recalling the time before remote entry, all the way back to when I had to put the key in the door and turn it. Assuming my shaking hands can make that happen.

Emotions jumble around my stomach like it was a trampoline. Excitement bounces around with the tingling blooms of first love. But, dread is a dead weight sitting in the middle, jarring in the realization that this dream is feeling more like real life.

CHAPTER 6

Turns out, it isn't that hard to get into my house. The house is as quiet as a church when I get home. Both parents' cars gone, no note, nothing.

I dig through my purse. I'll text Mom, see when…wait. No phone. That's right, in 1993, the best I can hope for is a pager, and according to Mom only doctors and drug dealers need those.

Throwing my clothes across the bed, I open my nightstand drawer. Tucked underneath college brochures is the blue velvet-covered diary. I didn't practice journaling religiously, but I did it enough to work through some of the big stuff.

I flip to the last entry.

August 1, 1993.

Mom and Dad are being so weird. Like overly nice, weird. To me and to each other. Maybe they are trying to butter me up to stay home for college. Or maybe they realize this is my senior year. I miss Daniel. He'll be back next weekend for senior pics, but I wish he'd been here all summer. Wish we could have had a picnic down at the springs. Gone swimming to cool off from the heat. Maybe he'd dunk me, I'd cough and tease him that he owes me mouth-to-mouth. Ugh! He's, like, one of my best friends. Maybe even more than Em and Sof because I can tell him things. Real things. But if I fall in love with him and we break up, then I'd have nothing. Maybe it's better to have friend Daniel in my life and be happy rather than lose boyfriend Daniel and be miserable. Because you can't be in love with your best friend, right?

"Oh, you poor girl, you are so, so wrong." I stroke the words written by my teenage hand, trying to make sense of the world with only seventeen years of experience.

How many times had I said if I could go back and tell my teenage self…?

I'd tell her to hold tight to the people she loves because they won't always be there. This was the last summer my parents were married. Was the split already happening?

I was shocked when they told me after Christmas that Dad was moving out. Experience told me falling out of love is harder than falling in.

I'd tell her that kindness is always the answer. Somehow one of my best friends was irreparably hurt and walked away from us.

I'd tell her the best love is with someone you consider to be your best friend. Because in relationships sometimes you're lovers and sometimes you're friends. You have to have someone who is your friend when you need him to be.

I slip the journal back into hiding and sit on the bench under my window. The sun shone behind the big oak tree at the yard's edge, casting my childhood into a soft glow. A rusty swing set stands sentry at the back of the yard, cast aside for the much cooler, and more dangerous, trampoline. No netting surrounding it, no pads cushioning springs that pinch until the skin breaks. How no one died is a miracle.

My gaze drifts past our yard, over the chain-link fence Daniel hopped with ease whenever he came over. Where our backyard was tended and filled with life, his was a forgotten wasteland.

If he wasn't home to mow the grass it would grow to Patricia-complaining heights. Plastic patio furniture was strewn about. A lone planter sat at the end of the patio, not housing plants but a year's worth of cigarette butts.

It wasn't that Daniel was poor. His mom worked as a nurse, and his dad was a Colonel in the Air Force before he was honorably discharged after the first Gulf War.

I sigh and hug my knees against my chest. It's still years until post-traumatic stress would be widely understood, but in the brilliant illumination of hindsight, it's obvious his dad struggled with it.

Is that what's happening to me?

I haven't gone to war, but maybe the stress of a divorce, learning my ex wants custody of our kids, and the fact that my business might be heading to bankruptcy caused a break with reality. Maybe Em is sitting with me, guiding me through some sort of hypnotic trance through my life, allowing me to repair my broken psyche.

Shortly before seven, a knock sounds at my door. I've been so lost in thought I hadn't heard the house-shaking rumble of the old garage door.

"Josephine," my name came out of Mom's mouth in that exasperated sigh all parents use. "Please tell me you did that after the pictures."

I smirk. "I could, but that would be a lie."

She plops down on my bed, studying my pink hair. "Well, if you used the box you've been hiding in your bathroom all summer, it's temporary and should wash out in a couple of days." Mom cocks her head to the side. "It looks pretty cute on you. Life is short, Josie. Eat dessert, do something that scares you, and dye your hair pink."

It's my turn to study her. At this point in her life, Patricia is several years younger than I am in real life, still in her late thirties, but she looks decades older.

"You okay, Mom?"

A sad smile crosses her face, but she quickly covers it with her usual perky brightness. "You're growing up faster than I realized."

"You're really not mad about the hair?"

She shrugs. "If I make all of your decisions, how are you going to learn to make them for yourself? It's hair. Years from now we'll look at your senior yearbook and laugh about it." My mother leans in and whispers. "Plus, your kids will think you're cool. Now, don't you have a senior party to get to?"

My mouth drops open. The mother I grew up with was never one to encourage me to go to parties.

"I was young, too. Once..." Her gaze drifts out the window, the waning sun casting a beautiful orange glow on her face. "A long time ago. I've got a pizza coming. Start getting ready and I'll shout when it's here. You're going to want to eat."

"Hey, Mom," I call before she closes the door behind her. "Dad having dinner with us?"

A sad smile brushes her lips. "Not tonight, sweetie," she says, the door clicking behind her.

Is it my fear of facing my dad that's keeping him from materializing in this dream? There's so much I want to say to him. Maybe my fragile psyche doesn't think I'm ready to confront the biggest regret in my repertoire.

This time, I'm more intentional in getting ready. The clothes in my closet are nineties chic. Lots of flannel, ripped jeans, shorts that graze the top of my knees. Aubrey would have a field day in this closet.

My heart somersaults. Is she freaking out? Does she even know? Is this a big enough medical emergency to cancel their vacation?

I push the concern into the back of my mind like last season's trend. I have to fix whatever's wrong with my brain. Just go with the flow. Emily will get me out of this when it's time.

After several minutes, the outfit I'm looking for comes into view. If I'm going to be a size two in my dream, I'm taking full advantage of it.

The light blue and red plaid pleated skirt is short enough that I'd never let my daughter wear it. Paired with a white tank top and black Doc Martens with every piece of random jewelry, pink hair pulled up in a messy bun to avoid the lake breeze and dark eyeliner and I am a nineties grunge queen.

I shove a slice of pizza in my mouth before Em pulls up. She doesn't need to honk or even come up to the door. The sound of Sonic Youth blaring from her Jeep is all the signal I need.

"One drink, a beer. Avoid anything that comes out of a trashcan. Skip the drugs. It's okay to say no." Mom runs through the speech while I slip my crossbody purse on. "And, Josie, have fun."

The cicadas greet me as I burst from the front door.

Emily and Sofia wait in Em's cherry red Jeep, a gift from her estranged father. "You are wearing that hair, *chica*," she shouts over the guitar solo. "I'm a little jealous."

As she drives toward party cove at the lake, I lean back in my seat, watching the clear night sky pass by. This area west of Austin is still several years away from development in the early nineties, and the dark, clear night is awash in pinpricks of light.

The party is in full swing by the time we get there. Some folks hit the lake as soon as they're done with their pictures. Using one rite of passage as a launching point for another.

Dark bodies are illuminated against a bonfire and milling about.

It's been years since I've seen some of these people.

My memory has been pretty damn spot-on so far, but what if I forget someone? What kind of glitch will that throw in this mind matrix?

"Hey, Em, I want you to know I trust you fully." If she is indeed leading me through hypnosis, maybe I'll mumble this out loud, let her know I'm with her.

She turns. "Thanks? Okay, weirdo, let's find something to drink."

We make our way into the thick of the party.

A few of the faces come back to me. Jeff Turner and Ian Phillips, the two stars of our pathetic football team, stand at the makeshift bar, pumping the keg or dipping into a lined trashcan.

"Ladies," Ian says, bowing as if he were a Shakespearean actor instead of a running back. "May I interest you in a beverage?" He hands Sofia a cup from the trashcan, but I push it away.

"Three beers, please."

With beverages in hand, we wander the lakeshore party site. It's still much too warm to hover near the bonfire, it's more for lighting the dark area.

The people I'd grown up with mingle, the cliques mostly hanging together in their own galaxy but now and then two star systems merge. The cheerleaders chat with the girl jocks, the football players laugh with the drama club kids.

At this point, it doesn't matter which group we've fallen in line with, we're all seniors. All standing at a precipice. In just nine short months, we'll cross the threshold from childhood to adulthood.

Some of us will go to college, others join the military and serve our country. Some will succeed, others will fail. Some will stay close to home; others venture across the world.

My feet lead me to the water's edge. How long will I be in this hypnotic state? It's been a full day in this dream time, is that how much time has passed at home?

"I take it from the change of clothes that Patty let you in the house."

I jump at Daniel's voice. "Even back out again. She didn't freak out nearly as bad as I thought."

"Cheers to parents being cooler than we think."

I meet his offered cup with the rim of my beer. "I think we forget they were young once. Our kids will do the same."

He coughs into his cup. Oh shit, that came out…well, possessive.

"I don't mean *our* kids…" I fumble for the words to right this verbal wrong. Wait, what if part of my healing is letting out the emotions I've bottled up my entire life?

I really wish Em would've given me some instruction as to how this works. I turn on him. "But would that be so bad? I mean, not anytime soon, because you know, college."

Even in the darkness, the fear in his eyes stares back at me like we're in the midday sun. "I, um, need a refill. Do you want another? Beer, right? Yeah, you should definitely stick to beer. Nothing stronger. I'll, um, be right back." Daniel runs from me like I'd let out the world's stinkiest fart.

Did I crap myself in real life?

Em will never let me live this down.

"Emily, can you tell me what I'm supposed to do here?" I say to the lake, hoping my voice is clear and commanding. I drain the rest of my cup. Is my alcohol tolerance aged forty-seven, or is it seventeen? Well, there's only one way to find out.

Trashcan punch.

I head back to the bar, skidding to a stop at the scene playing out in front of me.

Jessica Dawson, tall, blonde and tanned, full lips and perfectly arched eyebrows, leans against a tree. A white sundress fitting her perfect body like it was made for her. She spent her summers at her parents' house in the Virgin Islands, which is ironic because she was quick to tell everyone when she was no longer a virgin at the start of our sophomore year.

She didn't run in any clique, mostly because when she wasn't in class, she was running off to various modeling jobs. In a world of ducklings, Jessica is the swan, beautiful and aloof.

It isn't the sight of Jessica that stops me. It's Daniel, standing close to her, his forearm braced against the tree, leaning in close to whisper something to her.

Did this happen in real life at the senior bash?

Is that why I got so shit-faced I don't remember the night?

A cup is thrust in my hand. Whatever is inside it doesn't stay inside the cup for long. The bittersweet liquor burns my throat, pushing tears to my eyes. "Another," I croak in that Eartha Kitt husky sort of way.

After my third cup, the party pit sways like a ship at sea.

Can I get drunk under hypnosis? Daniel and Jessica are gone. Maybe they aren't, I'm not sure, all the faces blend together in the darkness like a Francisco de Goya painting.

All except for one.

Em's in a group of strangers that I used to know. I tug her arm. Her eyes widen at the sight of me.

"Wake me up." The words are a slurred sob. I rub my face, wiping away the hot tears. "I don't want to be here anymore. Wake me up."

CHAPTER 7

Em tucks me under her arm, holding me up as I stumble and mumble incoherent sobs.

"I don't know why I'm here," I cry as my friends heave me into the back seat of the Jeep.

"It's senior kegger, you came with Sof and me, remember?" Her voice floats from the front seat as the late summer wind blows around me.

Whatever happens next is a broken VHS tape of memories. Emily holding me as I cry for people she claims not to know. Waking up on the floor of her bedroom. The hangover. God, there is nothing worse than a trashcan punch hangover.

I slip out of her house as soon as the sky lightens. It's only a few blocks to my house, and a good old-fashioned walk of shame seems appropriate.

A warm, gentle breeze teases the tangled hair off my shoulders. None of the past twenty-four hours makes sense. If this were a dream, how can I still be asleep?

My dreams are usually less linear, jumping from one anxiety-fueled scenario to another. Leaving my kids somewhere. Forgetting to wear pants. Being halfway through a semester only to realize I never attended a class. The usual stuff of type A-person-alities.

This is different. This is—I burp and taste trashcan punch all over again—this is too real.

I slip my key into the front door and turn it with the gentleness that can only be mustered by hungover teenagers sneaking in. Even those dreaming.

I barely make it through the living room when a ghost emerges from the kitchen. Not an actual ghost, at least not in the Casper sense.

Clad in pajama pants and a T-shirt with an older-than-me cotton robe thrown over it, Dad stops mid-step, his coffee cup proclaiming him *World's Bestest Dad*, pauses at his lips.

"Hey, pumpkin, you're home early."

Part of me wants to run into his arms and have a long-overdue hug. The other part of me wants to fall to my knees and beg his forgiveness. Tell him how terrible I am for being angry. How I've wished I could call him over the years for advice. Or, to tell him about something Aubrey did. Or ask him how to make Ben play more.

Instead, I'm frozen in my spot and just gape at the apparition standing in front of me.

His reddish-auburn hair is mussed, standing up in the back. Soft blue eyes sparkle with humor as if he's in on the joke.

My hand instinctively reaches out and gingerly touches his arm. I'm met with warm, solid flesh. "Dad? Are you real?"

He pats my hand and laughs. "Are any of us real?" My father takes a sip of coffee. When he pulls the cup away, the smile is replaced with pressed-tight lips. "You okay, pumpkin? No offense, but you look a bit worse for the wear."

I drop my purse and fall into a chair at the kitchen table. The hang-over. Seeing and touching my long-dead dad. A dream that seems to have no end in sight. I'm starting to think Dad is right.

Is any of this real?

He sits next to me, admittedly less dramatically.

"Is there more where that came from?" I ask, nodding at his steaming cup.

A snort escapes his mouth. "It's like they always say, your children are babies one minute and the next they're coming in at dawn, smelling like a bar and asking to drink coffee. Yes, Josie, there's a fresh pot. And, we'll talk more about the smelling like a bar part later."

I instinctively reach for a *Mom of the Century* mug, but put it back because one, the person deserving of that is still asleep, and two, considering I have no clue where, or when, my children are, I'm barely Mom of the Hour. I instead grab a *Far Side* mug. The classic comic strip feels more indicative of my frame of mind.

With a fresh cup of lifeblood, I sit at my spot at the table and watch as Dad reads the paper.

How could I have gotten so angry at him to have cut him out of my life?

That's the problem with letting teenagers make life-changing decisions. The part of our brains that understands long-term consequences is too busy worrying about how life will be over if a certain boy never calls them back. Yet, we're continuously given ample opportunity to royally screw up our lives. Not to mention, others.

"I can feel you thinking over there," Dad says from behind the ink-stained pages. "Was the senior keg party that bad?"

Maybe this is the morality lesson I'm supposed to learn in whatever purgatory I'm in. Is this the chance to ask Dad for forgiveness, to absolve myself of a lifetime of guilt that has seeped into my marriage?

Em will be so proud of me for sussing out all this on my own.

"There's so much I want to say, I just don't know where to start."

Dad folds the paper and tosses it to the side.

Only then do I pay attention to the news on the front page. *Tropical Storm Bret ravages Venezuela.*

My panic attack happened before Spring Break. We don't have tropical storms in the spring now, do we?

Unless…

I don't even remember that happening, yet my subconscious must have filed it away for some reason.

What useful bit of information was tossed to the wayside to remember this? Probably where I stored the lid to some long-lost Pyrex container.

Unless…

"Josie?"

Unless this is real.

That can't be.

People don't just fall back into the past, right?

People don't also have hangovers in dreams that squeeze their heads, or have conversations with their deceased fathers. Or even lock away some useless bit of historical news to place on the front page of a newspaper nearly thirty years in the past.

Suddenly, the few sips of coffee threaten to gush up like one of Ben's science projects.

"Uh oh, I know that look," Dad says, obviously having too much fun at his daughter coming home hungover.

I'm sure he thinks a good morning after will be better than any lecture he could give me. I spring from the table and run to the half bath down the hall. The fact that throwing up coffee burned worse than drinking it just reaffirmed what I've already concluded.

This is not a dream.

I just don't know what the hell it is.

CHAPTER 8

Emily's waiting for me in the school parking lot, the backpack stuffed so full that she keeps swaying backward. "You doing okay?"

"Yeah, still a little nauseated, but I'll survive. And, I'll never drink trashcan punch again."

Her big blue eyes study me, looking for any trace of my Saturday evening breakdown. Is she checking my eyes for redness? Seeing if I'm sniffing too much? Making sure my teeth haven't rotted out from drugs?

"Josie, you really freaked me out. I think someone slipped you something. You were going on about an ex-husband, your business, kids even. Wanting me to wake you up?"

We approach the front doors of the school. Day three of being stuck in the past. Thoughts ping-pong around my mind. If I am in the past, what happened to my future/present self?

Did I disappear? Are my kids eating enough vegetables? Is Ben getting some sunshine? Has Aubrey put her phone down to just enjoy life?

I force a laugh. "Maybe I'm a time traveler?"

Em stops at my locker, her eyes as sharp as cut glass. "Well, if that's the case, can you tell me if I'm going to marry Kurt Cobain after he ditches Courtney Love?" She folds into the stream of students looking for their classes. In just a little over six months, she'll be inconsolable at the untimely death of her idol.

My first class is AP World History. I slide into the open desk next to Sofia.

She leans over. "How are you feeling?"

"Like I tucked the back of my dress into my tights, and everyone is laughing." My nose wrinkles at the flashback of coffee and trashcan punch making a duet in my toilet.

The teacher launches into his monotone explanation of what we'll cover for the year, but I can't focus. It's strange listening to a history of the world that won't include the last thirty years.

Three decades of making the same mistakes that humanity seems doomed to commit over and over again.

I sit up straighter. Time only flows in one direction.

What happens if a boulder drops into the timeline? Something that diverts the flow or even reverses it. Like a person.

Like me.

Alternate history is all the rage in modern times. What would happen if Kennedy wasn't killed? Or, what if the Axis powers won World War II?

I scribble in my notebook, stream-of-consciousness musings of how a disruption in history could change things in the future.

"Miss Berry, you are taking copious notes for the first day of class."

Only when Sofia nudges my foot do I realize the teacher's speaking to me.

"Oh, yeah, sorry. What do you think would've happened if President Kennedy wasn't shot?"

Mr. Lancaster's mouth opens slightly as if he were expecting a student to confess to writing a love note rather than debating alternate history on the first day of school. Then again, this *is* AP World History.

"Josie," he swallows hard, his Adam's apple bobbing. "I appreciate the initiative, but let's stick with the curriculum I've laid out. Perhaps we can find some free time to debate conspiracy theories."

An argument bubbles up my throat, but I hold tight to it.

"What do you have next?" Sof asks as we gather our belongings after the bell.

I study the schedule in the clear front of my binder. "AP Calculus. Hmm…I know for a fact I will never use this in the future. Think I may swap for something less math-y?"

Sofia furrows her brow. "But what about your class ranking?"

I shrug. "That's only important for when I walk across the stage. Trust me, no one will remember it after that."

"Josie, you okay? You're acting…well, you're you, but not you. Like an alternate you?"

I wrap her in a tight hug. Before Emily wakes me up, or I move on from this purgatory, I need to tell her how much I adore her, and no matter what happens in the future, I will be there for her. Even when she pushes us away.

The school secretary, Mrs. Fry, is just as I remember her. Bright red hair piled high on her head, a grandmotherly figure that could either squeeze the life out of you or make you feel safe from the storm of teenage hormones.

"Welcome back, Josie," she says when she sees me standing at the office counter. "I can't believe this is your last year. Once we get you kids trained, you graduate on us. What can I do for you?"

"Is it too late to swap out my second-period class?"

She jabs her glasses on her face and shakes a huge mouse, bringing to life an ancient IBM computer.

"Let's see, you're supposed to be in AP Calculus. Is there a problem with the class?"

"No, I just won't be using any of what I learn anywhere in my future. So, I thought maybe I'd switch for something that isn't as… hard."

She presses her bright red lipsticked lips into a thin line. "Well, if you say so." She motions for me to come around and join her at her desk. The old dark screen with green pixelated text stares back at me.

"Well, luckily, you've satisfied all of your core class credits, unless we shuffle everything around…" The old keys clack as she strikes them with long nails. "Looks like your choice for second period is either Home Ec or Intro to Agriculture, but you'll have to buy a calf to enroll in that one."

I stare at my choices in green boxy type. The feminist in me wants to scream that a class in home economics in the early nineties is incredibly old school, but then again, maybe I can test out some new all-natural cleaning formulas that have been rumbling around in my brain. Just because I'm locked away in my past self doesn't mean I can't keep working.

The class is well underway by the time I make it out to the vocational extension building. It's weird to think about how the walls of a box form early around kids.

Not long ago, we started sectioning them off, telling them their only path was learning to sew, or fixing a car. They're put behind the main high school, hidden away from the other aspects of academia when, in reality, there was a hell of a lot of math in sewing and cooking, and not to mention in just a few decades cars, will be more computer than combustible engine.

"May I help you?" The Home Ec teacher, Mrs. Wheeler, stares at me through the open door.

How long was I standing there fuming about injustices?

Too long.

"Hi, I'm Josie Berry, I just transferred into this class." I hold out my transfer slip. While she studies it, I glance around the room. Judging by the wide eyes and youthful faces, this class is predominantly filled with freshmen with the odd sophomore thrown about.

The teacher hands back my slip. "We don't get many seniors." Her cheeks are drawn in tight like she'd just hit the sour core of a gumball.

I grin the most peace-making smile I can muster. "Well, guess there's no time like my senior year to learn to cook for myself."

The rest of the class passes quickly. A rundown of what we'd cover; cooking, household budget keeping, sewing. If I didn't have more important things on my mind, like how to either pull myself out of this coma or time warp, I'd ask why this class is only filled with young women. It wouldn't hurt equality to start a few years earlier.

I'm the first one out the door at the bell. Physics, which might be my most important class of the day, is up next. If my memory is correct, it's on the other side of the main building on the third floor.

My heavy backpack bumps against the top of my butt as I jog. The breath fills and leaves my lungs with ease. Gone is the hitch in my left knee, the shiv of pain that usually pulls at my hip. The tiny leak of my bladder from two healthy kids playing kickball on it. Instead, I take the stairs two at a time like, well, like a healthy seventeen-year-old.

The second bell is ringing when I round the corner into the half-full classroom. Physics is a class that's only taken if you need the extra weighted credits or are most likely to be a rocket scientist.

I fall into a seat in the middle of the room. Em and Sofia are sitting this one out, it's all me trying to get my GPA as high as possible for a few coveted scholarships. Sadly, setting up college funds for kids in utero didn't become a thing until I was pregnant with Aubrey.

Aubrey. How can my body feel so young, yet my heart feels an ancient ache?

A new thought backhands me like a soap opera vixen. If I'm here in 1993, do Aubrey and Ben exist? Did my rolling back in time erase them as simply as the wrong answer on a test?

I clutch my lower abdomen. A stat from last year's, or was it twenty-something years, biology class crosses my mind. Women are born with all the eggs we'd have in our lifetime. Does that mean my kids are back inside me? Hanging out in my ovaries? I imagine Aubrey's egg furiously pecking and swiping at a tiny phone.

Ben's egg has a pair of his thick glasses, drinking out of a tiny coffee cup. Half-listening to the teacher's droning voice, I sketch out a picture of my kids as eggs, giggling to myself at how perfectly absurd they look.

With ten minutes left in class, I take a deep breath and raise my hand.

"Yes, Josie," Mr. Davies says, cutting himself off mid-sentence.

"Do you think time travel is possible? And, if so, do you think in say twenty-five, thirty years we'll have the ability to maybe travel back to the past?"

If we were in a nightclub instead of a physics class, the record would've scratched. It's that same uncomfortable silence.

Like someone laughing at a funeral.

"Sorry, I, uh, read this book, um, this summer…" I stammer for a suitable excuse.

Mr. Davies finally blinks and perches one butt cheek on the edge of his desk. "Well, as you can imagine, many scientists and innovators draw inspiration from science fiction."

"Like cellphones." The words leap from my mouth before I do a mental check on the prevalence of cellphones in the early nineties.

Did we call them cellphones then? Or were they still car phones?

The teacher gives me a withering look, like he isn't prepared to think this hard on the first day.

"And flying cars," I add. *Back to the Future* promises we'll have them in the next millennium, right?"

The bell rings, saving Mr. Davies from having to dignify the fiction part of science fiction with an answer. I pack up my books slower this time. My next class is Yearbook. The only class that Daniel and I share. Maybe its teenage hormones flooding my body for the first time in three decades, but I seesaw between wanting to see him and wanting to hide from him.

I pass through the open door by three boys staring at me like I'm either the most beautiful creature on the planet, or I have a booger hanging out. Since Jessica Dawson already claims the former, it has to be the latter.

Rubbing my nose, I stop at them. "Did I get it?"

Their faces morph from adoration to she-actually-talked-to-me to what-the-hell. Without waiting for their response, I head out the door. Booger or not, I have to face Daniel.

CHAPTER 9

My gaze fixates on the floor as I hurry into the Yearbook room. I already know where he'll be sitting. That his backpack will lay claim to a spot he saved for me. His face will be set in keeping-it-cool mode, but his green-golden eyes will crinkle with anticipation. Just the thought of seeing his eager yet chill face twists my stomach like my ex's new girlfriend in one of her impossible yoga poses.

Peter. If I'm thrown back in time, does that mean he met someone else that night at the bar? Someone else who'll see the rock of who he'll become under the pudgy softness of his computer engineer exterior?

My insides never reacted when I saw him. Never squeezed like a juicer trying to get past the scar tissue of teenage heartbreak. Never sizzled like a piping hot plate of fajitas. Instead, seeing Peter warmed me like the gradual heat of the rising sun. He was the gentle rain that followed the thunderstorm of Daniel.

"Josie Berry, did you become a vampire during the summer?" The Yearbook teacher, Mrs. Mitchell, stands at the front of the room with her glasses practically dangling off the end of her nose. If it weren't for the ornately jeweled eyeglass chain they'd fall off. "You don't need an invitation to enter, dear. Especially if you have Lestat behind you." She giggles at her joke. There's something incredibly creepy about sharing a book crush with a teacher.

"Just getting a feel for how the undead roll."

Daniel straightens at my voice. His gaze drops to the empty seat beside him. A simple look that says so much.

Sit with me. I'm worried about you. We need to talk.

"Em, can I wake up now, for real?" The words are tucked into an exhale.

"What's shaking, Berry?" His words are cool, nonchalant.

I take a deep breath, chastising the image of Jessica's impossibly long legs wrapped around Daniel's toned and tanned back. We aren't dating. He's not mine to possess. At that thought, an adult Emily hisses in the back of my head, *'yes he is.'*

Is that real or imagined?

"You know, world domination," I try on my brightest, airiest, not-a-damn-thing-wrong voice. Luckily it still fits. "You?"

He turns in his seat and leans in. Golden flecks twinkle in his eyes like the sun bouncing off Lake Travis. "That's funny; I'm also pursuing world domination. Hmm…what happens if it comes down to us and we have to battle it out?"

"Well, if you surrender, I promise to make you my most treasured subject." Did I so overtly flirt with him like this in high school? If I did, yay me. I'm even more badass than I give myself credit for.

Somehow it feels different. Like the time I finally lost all the baby weight and could slip back into pre-pregnancy jeans. They fit, but they didn't. As much as sitting here with Daniel in Yearbook class feels like near-*déjà vu*, something was still different. Like royalty-free music that's just a beat off from a major hit.

The twinkle in his eyes dulls to a concerned glow. "You okay, Jo? You look like you spaced out. Where'd you go?"

Maybe I'm looking at this all wrong. What if this is real and the last twenty-something years was a dream?

"Sorry, was trying to think of all the ways you can prove your loyalty to me."

How could that be? I know things. I know Kurt Cobain will take his own life, devastating an entire generation. I know that at the end of this decade we'll all think we'll face a computer-generated apocalypse, only to realize when we wake up hungover on January 1, 2000 we're all fine.

I know we'll face global tragedies that equally pull us together and break us apart. Not to mention, I know I'll find an all-consuming love when the nurse hands me a red-faced, swaddled baby girl, and again when my serene, watchful son is placed in my arms for the first time.

I know all this as surely as I knew my name is Josie Berry. That I'll become Josie Gardner in a sunset ceremony. That instead of my father walking me down the aisle, my mom grips me tightly, and we held each other upright.

I know the day after graduation, this beautiful boy sitting next to me, the one I trust with my most precious secrets—secrets I didn't tell anyone, secrets I barely tell myself—will walk out of my life, never to be found again.

"Josie?" Daniel's voice is far away. Across space and time. "Are you okay?" He never calls me Josie, or even Josephine. It's either Jo, CuppaJo or my last name. "You look like you're going to be sick."

I push a strand of faded-pink hair off my clammy face. The room wobbles. Relics of nineties computers lining the wall bounce in my vision, like the bouncing white ball of a kids' sing-along show.

Mrs. Mitchell speaks disjointed words. Something about designing a yearbook we'll be proud of, that this is our legacy to the school.

Maybe this is it. Maybe Em is calling me out of whatever psychotherapy get-in-touch-with-your-infant-self BS she put me under.

I grip the edge of the desk, bracing myself to get whooshed into the present. If this is really happening, if I'm going to end up back in my normal life with my stretch marks and saggy breasts, broken marriage, and crumbling business, with only one of my best friends still speaking to me, I have to say it.

I have to tell Daniel what I've kept locked away in my heart for so long that it stole the love I should have given to my husband.

"I don't know how much time I have." My words come out low

and breathless. The edges of my vision grow dark, like speeding toward a dark tunnel. I can only see his eyes around the approaching maw. "I'm sorry. For whatever I did, will do. Don't leave me. And, I l—"

The darkness snatches me in its talons like prey.

CHAPTER 10

The thing about realizing you passed out is how thoughts fly through your head like they're spun up by a tornado. Did I hit my head? Does Daniel think I weigh a ton? Did I drool? Or worse, did I pee on myself?

Apparently, Daniel carried me down to the nurse's office after my fainting spell, but he's nowhere around when I wake up. Just a nurse who lobs question after question at me like I'm the lone dodgeball player left on the opposing team.

"What drugs have you taken? Do you smoke? If so, how many packs a day? Do you drink? Are you sexually active? Have you eaten breakfast?"

The questions come so quickly that I can't manage to break in with an answer until the nurse sneezes. "None. No. Not really. No. Yes."

She looks at me, blinking behind thick glasses. Maybe this means I passed some sort of test.

"When was your last period?"

I gnaw on my lower lip, pretty sure 'thirty years from now' isn't an acceptable answer.

Voices outside the door save me from an answer that would send me to a home for troubled teens. Relief loosens Mom's face when she sees me sitting upright.

"Josie, I'm so glad you're okay." She wraps her arms around me, effectively turning on the eye spigot.

The sob croaks out and my shoulders shake with each wave of tears. This isn't where I belong. Not anymore. I belong with my kids.

I should have woken up. Should be comforting Aubrey as she adjusts to being just another teen with divorced parents. I should be telling Ben that life is short, but childhood is shorter, and he just needs to be a kid for God's sake, and telling Peter to shove his custody papers up his butt and reminding him that dating someone half your age doesn't make you feel younger, it just reminds you how old you really are. I should be reassuring my team we're going to be okay, that this was just a blip and we'll come out the other end stronger.

Mom holds me until the tidal wave of tears ebbs to a trickle. The nurse slips away. The deluge must have made her think this is more of a job for the school counselor.

"Josie-bear," my mother coos, tucking a strand of hair behind my ear. "What hurts?"

My heart, but I'm not prepared to explain any further. I open my mouth to breathe life into a non-committal lie, but she cuts me off.

"I know, it's overwhelming. All the changing. Sitting at the beginning of an ending and the edge of a beginning. It's exciting and terrifying at the same time. We tried to prepare you for it, but something about becoming a parent makes you forget what it's like to be a kid." Mom takes a deep breath and pastes on a smile that doesn't touch her eyes. "No matter what happens, your father and I love you. We are proud of you and will always support you."

"Thanks, Mom."

We sit there for several minutes.

Me studying a younger version of the woman I talk to every day on my drive home. Kids growing up is so in your face, but parents aging is much more subtle. Like the sun moving across the sky. We come into the afternoon of their lives and stay as they gradually age into the night.

"Well, since you gave them quite a scare, I think the school would happily send you home for the rest of the day. What do you think? I'll make grilled cheese sandwiches. We can watch some soaps. Pretend it's summer one more day? Why don't I drive us, and Em can take you to school tomorrow? Just in case it happens again while you're driving home."

"Sure, Mom." Before, I would've argued I was fine. Call it a maternal courtesy, but I would've said the same to Aubrey. "That's a great idea."

I heave my backpack on my shoulders and follow my mother out of the room. We're nearly to her car when Mom speaks again.

"I almost forgot. Mrs. Fry told me you dropped AP Calculus for Home Ec?"

"Yeah, I don't think I'll use Calculus much in my career."

"Okay, but Home Ec? I guess I always saw you as a CEO instead of a homemaker."

The thing is, I didn't actually pass out on the first day of my senior year, not the first time around. I didn't switch to Home Ec. I suffered through AP Calculus the whole infuriating year. If this were real, if I did fall through some sort of quantum-leap-space-time-wormhole that propelled me back to the start of my senior year in high school, am I doomed to repeat my same mistakes? Is the past set in stone, ready for me to fall into the same path like ruts in a road?

The soap operas barely register in my mind. The first panic attack, the one in my office, replays on slo-mo. The pressure of feigning normal with my kids, of keeping it cordial with my ex, of not just running but growing a small business.

All of it pressed down on me until I was nothing more than a heap of tissue and bones. Tissue and bones and eyes that locked on a drawing Daniel left on the windshield of my car the morning he disappeared.

After doing some homework, not that any was assigned, but I should at least practice what I always preach to my daughter, I came downstairs to find that Mom had the table set for two.

"Where's Dad?"

"Oh, he has this thing." She doesn't look up from the casserole she's plating, not giving me a chance to see the lie in her eyes.

If I am here, truly back in my seventeen-year-old self and experiencing my senior year of high school again, can I stop my parents from divorcing?

Can I help them remember the love they have for each other? If so, maybe Dad won't die of a heart attack just two years from now. A heart attack brought on by his only child blaming him for the end of his marriage.

After dinner, I sit in my window seat, the blank page of my journal open in my lap, a pen waiting to share something meaningful, the dying sun to my right. Movement across the backyard snags my attention.

Daniel pulls up the aluminum blinds of his window. With one side of his mouth tugged into a crooked grin, he holds a large sheet of sketch paper to the glass.

I lean forward, forgetting that my seventeen-year-old eyes still have perfect vision.

It's a drawing of us. Me draped across his arms, head resting against his chest. His face pinched tight with worry. If I drooled, he was kind enough to leave it out of the picture.

My window sticks, a hitch Dad always promised to fix but never got around to. I finally slide it open. Warm air, heavy with the dying embers of summer trickles in, mingling with the air conditioning like kids from differing cliques hanging out together at the school dance.

Daniel takes the picture down and slides his window open.

"Hey, thanks for taking me to the nurse."

The other side of his mouth pulls up. "I think this means I win. You know, world domination."

"How so?"

"Well, obviously, you were just so freaked out that I might beat you, you passed out."

I straighten, leaning my elbows on the grimy windowsill. "What if I were just testing you? To see if you can carry me around. By the way, I hope you didn't throw your back out."

He laughs, a sound as crisp and clean as cotton sheets. "I'm only two months older than you, Berry. Don't put me in an old folks home yet."

The tree rustles between us, throwing daggers of dying sunlight across his tanned face.

Why did it take us all school year to finally admit how we felt?

Strike that.

Daniel admitted it.

I freaked out and ran in the other direction.

"How are you feeling?" he asks.

"Tired, but mostly okay. How was the rest of Yearbook?"

He shrugs. "You know, Mrs. Mitchell reminding us this is the time of our lives, and we have to design a yearbook to remind everyone how important this moment is when in reality, we're going to forget it all in just a few years."

"Sounds like I didn't miss much."

The sun sinks lower, in about as much hurry to end the day as I am to say what's on my mind. "Daniel…"

"Berry," he says over his name.

Nervous laughter hangs in the air like summer humidity.

"You go first," I say. "You're currently dominating the world."

Daniel shakes his head, sun-kissed waves moving like a wheat field in a gentle breeze. "Nope, ladies first."

I take a deep breath. Can I do it? Change everything with a single admission?

If this is real, if I did travel back and tell Daniel how I felt, what happens next? We could spend the year as a couple.

Maybe go to college together, get married, build a life.

A pain kicks in my gut, like Aubrey when she was in my womb. My little tap dancer. That's what Peter and I called her. The child was so anxious to be in the world she kicked me the entire time I was preg-nant. Then there was Ben. He'd only move if I poked at my belly.

If I say what's in my heart, will I lose my children? They may not exist at this moment, but they will one day, and the promise of them, of getting back to them, is the only thing keeping me sane.

The words perched on the tip of my tongue crawl back down my throat.

"Did we have any homework?" It's the most chicken-shit cover-up.

He agrees; it's written all over his face. Daniel opens his mouth, but a shout from deep inside his house covers up whatever he was going to say. The shout is followed by a bang, either a fist to a wall or the slamming of a door.

His handsome face flashes rising-moon gray. He glances behind his shoulder. "Umm, not really. I'll see you tomorrow. Night, Berry." The window slams shut, the blinds crashing down.

The late summer frogs squawk what a fool I am.

CHAPTER 11

It's funny how people think fainting in class is contagious. The sea of students part as I make my way into the building, like I have a particularly deadly strain of leprosy.

The morning classes fly by like clouds passing outside a plane's window. When I make it back to Yearbook, Mrs. Mitchell is especially attentive.

"Josie, do you need some water, dear? Is it too warm in here? You'll let me know if you start feeling dizzy, won't you?"

"Of course, Mrs. Mitchell, it was just all the excitement of the first day."

The second bell is ringing when Daniel slides into the room. He keeps his gaze on the floor and falls into the chair next to me without glancing in my direction.

With the teacher focused on the blackboard, I nudge him with the toe of my sneakers. "Hey, everything okay?"

He perches on the stool at the desk, his body taut, as if he might spring into action at any moment. Daniel's gaze is on the notebook paper in front of him, his hand making quick, dark lines; nothing that forms an image. Just darkness. Golden brown strands hide his eyes, but his jaw is rigid, his full mouth a thin line. "Oh, sorry, did you say something?" He jerks his head up only slightly.

Did I see all this clearly at seventeen? How he would retreat into himself, only to slowly crawl out of the hole. It wasn't a secret his home life wasn't great, but something about looking at him with an additional thirty years of life experience parts the rainclouds of youth.

"Just said hey." I want to encourage him to talk to me, but I know it'll only scare him off. I'll have to talk to Em about how to approach the subject.

Shit. The Emily I have lunch with next isn't a therapist yet. Maybe the skills are already there?

"Hey," he whispers back. Daniel straightens suddenly, as if remembering it's me, that I have a bird's eye view into the distinct differences of our fathers.

There's nothing he can hide from me.

"What about you, Berry? Am I going to have to catch you and throw you over my shoulder again like a hay bale?"

"You didn't carry me like a hay bale?" I act affronted, rearing back.

A ghost of a smile slips across his mouth. "How do you know? You were too busy drooling."

"I did *not* drool." At least, I hope I didn't.

"Ms. Berry, Mr. Palmer, would you like to share your thoughts on the theme for the yearbook with everyone else?"

The silence of everyone looking at us is as thick as a Houston summer.

Laughter dances in Daniel's eyes. He isn't necessarily a rule follower, so getting called out doesn't bother him.

It shouldn't bother me, but heat radiates from my core as if a bomb had detonated. I clear my throat and give him one last pleading look. "Well, yeah, we were thinking about, well, how about a *Back to the Future* theme, where we make predictions and stuff."

Chalk scratches out my words, and the room exhales.

"Do you think we'll all have flying cars in the 2000s?" Daniel whispers on a light chuckle.

"Yeah, that doesn't happen. The best we get is a car that backs into a parking spot." The words fly out of my mouth before I can stop them.

His stare probes me, checking for antenna growing out of my head or anything else that might label me as crazy. "Maybe I should catch you quicker next time you faint."

The end of class bell rings, and students pop up like zits before homecoming.

The cafeteria buzzes, a hive of hormonal bees.

Emily and Sofia are already at our spot, the end seats of a long table with a view of the outside common area. This table is reserved for seniors, with freshmen starting at the far end, tables closest to the tray drop off and trash bins. With each passing year, we're elevated away from the powerful stench of half-eaten food and toward the utopia of picnic tables, shade trees and blue sky—a literal progression to our freedom.

"Do you know how many girls want to faint in front of Daniel Palmer today?" Em says through a mouthful of iceberg lettuce. "Poor guy will have his hands full. Literally."

I open the bag Mom packed for me. It's the epitome of a nineties lunch. Lunchables. Snackwells. String cheese and an apple. I guess I shouldn't feel so bad about forgetting my kids' lunch occasionally.

"Are you feeling okay? Should you have your blood sugar checked?" Sofia asks.

Did she become a doctor? She was always trying to diagnose things, quick to patch up scrapes and cuts, bandage turned ankles.

My gaze at her must be as heavy as a two-ton truck.

She narrows her dark eyes, a harshness faintly crosses them before she dashes away.

Has it begun? The fracture of a friendship.

I peel back the plastic film of my Lunchables and make a cracker sandwich. "I'm feeling much better. Nothing a little processed meat and cheese can't cure. Hey, Sof, are you thinking about medical school?" Maybe I can plant the seed, see what it grows into.

Her eyes brighten and dull like a flickering light. "I dunno, we'll see."

A memory peeks around the corner of my mind. Money was

always tight in Sofia's home. Her dad worked odd jobs, and her mom was a cashier at the local grocery store. Luckily our town is still more small town than suburb in the nineties, so the battle for parental professional dominance isn't a thing.

Which means that my insurance broker parents sat squarely in middle class. Emily is an anomaly of the time. After her parents' divorce, her dad moved to Houston where he set up a successful plastic surgery practice, and her mom is one of the few real estate agents in town.

"I can help with scholarship applications if you want," I offer Sofia.

That lands me another hard look and my friend diverting her attention to her bowl of cottage cheese.

"Have you ever thought about hooking up with Daniel?"

As much as I want to kiss Em for breaking the building tension, I don't want to pick at the scab of my secret crush.

"I swear that guy comes back hotter every year. If you hadn't dropped calculus, I bet we could've come up with a formula to determine his peak hotness." Em winks.

Is forty-something Daniel as hot as seventeen-year-old Daniel?

He'd have filled out some, maybe even added another inch or two to his already six-foot frame. His hair could've gotten cut short, but I hope not. Light lines would radiate from his eyes, not deep, just enough to add a bit of interest, to make him sexy.

"The way you're making out with that cookie means you agree with me."

The piece of meat I throw at Em slaps against her cheek. Her blue eyes widen for a second before she flicks a leaf of iceberg at me.

"Ladies, I'm so glad to see you haven't grown up too much over the summer," Mr. Martinez, the principal, wanders behind my friends, hands clasped behind his back. "Just a reminder, you're seniors. Role models now. With great power comes great responsibility."

We sit up straight and clasp our lips tight. Emily and Sofia's faces turn red from holding back laughs.

"With great power comes great responsibility." Em mocks as soon as he moves on from his drive-by chastisement, and we erupt into another fit of giggles.

The bell rings, ending lunch. I hurry to the center of the high school for Library Aide period. The much-coveted credit is usually snatched up by seniors. The job is pretty simple, help peers find resources, re-shelve books, and when all that's done, get a head start on homework.

I find the librarian in her office behind the check-out desk. "Good afternoon, Mrs. Patel. I'm so sorry about yesterday. Hopefully, I didn't put you too much in a bind."

She smiles warmly. Her gray-streaked hair is pulled into a low bun, the gray-blue kurta with a beautiful paisley pattern draws me in and calms my racing heart.

I've been waiting for this period since I woke up four days ago. Somewhere in the rows and rows and shelves and shelves of books has to be an answer as to why I'm here, how I got here, and most importantly, how in the hell I'm going to get back to my time.

Mrs. Patel wraps me in a tight hug. "It's so good seeing you, Josie. I'm glad you're doing well. And, lucky for you, you have a partner this year."

"Hi, Mrs. P." Ruby Bell huffs into the room and drops her heavy backpack. The girl's dishwater blond hair hangs limply down her back.

Just one click away from being pretty, Ruby has a broad face, still beet red from a sunscreen-less summer. She's tall, but not in a Jessica Dawson fashion-model sense, and boxy, as if genetics drew a rectangle for her body type and shoved her inside.

Ruby and I were best friends during second grade, or at least part of it. Mostly because we ended up in a class of almost all boys and we had to band together. Even during that year, the friendship was built on a foundation of discomfort. Ruby always wore clothes two sizes too small and two seasons out of date. She laughed at inappropriate times. Made jokes that missed the mark like a blind boxer.

The failure of our young friendship cranked up the tension to DEFCON 2, an exposed wire on our uneasy truce just waiting for a spark to set it off.

"Ruby."

"Josie."

I drop my backpack in a cubby behind the checkout desk and grab an armload of books that need re-shelved.

What became of Ruby after high school?

Maybe prison. As either a warden or inmate. Or, she could've become a door-to-door solicitor. She had a knack for showing up when you didn't want her.

"Josie, Ruby, let me show you something we got over the summer," Mrs. Patel calls us over to a desk shoved against the wall.

A behemoth computer takes up half of it. Hard beige plastic holds a thick black screen. A floppy disc drive sits open, like a hungry cat begging for food.

"We were awarded a grant to digitize the library. We'll be one of the first in the state. In just a few years, we won't even need a card catalogue." The librarian beams like a proud momma. "I'll show you how to use this later, but this will be our project for the semester. Ruby, I need your help shelving some books up high."

She skulks away with Mrs. Patel, leaving me alone with the ancient machine.

"What are the odds you have internet?" I whisper to it.

A quick shake of the mouse and the screen slowly wakes. A green cursor blinks. Crap, what are the old DOS commands?

I click a few random keystrokes. The computer responds with a judgmental tone. I move the mouse around the screen, hoping a start menu will pop up. No dice.

"Shit. What am I going to do? Google how to go forward in time?" I whirl around, making a mental note that I'll try again once I know how to do more than make the computer judge me.

Three boys stand in front of me. Shoulder to shoulder to shoulder, like denim and cotton T-shirt-clad soldiers ready to wage battle against the gorgonzola monster, or whatever the hell that was called in Dungeons and Dragons.

One is tall and reedy, with the sharp angles of someone who grew quickly, and his muscles are trying to fill in the gaps. His dark hair is long on top, bangs grazing his eyes.

How often did his mother tell him to get a haircut?

His Michael Jackson Thriller T-shirt grazes the top of his jeans. A treasured shirt he's going to hold on to until it became a Britney Spears-era belly shirt.

The boy in the middle is shorter, with dark skin and warm dark eyes. He, too, seems to have had a recent growth spurt, but instead of a too-short shirt, his jeans are two inches above the tops of his white Air Jordans.

The last boy is somewhere between the first two in height, but he probably outweighs the other two combined. His vintage Atari T-shirt stretches across his wide middle, the already-faded screen print cracking and peeling.

"So it's true, huh?" The heavier one says.

"You're into time travel." The tall one adds.

"Quantum mechanics, wormholes. I bet you're even into quarks." The short one says, his brown eyes wide with awe.

Are they speaking as a collective brain?

"Em, seriously, this would be a good time to wake me up," slips out the side of my mouth in case this is still hypnosis. "Can I help you find something?" I add, louder.

"How was a googol going to help you?" The short one asks. "Are you writing an algorithm?"

"You weren't exactly asking typical first-day-of-school questions in Physics yesterday," the tall one says.

Ah, yes, that's where I've seen them.

The boys who'd stared, as if I'd suddenly sprouted a horn from my forehead and had a rainbow trailing from my butt as I walked out of the classroom.

I brighten like the sun on virgin snow. "Well, just getting ahead of college admissions. It's competitive out there, you know."

They trade glances.

"Okay, but you're a girl," the heavier one is the unfortunate soul to speak.

I hitch one hand on my hip, going full Mom-mode in zero to sixty. "I will have you know that Neanderthal thinking like that has cost us a generation of brilliant, young *female* scientists. We are more creative and intuitive. There is no reason that girls, women, can't do *exactly* what guys can do. It's institutional thinking like this that holds us back." My voice echoes around the library.

Mrs. Patel clears her throat. "Josie? Everything okay?"

I tamp down the fire simmering in my gut. What if these guys hold the key to returning me to my time?

My kids. I dropped Calculus for Home Ec for goodness sake. I'm not exactly a beacon for feminism these days.

"Sorry, Mrs. Patel, just helping these guys with a research project." I turn my attention back to the trio. "Okay, we can talk after school. I have cross-country practice at four, so it'll have to be quick."

The guys look at each other.

Atari T-shirt nods. "Let's meet in the computer lab."

CHAPTER 12

The computer lab is as dark and quiet as a tomb. In some ways, it's an appropriate atmosphere for a room holding the ghosts of technology past. A life of mistakes past.

I glance at my watch. Three-twenty. If these guys don't show up in the next ten minutes, I'll have to bail for practice.

Ugh, cross-country practice. My fainting spell got me excused from yesterday's practice. Would my seventeen-year-old body, six-pack included, be able to complete the grueling run in the late-August Texas heat with a forty-something's mentality? Or will all those aches and pains project onto my lean and lithe body?

"Josie, thank you for coming." Atari guy speaks as he enters. His voice has the same serious timber as a doctor doling out a death sentence.

I fold my arms over my chest. "So, you know who I am, but forgive me, I don't believe I know your names. It's been a bit of a…well, crazy week."

"Of course, you probably don't know. I mean, you being a girl; which is not a sexist statement, it's just that you probably don't look at guys like us," the tall one says, holding out his hand, his voice as soft as Ben's blankie. "Jake Beebe."

The boy in the Air Jordans holds out his hand next. "Matthew Fraser."

"And that would make me Stuart Lohenstein, but you can call me Lowey." Atari T-shirt chimes in.

"Nah, I'm good with Stuart. I'm Josie Gar—" I hide the near slip in a cough. "Josie Berry. Okay, so first of all, this is all hypothetical. Repeat anything I say, and the entire football team will descend on you like an all-you-can-eat pizza buffet." I hate pulling the hard-ass card, but it's been four days since I put the fear of God in anyone. I'm long overdue. "Got it?"

Three heads nod.

"Okay, so yeah, I'm interested in time travel." The admission feels like an elephant getting off my chest.

"Is this applied or theoretical physics?" Matthew asks.

I shrug. "Which is more real?"

"Okay, so are we talking interdimensional time travel?" Jake's hand cups his chin, reminding me of Ben.

"I have no clue. I just—" The words snag in my throat.

Can I say it?

Confess to them what I've barely been able to confess to myself. That Emily isn't going to wake me up. Either I'm doomed to repeat one of the hardest years of my life, or I'd suddenly been thrust back into the beginning of a *Choose Your Own Adventure* book, and I'll have to try a different path in life.

I sit on the edge of a desk; not trusting my legs to hold me up if I breathe life into what I need to share. Also, I'm not sure any of these guys can carry me down to the nurse's office.

Or that I'd want them to.

"I just want to go home." My voice shatters like a dropped plate. "And, not my parents' house, but mine, thirty years from now. With my two kids and husband who's divorcing me because he got tired of loving me more than I loved him, and who can blame him?" I push off the desk and cross the room to look out the window, feeling the need to move from their wide, judgmental eyes.

The marching band is practicing a formation, the sun glinting off their brassy instruments.

"I need to go home to fight for my kids, for my business." I turn back to the room, half expecting it to be empty, but the guys are still there, each wearing a different mask of disbelief on his face.

"How did you get here?" Jake asks.

I throw my hands up in the air. "If I knew I wouldn't be here with you, I'd already be reverse engineering my way back."

Stuart cocks a thick eyebrow. "We're going to need some proof. Like lottery numbers."

"Seriously, you expect me to remember some random group of numbers? I routinely forget where my keys are."

"Okay, will the Cowboys win the Super Bowl again?"

"I dunno, maybe?" I search my memory for something I can give them to prove I'm not crazy. Prove to them and myself.

"How about this? We have the opening football game this weekend. The team will lose. Badly."

Stuart snorts. "You have a fifty-fifty chance of getting that one right. And that's generous. Our team sucks."

The big controversy at the start of my senior year floats to the top of my memory. "The team won't just lose; they'll be obliterated. Jeff Turner's dad will be so pissed, he'll demand the coach to step down immediately. There'll be school board meetings, drama. It'll be quite the thing."

The trio exchange looks heavy with a silent conversation. The kind of conversation that could only be had with lifelong friends. Emily, Sofia and I did the same many times.

"Do you know who'll be valedictorian?" Matthew asks.

"I'm pretty sure it's one of you?" I roll my eyes with such enthusiasm that my daughter would be impressed. "Guys, please, I want to get back to my time. I promise if you can help me, I'll give you some good insight into the twenty-first century."

"Okay, if the game is an embarrassment and Jeff's dad does what you say, we're in," Stuart said.

I glance at my watch. I'm going to have to sprint to make it to practice. "You guys are awesome. I have cross country, but let's catch up Monday in Physics." I jog past them and out the door but stick my head back inside. "Remember, not a word." I give them my best mom-eye, but it's probably not as effective coming from a seventeen-year-old's face.

I'm the last at the track for practice. Daniel searches over the heads of the other runners, his gaze brushing against mine, lighting up his lopsided smile. "Hey, was starting to worry that you'd passed out again." He grips my shoulder for balance as he stretches a quad.

My skin pulses under his warm touch.

"Sorry, got hung up with something. What's the route today?"

"Hitting some hills."

Great, nothing like blowing out a hamstring on my first run back in my teenage body.

The coach calls us into a huddle and reviews the route he'd set up for us. Three miles out, nothing but hills, and then three miles back, also nothing but hills. Punishment disguised as exercise.

We start with a light jog. Daniel holds back, running beside me when he could easily kick it in and lead the pack.

"Hey, so last night…" His voice trails in a series of heavy huffs. "I'm sorry I disappeared like that."

I barely hear his words. My mind is focused on the weightless feeling of my feet striking the ground. The hitch in my right knee is gone. My hips are as loose and free as a bird fleeing its cage. Hell, as far as I can tell, I'm running without my bladder leaking.

I kick it up to a faster run.

Daniel calls after me and catches up. "What are you doing, Berry?"

I can't contain my excitement. "Running! This is awesome!" I turn up the speed again.

Heavy breathing trails after me. "Careful, or coach will think you're on speed or something." Daniel lowers his voice. "You're not on speed, are you?"

Why does everyone think I'm on drugs?

Probably because it's much more likely than being a time traveler from thirty years in the future.

The first hill looms. A steep one I'd run and cursed many times during my high school cross-country career. "Race you to the top." I turn my imaginary gear shift into overdrive and shorten my stride and quicken my steps.

Daniel comes into my periphery. Sweat glistens on his tanned skin, his tank top is cut nearly to the bottom, the muscles of his stomach flex as he pumps his arms. "I'll always catch you, Berry. Running or fainting." With a laugh, he blows right by me.

I watch him run ahead, admiring the view when dread expands in my stomach like I'd inhaled a bag of popcorn with a soda chaser.

Am I now officially a dirty old lady? Is my ogling of Daniel creepy?

Because while my body is seventeen, I'm having very mature thoughts about him right now.

Is being a cougar a physical thing or mental?

I slow my pace, letting the guys pass me to catch up to Daniel and I take my place at the front of the pack of the girls.

The feel of my feet striking the concrete, the late afternoon sun warming my face, the fluttering in my stomach when Daniel looks at me; all of it feels as real as the moment when Aubrey rode her bike without training wheels.

What if I'm not really hypnotized, or dead?

What if by some strange turn of the screw I actually fell back in time.

The long shadows of the trees thrust the runners ahead into darkness before they blink back into the light. Summer lingers in the air like a teenage boy with heavy-handed body spray.

We crest the next hill, and only part of the road ahead is visible, the other obscured in valleys and curves. Country roads jut off to the side, leading to another path, another option for the driver.

This is a down-and-back run, but I don't have to live a down-and-back life. If this is a gift and not a curse, maybe this time around I can take a side road, a different, better path. One that won't end in a broken family, death, or a broken heart.

This time around, I can be the detour.

The sign that diverts the people I love from making terrible mistakes. That keeps the people I love in my life.

CHAPTER 13

The van carrying the cross country team from our meet swings into the high school parking lot late Saturday morning. The upside to cross country is that we're usually done by noon. The downside is we start at the ass-crack of dawn the morning after football games.

The team piles out, dragging duffel bags, muddy running shoes, and, for everyone but me, dragging ass. It about killed me, but I'd placed first in the meet. My first time around, I was never motivated enough to do better than middle of the pack. This time, there was nothing better than kicking much younger butt than mine.

With a wave, Daniel hops in his old farm truck for his part-time job. Everyone else scatters to likely crawl back into bed and sleep like normal teenagers, leaving me alone with an old-enough-to-buy-beer El Camino.

Once the parking lot clears, the doors open, and Stuart, Matthew, and Jake emerge.

"It was 50-0," Stuart says as if it were the first time I'd heard the final score of that horrendously embarrassing game.

"My grandfather said this morning at the donut shop Jeff's dad was telling anyone who'd listen he would get the coach fired," Jake adds.

"We believe you," Matthew says. "We'll help you."

Those simple words, *we believe you, we'll help you,* carry the weight of a tugboat.

I slump against the side of my car. I have no clue how I got here, and no clue how I'll get back to my time, but hopefully these three small-town geniuses can figure out something that no one in my present time has mastered.

I nod, swallowing my urge to shout and crush them in hugs. "Thank you. I can't tell you how much it means to me."

Stuart plays it cool, lifting one shoulder as if it's an everyday occurrence for a teenage girl to admit to him she's a time-traveling middle-aged woman. "Can you meet us back in the computer lab Monday after school?"

"Do we have to wait until then? Can't we start today?"

Stuart tosses his keys into the air while keeping his gaze on me. Instead of catching them, they fall to the cracked asphalt with a clang.

I stifle a groan. Why in the world did I think these teenagers could have any grasp on time travel when they can't even handle gravity?

"As much as it appears we have all the answers, my crew and I have to do a little research this weekend. But don't worry, you've come to the right people."

The threesome climbs back into Stuart's car. It isn't so much that they're the right people, they're just the right-now people. The right in front of me people, even.

When I get home, the house is as quiet as an uncomfortable dinner party. It's not unusual for Mom and Dad to go into their insurance office on Saturday mornings to meet with clients who work during the week or get caught up on paperwork. However, this feels different. As if the entire house is holding its breath.

The answering machine's red button flashes like a spoiled child needing attention. I click the button, and Dad's voice fills the air.

"Hey pumpkin, we're going to be out for a bit so if you don't have plans with the girls, feel free to order a pizza. We left cash in the cookie jar for you. See you later, love you." His voice sounds tired, but there's also a lightness to it.

Could he and Mom be off on a romantic day date? Trying to find themselves and who they were before I came along?

I wasn't a hard kid, didn't demand much attention. This was a time before kids were over-scheduled and parents developed rotors to hover over their every action.

I grab a non-diet soda and a bag of full-fat, high-sodium chips, because yay metabolism, and head to my bedroom. It could be a week or, God forbid, a year before I return to my time, but no matter how long it is, I can use this time for good. Accidents can be prevented. Lives can be saved.

Hearts don't have to be broken.

I grab my journal and settle into my window seat. Movement in the yard behind ours catches my attention.

Daniel's dad is bare-chested, a cigarette barely clinging to his mouth as he pushes a lawnmower. He's not as tall as his son, and his hair still military short. He's lean, with just a paunch of a belly.

His dad would mow a line down the small backyard, stop, and take a drag. Back up the other way, limp over to the metal table on the patio for a pull of beer. At this rate, it'll take him all day to mow the yard.

It isn't so much the sins of the father that's the concern, but the unfulfilled destiny. How many sons feel the need to finish what their fathers started?

How many daughters fall into a tedious existence because it's what their mothers did? Is that what happened to Daniel? Ran away to join the military like his father?

Is this what's happening to me? Finding myself on the downward slope of a failed marriage?

I pry open the locked vault of my memory. My parents' divorce was finalized after I graduated. Dad had already moved into an apartment on the other side of town, and Mom started talking about moving to another area for a fresh start.

Daniel left his portrait of me—the one that hangs on my office wall—as a bittersweet goodbye after I stupidly rejected his declaration of love. Anything before that was lost in a haze of senior pranks, traditions to mark the end of a twelve-year journey, and rites of passage.

I flip to a blank page in my journal and scribble across the top. *Bad stuff that happens.* Not exactly eloquent, but it gets the job done.

Mrs. Patel breaks her ankle. This dominated my memory for some time after it happened. The librarian was up on a ladder, shelving an armload of books when she lost her footing and fell.

I was on the other side of the bookcase. There was no sound, just the snap of her bone as she fell. The break was bad and never healed correctly. The last I'd heard, Mrs. Patel had to use a cane, but worse than that, the light that drew us to her like moths was snuffed. If I can stop her from climbing that ladder, the break will never happen.

I'm sure in some philosophy class they'd argue that this would be the equivalent of clipping a butterfly's wings, but I'll risk it for Mrs. Patel.

Mom and Dad's divorce. This I can change. I can make my parents realize they still have so much love between them, that whatever they're going through, this silent war that hasn't broken any dishes, rattled any walls or made their teenage daughter cower in fear, isn't worth ending a life they'd built together.

Problem with Sofia. I still don't know what's broken, but regardless, I have to do everything in my power to protect our friendship.

I lean my head against the wall and watch the waning sun slip away into the night. My whole body tingles, as if I'd finally stretched after a long, uncomfortable flight in the middle seat of the middle section with the person in front of me reclined into my lap.

The more time I spend in my past, a past that feels as close as the moon, the more I fall into the gravitational pull of my former life.

Memories I thought were as lost as my waistline after my second pregnancy float past like dandelion seeds. They aren't as solid as the memories of Aubrey's last dance recital, a cynical teen miraculously turned into a graceful swan as she swept onstage. Or Ben having a very grown-up conversation with me after Peter moved out, reassuring me that he had no problem stepping up to be the man of the house.

Those memories are solid, but these have the wispiness of passing clouds taking a shape I recognize before morphing into something else.

A flood light from Daniel's house flicks on, illuminating the half-mowed yard. His waif-like mom slides the backdoor closed behind her and stands barefoot in the middle of the yard, arms wrapped around her body. Even across the distance, I can make out the tears streaming down her face.

Did I ever pay much attention to Daniel's mom when I lived behind her?

Sure, I'd see her occasionally, but she was a nurse and worked odd hours. Did it take becoming a wife and mother to notice all the wives and mothers that had passed through my life in need of a smile, a kind word, or even a safe place?

I turn back to my list, needing to get it completed before the clouds of memories clears and my mind fills with nothing but an unblemished future.

Ian Phillips dies. Our senior class tragedy. I remember hearing warnings of this as a kid growing up. It usually came with a reminder to always wear a seatbelt, don't do drugs, make sure you're wearing clean underwear, and never drink and drive. They should've also told us to never swim in the cold lake while drunk.

I take a deep breath and with a shaking hand write the final item on my list.

Tell Daniel the truth.

That's the easy part.

The hard part is to figure out which truth to tell him.

CHAPTER 14

Monday tests the law of time, and not in the way that will send me back, forward, to my kids and the twenty-first century. Words flow out of the teachers' mouths like they rode on a tide of frozen molasses, and the class periods move as slowly as the world under a hot Texas summer sun.

I find myself fidgeting, fighting the urge to hop to the front of the classroom to help speed the teachers along.

Finally, the dismissal bell rings. While the student body rushes to leave the building, I race up the stairs to the computer lab, to meet my team of mad scientists.

The guys are already there. Stuart gnaws on a pock-marked pencil and leans over a spiral-bound notebook that already looks like it's been around the block a few times this semester. His dark hair is mussed, but not in the hot-actor-pretending-to-be-above-caring sort of way. Continuing his affinity for video game shirts, a *Donkey Kong* shirt stretches across his middle.

Matthew drums an anonymous tune on the cover of his Trapper Keeper. His gaze planted out the window, as if trying to make sense of the bright blue sky.

Jake paces at the back of the room, one hand hitched on his hip, the other tracing imaginary symbols in the air as he mutters either mathe-matical equations or religious tongues. A lock of his dark lanky hair flops over his left eye.

"Hey, so you guys have it figured out?" I ask.

They freeze, as if I'd caught them with a dirty magazine, a bottle of lotion, and a sock.

Stuart straightens and puts his pencil down, changing his posture from geeky teenager to austere adult. "Before we begin, we'd like to discuss our terms."

I cross my arms in front of my chest. These guys have no clue that I've spent the last few years negotiating with ornery kids. "Oh? But you've already agreed to help." I pause, waiting for the flinch of capit-ulation. "All right," I drop my arms and hold back an eye roll. "What are your terms?"

His gaze flicks to his friends. "Stock tips." Stuart adds a shrug as if it isn't a big deal to ask me to commit fraud.

"It's illegal for me to give you stock tips. Insider trading. Martha Stewart went to jail for it."

Jake perks up. "Martha Stewart goes to jail? I can't wait to tell my mom!"

I pinch the bridge of my nose. That's right, it's still a good decade or so away before the lifestyle icon spends time in jail. Trying to keep timelines straight between what's happened and what will happen is giving me a migraine.

I pull out a chair and sit. "Look, we need to have an understanding if this is going to work. I don't know if I'm already influencing the future, for better or worse, by just confiding in you guys. You have to promise me, anything I do or say stays between us. You're the only ones who know. Not Emily or Sofia, my parents, or even Daniel." My eyes burn with the realization that I can't trust the people closest to me, but I can trust these guys—faces in a yearbook I barely knew.

Then again, how many deepest, darkest secrets are spilled to a stranger on an airplane?

I take a deep breath. "How about this, at a future date, maybe as we're getting closer to figuring out how I can get back to my time, I'll give you three things that can help you in the future. I need to have time to think it though." I narrow my eyes, "And, you guys need to prove that you know what you're doing."

Stuart pulls up the chair across from me and folds his body into it. He leans forward, forearms on his thighs, and lowers his voice. "Answer me this, do we," he motions between us, "have a chance in the future?"

I meet his posture. "Not on your life," I add a wink, hoping it would diffuse my words. Quite frankly, I'm not sure what becomes of Stuart. For all I know, he could've gotten as hot as Matthew McConaughey. I'm almost single, I might as well keep all my future options open. I lean back. "Not yet, at least. We good?"

The boys look at each other, another silent conversation, and they nod simultaneously.

Stuart sticks his hand out. "Your terms are acceptable."

I meet his palm with mine, almost expecting it to be clammy but I'm pleasantly surprised to find it warm and strong. Hell, maybe Stuart and I do have a chance in the future.

"So, what have you guys come up with?"

Matthew clears his throat. "This weekend was filled with researching time travel, more specifically the possible types of hardware, vessel if you will, that might be required to make an interdimensional time jump."

"Ohhh-kay, but I didn't arrive in a *vessel*. I woke up in the bedroom of a home my mother sold nearly thirty years in my past. There was no spaceship or time machine."

"We're gathering all the information we have access to in order to formulate a hypothesis on how you got here and how to get you back in your time." Jake jumps in to rescue his friend.

I exhale a deep breath. "Fair enough. So, did y'all go into Austin to use the libraries there? There's got to be good science-y ones at UT, right?" Even though there is a nascent Internet used by the military at this time, I have serious doubts these guys had any sort of clearance to access it.

Instead of answering, they each employ a different avoidance tactic.

Stuart studies his cuticles.

Matthew toes a crack in the linoleum with his immaculately clean sneakers.

Jake picks at a piece of the veneer of the desk that was flaking away.

"Guys, what did your research entail?"

The honking of the marching band practicing outside the window answers.

"I have a fifteen-year-old daughter. My ability to wait is off the charts. I've also honed my BS sensor, so out with it."

Stuart caves faster than a dropped soufflé. "Let me start by saying many scientists look for inspiration from unconventional places."

"Stuart."

"And many of the greatest inventors in history didn't just sit around and wait for an idea, they perused books and such."

Seriously, this kid might even beat Aubrey at her own game. "Okay, so you went to the library and read some books."

"Well, not exactly the library-library."

I inhale, hoping it'll fill me with patience and push away any murderous thoughts. "Stuart, so help me, if you don't spit it out, I'll sic the entire football team on you. And yes, they had their asses handed to them, but my guess is they could still inflict some harm…plus, they're probably looking for a way to get out some aggression." To punctuate my point, I take two steps toward the door. "I can probably catch them at the end of practice, and you know that was rough."

"Josie, wait." Stuart hangs his head. "Maybe it was more videos than books."

"Videos."

"*Back to the Future*," Jake says. "The whole trilogy."

"And, *Doctor Who*," Matthew adds. "But then we realized that wouldn't help since we don't have police boxes here."

I fold my arms again, not to have *the mom* stance, but to stop myself from shaking with fury. "Let me get this straight, you spent the last two days watching a marathon of movies?"

"Well, we watched a few episodes of *Quantum Leap* I had taped—" Jake says.

My barely contained anger breaks through the thin barrier. "Do you think this is a joke? I am *not* meant to be here. I'm supposed to be thirty years from now fighting to have custody of my kids, trying to figure out how to keep my business afloat after a disastrous deal, and I'm supposed to do all of that with a smile because that's what good mothers do. We put up with a swirling shitstorm in skinny jeans and heels and blowouts that still look good three days later."

The edges of my vision grow fuzzy and the marching band sounds like they're being carried off with a tidal wave. I grip the edge of the desk to stay upright. "Look, I have people who depend on me, and I don't know if my timeline just stopped or if they are going on without me. I'm afraid the longer I'm here, the more likely I'll wake up and have lost everything: my kids, my business. My sanity."

My breathing slows, and with it the dark edges of the room recede and the brass horns of the band bleat like sheep. It's only once my awareness fully floods into this body that is mine but feels as foreign as a faraway land that I feel the wet heat from tears streaming down my face.

Matthew moves first, wrapping me in an embrace so tight my arms are glued to my side. Jake moves in next, followed by Stuart. We sit there, a huddled hug of teen angst before their over-done body spray burns my eyes.

"Okay, thank you, but I kinda need to breathe now."

The guys disperse and fall back into their seats; their faces pinched in focus and concern.

"Tell us everything you remember," Jake says.

I recall being in my office, the pressure of fighting for my kids, and the contract with Bixby's falling apart. I leave out the picture from Daniel hanging on my wall. It's a part of my past—my future—that's still too raw.

Matthew straightens. "It could've been a medical event. Sounds like a panic attack. I used to get those before tests."

I nod slowly. "Yeah, that's possible. If that's the case, is this real? Did anything like this happen to you?"

He stares at me for a second before shaking his head. "No, I'd just get really freaked out. Couldn't breathe, heart beating fast."

"And you've never had any weird time-space portal issues at your office before?" Stuart asks.

"We had some mice when we first moved in, but no, no random portals to another world," I say.

Jake flicks his pencil against the side of his head. "This could be philosophical, a test of some sort. The Greeks always put their heroes through excruciating tests to ensure they were worthy."

The guys exchange glances again. Maybe one of these days I'll figure out their silent conversations. Then again, I hope not to be here long enough to pick up on it.

"This is what we'll do. We'll tackle it from different angles," Stuart says. He points at Matthew. "Medical." Then Jake, "Philosophical," and then himself. "Physics. Give us a few days to research and let's meet back here Thursday."

The boys stand, but I'm not convinced my legs are ready to carry me out of the room.

"Josie, we're sorry this happened to you. And, for what it's worth, we'd do it even if you didn't have anything to tell us about the future."

Only after their squeaking sneakers recede, the last of the horns from the marching band fade away, and the roar of the floor buffer fires up that I let go of the sob that threatens to strangle me.

CHAPTER 15

The exchange with Stuart, Jake, and Matthew played through my head well into the next day. What sort of voodoo propelled me back to the start of my senior year? Am I bound in a coma replaying a pivotal year in my past?

A year when everything seemed possible, but adulthood smacked into me with a tidal wave of responsibility, regret, and the realization happiness that's only on the surface can't support the weight of a marriage.

That's just as plausible as the fact that this is real, I had somehow gotten sucked back into the early nineties. What will it be like to face the same decisions with the knowledge of one path? Do I explore others, or hold steady to the path I'd taken with a clear view of the potholes and bumps?

Possibilities and questions play through my mind like a basket of kittens, darting one way and then the other, hissing and booping their way to the surface, only to be pulled down by another thought-kitten.

If I'm here for philosophical reasons, what's the decision to catapult me back to my present? I mentally go down my list, tucked away in my journal buried at the bottom of my backpack. Is it something as simple as keeping Mrs. Patel from breaking her ankle? Or could it be something bigger? Something like keeping my parents together or saving my friendship with Sofia. What about something as huge as pursuing a relationship with Daniel?

I chew on the inside of my cheek. Is it worth sacrificing my children for that? Whatever force sent me back wouldn't make me choose between the children I have and those I might have with Daniel.

Right?

"Josie, you're welcome to stay for another round of Physics, especially since you weren't paying attention during the first go at it." My teacher's voice throws a bucket of ice water on my musings, pulling me back to an empty classroom.

"Um, sorry, I'll be going." I grab my backpack and hurry by my locker to pick up lunch before meeting the girls in the cafeteria.

I drop my lunch bag at our spot at the senior table.

Emily is already there, absentmindedly munching on a celery stalk, her gaze laser-focused on Jordan Chambers. "Em, you're drooling."

My friend runs her hand across her mouth, red touching her cheeks like a fleeting thought. "How did we not notice how hot he is?"

A memory bubbles up from the depths of my mind. Emily had developed a massive crush on the basketball star after he'd shot up nearly half a foot during the summer. It was a crush unrequited. Like most teenage boys, Jordan didn't have a clue that the petite brunette with huge crystal blue eyes was in love with him.

I study the boy. Golden blond hair that's just shaggy enough to look cool when he needs it to, but can still comb it back for church. In addition to shooting up several inches, his body broadened about the same. A deep tan makes his blue eyes look as deep as the sea.

Emily could, and will, do much worse. Maybe I can encourage her to do what she'd been too afraid to do the first time around. If I can encourage her to go after Jordan, to do more than stare at him like he's a glass of water and she'd been wandering the Sahara, then maybe I can save my best friend the heartache of a terrible college break-up and a lifetime of meaningless flings.

"You should ask him out," I say, returning my focus to Em.

"Are you freaking kidding me? He'll think I'm desperate." She shakes her head, her long hair whipping her face. "Nope, not gonna happen."

"He could be *the one*."

Emily lifts a shoulder. "Well, he needs to figure out that *I'm* the one. I don't chase boys, I run from them."

I can't stop the laugh rushing from my mouth. "I'll remind you of that in a few years."

Sofia hurries into the cafeteria. Instead of lunch, she carries three bigger-than-she-is textbooks. "Hey, what did I miss?"

"Emily discovered that Jordan Chambers is a Greek god but also developed a sudden case of shyness," I say. "Where've you been?"

Sofia reaches into Em's bag of celery and pulls out two stalks. "Just had a few things to do. Stopped by to say hey before running to my next thing. See you after school?"

She pushes herself up, but I can't let her disappear as quickly as she appeared.

"Sof," I grab her hand, not just holding her back from escaping the lunchroom table, but from escaping my life. "You know if you need anything, we're here for you." I add my other hand to the grasp. "Anything."

"Ohh-kay." My friend's brown eyes flit around the cafeteria, either afraid we'll cause a scene, or unwilling to let me see the truth. She pulls her hand free. "I gotta go. Later."

I watch Sofia's retreating back. Her wavy dark hair swishing with every step away from me.

"Okay, freak, what was that all about?" Emily pulls me back from the past—the future—into the present.

"Do you think something's...odd about Sof?" I hate what I'm doing. Breaking a sacred vow to never talk about each other behind our backs. It's how the three of us retained such a close friendship for so many years. We're all equal. If someone has a problem, we all three talk about it.

I have to do it. I have to call attention to the cracks in our friendship that result in Sofia severing all ties. Maybe I can save it.

As a forty-something, I should have the emotional mortar to cement a crumbling friendship from my teenage years.

At least, I hope.

Emily stares at the door where Sofia escaped. "I dunno, maybe? She has been pretty busy lately. What do you think it is?"

I study the white Formica-top cafeteria table, searching for the words that will plant a seed of hope, of bonding, rather than something that will grow and fester and divide us.

Maybe I don't have this magic bullet. Maybe it doesn't matter if I'm forty or fourteen; the words to save a friendship before it disintegrates are hard to come by, not because of how they leave my mouth, but how they might land in Emily's ears.

"She's been…distant." I test the verbal waters, checking to see if it's freezing cold or if I'm on to something.

Emily's teeth snap another celery stalk. "You know, you're right," she says between crunches. "I can do some investigation, like *Murder, She Wrote*, but without someone dying, you know."

I withhold a cringe. Despite her small stature, Em is about as discreet as a drunk elephant. "Maybe nothing quite as covert, but let's keep an eye on her, just to make sure she's okay."

With the subject of Sofia pushed aside, we spend the next several minutes of lunch strategizing the purchase of Pearl Jam tickets, including an incredibly complicated plot claiming to spend the night at each other's houses just to have an alibi to camp outside the ticket box office.

"There'll be a day when we look back on this fondly as we click a button to buy tickets on our phone without the need for sleeping on concrete with questionable smells around us."

"And get stuck in busy-signal hell?" Emily says. "No thank you. I'd rather spend the night among the homeless to make sure I'm as close to Eddie Vedder as possible."

I hide my near-flub in a long pull of my soda. My gaze darts to the food line.

Daniel stands in profile with Jessica Dawson next to him. His tray loaded down with square slices of pizza, and Jessica carries a single baked potato.

"Now who's drooling?" Emily's voice is full of sass and understanding.

Daniel turns and catches my eye, nodding in acknowledgment and heading my way.

"He's like a brother," I say.

"But he's not. He's the hot guy who looks at you like you hung every star in the sky."

Daniel drops into the seat next to me. His hair is tousled, like he constantly runs his hands through it.

Does he still have this thick head of hair wherever he is three decades into the future?

"What's up, Jo? Hey, Emily." Daniel tears into a slice of greasy pizza.

Does he still have a youthful metabolism and six-pack abs in the future?

"Fueling up for cross country?" I ask.

"Gotta keep up with you, Berry," he says through a mouthful of food. "Speaking of fueling up. There's a new Italian place in town, and I'm thinking of carb-loading Friday for Saturday's race. Wanna join me?"

I swallow, my mind racing to remember what I'd done thirty years earlier. Sure, Daniel and I had eaten together plenty of times, but never when I knew he was in love with me.

Never when I had the opportunity to change the trajectory of my life.

Of everyone's life.

"Su-sure, yeah, I can do that," I stammer over a response. When did I start being nervous around Daniel?

"Cool." He shoves the last slice of pizza in his mouth, his cheeks puffing like a squirrel with a face full of nuts. "See you at practice." Daniel pushes up from his seat and carries his tray to the conveyor belt.

"One day, you two will make beautiful babies." Emily punctuates with a carrot stick.

I watch him leave, my eyes trailing him, so my best friend won't see the tears building up like rain clouds on a hot, humid day.

CHAPTER 16

The next two days fly by in a blur of college-ruled paper, ringing bells and lots of unanswered questions. Both in class and in my life.

I sit in the sprawling library in the center of the high school, a place where I find peace and solace in the crush of teenage hormones and a pre-menopausal brain. Maybe it's because the librarian, Mrs. Patel, feels more like a kindred spirit than a teacher. Or the fact that among the stacks I feel timeless. It doesn't matter if my brain is forty-seven and my body is seventeen, I'm all the same inside.

I'm shelving books when a *psst* cuts through the silence.

Stuart, Matthew, and Jake cluster around the small physics section, each loaded down with books.

"Hey guys, did you find my way home?" I keep my voice so low it can win a limbo contest.

Stuart tilts his head toward mine. "We think you could be dying." Where my voice is conspiratorially low, his is a theatrical stage whisper that echoes around the library.

"I can assure you I'm not dying."

Jake jumps in. "But can you be *sure*? You said it was a panic attack or something. A medical event, like a heart attack or an aneurysm."

"Yes, but I think I'd know if I were dead."

"It could be purgatory."

I take a deep breath. "For some, reliving high school could be purgatory, but it wasn't particularly hellish the first time around. Just… there might be…" My voice fades like the dissolving contrails of an airplane. The words sit there, perched between my heart and my head.

Can I push them over the edge, tell these teenage boys I barely remember, who may or may not be a figment of my imagination that I might have accidentally flung myself back in time because of a boy? Way to be a beacon of girl power.

"Look we need to know all the variables." Stuart crosses his arms and levels a heavy gaze on me.

Somewhere in the future—present—he'd be a formidable dad.

I look over my shoulder. The library is mostly empty. A couple of flannel-clad freshmen sit at a desk, their jeans slouching into a pair of Doc Martens like teenagers with bad posture.

Ruby sits at the large check-out desk. Her stringy dishwater blond hair hangs free, curtaining her face from the world as she bends over a spiral notebook.

Somewhere nearby, the faint humming of Mrs. Patel wafts through the rows of books like a lilac-scented perfume.

I beckon them to the political science section, an area that's as appealing to teenagers as an early curfew.

"I have a working theory. What if I came back here to do something different?" I whisper. "What if I have to change the past to change the future?"

"That could be seriously catastrophic," Jake says, shaking his head. "The Doctor was always careful to not change history."

Obviously, his *Doctor Who* marathon proved useful.

"I know, but I made a list of things that happened, *will* happen." I stretch up, looking over their heads to make sure no one is coming. "Maybe one of them will be the key that sends me back to my time."

"What's on the list?" Stuart asks.

Jake throws an arm across the other boy's chest, mom-arming him from whatever might come out of my mouth. "No, you can't know."

"Right, messing up the order of the universe," I say. "Little things." I shrug. "Big things."

Mrs. Patel comes around the corner. A stepladder hitched on one shoulder of the diminutive woman, an armload of books weighing down the other. The librarian lowers the stepladder, kicking its legs apart.

The hinge opens, not quite locked into place, glinting in the overhead fluorescent.

Is this when Mrs. Patel shatters her ankle?

The woman takes the first step on the ladder, and it shimmies like that pooch on my stomach that never disappeared after having Ben.

"Things like this," I whisper. "Mrs. Patel, wait," I say louder, hurrying down the aisle. "Let me."

I take the books from her hands and lock the ladder in place before climbing up to deposit them.

"Oh, goodness, Josie, that could've been bad. Thank you." The woman continues down the row, her humming fading.

I turn back to the boys. Their faces convey a rainbow of thoughts.

Stuart's skeptical.

Jake's pale complexion seems almost translucent.

Matthew furrows his brow. I can almost see equations flashing behind his eyes.

"What was supposed to happen?" Jake asks.

I take a deep, steadying breath. They've believed me so far. Or, at least pretended to. "Sometime during our senior year Mrs. Patel falls off a ladder and shatters her ankle. It never healed right, and she eventually had to retire early. It was tough for her and her family. This may have been it, or it could still happen. I don't remember exactly when she fell. You know, thirty years ago, things get fuzzy."

"And, yet, you're still here," Stuart says.

I look around. The Dewey Decimal System stares back at me. "I'm still here," I sigh. It's silly, really, to think that saving a teacher from breaking her ankle is the catalyst to my impromptu time travel. A forty-something girl could wish.

Matthew straightens, lifting his chin to almost be at eye level with me. "We got your back, Josie. We'll figure this out, one way or another."

A loose smile tugs at my cheeks. Wherever my kids are, I hope they can be this kind to someone who pops into their lives with a crazy-ass tale. "Thanks, guys. I don't even begin to know how to thank you."

Stuart shrugs. "Stock tips."

The boys leave, lugging their heavy books and oversized egos out of the library.

I put away the last few books in my arms and return to the checkout desk. Ruby's chair is vacant, but the heavy scent of her shampoo hangs in the air. It's an overly sweet smell covering up something with a chemical tang, like people who put on too much perfume to cover up the smell of smoke.

I pull my backpack from under the desk and rummage around until my hand hits the crushed velvet cover of my journal. I thumb to my list. *Bad stuff that happens.*

The words 'Mrs. Patel's ankle' stare up from the list. In the silence of the library, my number two pencil makes a checkmark next to them.

I keep my gaze on the list. Did that do it, or will I need to stay vigilant throughout the year? Did I simply kick the can of destiny down the road?

As my eyes study the list, searching for what I need to fix next, my skin tingles with the sensation of a thousand ants crawling over me.

I jump, jerking my head up and rubbing my arms, just in case a thousand ants are crawling on me. Instead of finding insects, I find Ruby staring at me from the card catalog.

Her gaze is hard, her mouth set even harder.

Without breaking eye contact, I slide my journal back into the backpack. Hoping that my actions are completely natural, even though my heart and mind fidget like a sprinter at the starting line.

CHAPTER 17

I stare into my closet. At a time in my life when I really need couture, I'm faced with early nineties teen angst plaid, flannel, and denim. Then again, wearing any of my current, well, future, clothes will look sorely out of place.

The weather is cool, back when October nights were filled with the chill of autumn and the heat of teenage hormones. My time-traveling abilities can't will forward my favorite silk top, which, quite frankly, will be two sizes too big, so I pull out a knit T-shirt with cap sleeves to pair with wide-legged jeans and a corduroy jacket. My well-worn and frankly, much-missed, Doc Martens round out the outfit.

I pause, studying my reflection. The girl staring back at me has Ben's nose and Aubrey's mouth. She has thirty years of love and loss, heartbreak, and happiness, packed tightly into a body that still has a lifetime ahead of her.

My long strawberry blonde hair is thick, shiny, a long way from that first gray hair that'll accost me early one morning shortly after Peter and I started sleeping in separate rooms.

The face in the mirror is smooth and taut. That little bit of discoloration across the bridge of my nose from too much sun is still a few years off.

"Maybe I came back just to remember to wear more sunscreen," I say to the reflection of my younger self.

I've been back for just over a month now. While I ache to get back to my time, there's something nice about being back in a time of my life I can never revisit, in a place I can never revisit.

With people I can never revisit.

Instead of this being something to run from, maybe I need to settle into it. Remember who I was thirty years ago. Spend time with my friends. Enjoy the gift of spending time with Dad. I need to appreciate it, even if I don't understand why it was given to me.

I roll a bit of lip gloss on my lips and grab my purse.

The house is darker than expected when I get downstairs. The kitchen is clean. The countertop scrubbed down like Mom does at the end of the day. A subtle signal I picked up with my kids. If the counters are clean the kitchen is closed. Go to bed. Except it's just a little after six-thirty on a Friday night. Mom should be bustling around the kitchen making sure Dad and I get all our food groups in.

The tinny echo of voices pulls me into the dark den. I study Dad's profile, his face lit by the blue-white light of the television. His auburn hair, more red really, reminds me of Aubrey.

Childish laughter draws my attention to the television. A toddler plays on the ocean's edge. Giggling and chasing the receding waters, only to squeal and run back toward the video camera when the next wave comes in.

It's me. A home movie I'd seen more than a few times growing up. Back when taking video was the exception, not something I've done from the inside of my purse by accident more than a few times.

The camera leaves me and finds Mom. Her hair blows across sun-kissed cheeks.

"I love you, Patty," Dad says in the video. "You've given me the world."

Mom shyly looks down and then back out toward the ocean, likely checking to make sure I'm still fine.

"I love you, Alan. I love our little family." Mom looks at the camera. A soft smile, reserved for lovers, full of secret language and stolen moments, kisses her mouth. Her eyes soften, no doubt studying the man on the other side of the camera.

A sniffle followed by a shuffling on the couch pulls me from the video.

Dad stands but pulls up short when he sees me.

"Hey, Josie Bear. Didn't see you there." He clears his throat. "You look nice. Going out?"

"Yeah, Daniel and I are grabbing some food. Carbing up before tomorrow's race. Where's Mom?"

My father rubs his chest.

Is this where it starts? Maybe his first heart attack is when his marriage begins to crumble, not when his only child, his whole world, blamed him for the end of a relationship.

"Oh, she's out." His voice is as thin as skim milk. "With some friends, I think."

Heat flares through my limbs. My mom's friends are the same as Dad's. Sure, there might have been nights where Dad would play poker and Mom had book club, but it was the same circle. They never did something if the other didn't have plans.

Is Mom straying?

No wonder Dad died. His whole world, his wife, and his daughter, rejected him. How do you will your heart to keep beating in the face of that?

"I can stay in, if you want some company." Suddenly I want to be there, with Dad watching old home videos, asking him to tell me silly jokes, dole out life advice, and to keep talking until his voice wears out.

"No, pumpkin, you and Daniel have a good dinner out." He grabs a folded-up paper from the coffee table. "I've got the Sunday cross-word to finish before it's Sunday again."

"I love you, Daddy. You know that, right? No matter what kind of jerk I am." I lean over to wrap my arms around him, committing his spice and woodsy scent to memory.

"Always, sweetie. And you know what, Josie, when you're a jerk is when I love you the hardest."

I turn to leave, pausing halfway down the hall to see if Dad starts the movie again, but the house stays as silent as a grounded teenager's phone.

Daniel pulls up to the curb.

Whatever spring I'd had in my teenage step earlier in the evening quickly turns into middle-aged aches and pains as I trudge down the front walk.

"Chin up, Cuppa Jo," Daniel shouts through the open passenger window. "It's Friday night, and you're walking like it's Monday morning."

"Sorry, it's just…" I pull his door shut, but it barely clicks. Damn new cars and their gentle frames, it'll take me forever to learn to slam a car door. Like twenty-first century cars, I'm too soft to live back in the past. "My parents. I think they may be fighting. They could divorce."

He turns in the seat, left hand still draped over the steering wheel. The dying daylight brings out the golden flecks in his eyes and makes his sun-streaked hair warmer. "My parents never fight."

"Well, I'm glad one of us has a stable home life." The words come out with so much bitterness they should be chased with a handful of anti-acids.

"No, what I'm saying is, they don't fight because there's nothing worth fighting for." Daniel grips my hand, squeezing it before letting go to put the truck into gear.

On the drive to the restaurant, my mind chews through the revelation. Have we had this conversation before? Is it possible that Daniel handed me a nugget of advice at the ripe old age of seventeen that could've saved my marriage, but I'd forgotten as quickly as what I had for lunch?

Peter and I hardly fought. Sure, there were a few disagreements over child rearing, or one would always make a big purchase without checking with the other, resulting in a few chilly days and even colder nights. However, as far as drop-down, drag-out, sell-ringside-seats-because-this-is-a-doozy, never.

Daniel clicks the column gear shift into park, rocking the old truck back.

I barely pay attention as we drive, my mind drifting through the ephemera of my failed marriage.

A waitress much closer to my actual age than the teenage body I inhabit tosses oversized, laminated menus on the table of a booth. "What can I get y'all to drink?" Her haughty actions and pursed lips clash with her relatively congenial tone.

Obviously waiting on a couple of teenagers isn't going to line her pockets with tips.

"A glass of your house red, oh, and a water, please." My gaze scours the carb and cream heavy food on the menu.

Daniel bites back a laugh and the waitress's face sours like a forgotten apple.

Damn, seventeen, not forty-seven.

"Haha, just kidding, April Fool's," I say. "Water's fine."

"About six months too early," the waitress drawls. "And for you?" She turns to Daniel.

"A rum and coke but hold the rum." He winks to reinforce the punchline.

"Thanks for covering for me," I say as soon as the waitress is out of earshot. "It's just been a day, and week...hell this school year has started off...strange. Don't you think?"

What I really want to ask is if he's noticed any changes. If the girl sitting across from him is different than the one he saw when he left for his summer with his grandfather?

Do I seem wiser? Does regret roll off me like an early morning fog? Is it clear that I live in two times, that present and future clash within me?

Daniel laughs nervously. "Yeah, I mean, that's part of the reason I asked you to dinner tonight."

The waitress drops off our drinks with a healthy dose of side-eye.

He takes a long drink. "Anyway, so yeah, you know when I came back from my granddad's, I found myself having, well, I guess feelings that I really thought were maybe just one-sided."

I sit up straighter and take a long drink of water. If there's ever a time to develop Christ-like superpowers this would be it. A glass of wine might be the only balm to calm the *bom-bom-bom* of my heart.

"So, I was thinking," Daniel says. "With homecoming in a couple of weeks…I'd really like to ask Jessica Dawson to the dance, but I kinda want to make it special. Maybe you can give me some ideas?"

Bom.

The sounds of the restaurant fade away. No murmuring guests. No clanking of bussed plates. No swoosh of air with the arrival of new patrons.

The only sound filling my ears is an audible exhale.

I scour my memory, trying to pull up any indication of what I should say. Is this why Daniel waited until graduation night to confess how he felt?

I recall Emily's crush on Jordan Chambers perfectly. How can I forget something like this?

Unless…just the presence of my forty-something mentality is already changing things. If that's the case, am I driving Daniel further away?

Maybe that's the way it should be.

"Jo?" The sound of his voice snaps the restaurant back into place.

"Sorry, yeah." I straighten and lean forward on the table. "Yeah, I can help you with that."

Too bad I can't drown my heartache in a bottle of wine.

CHAPTER 18

It's a good thing my parents never drink anything stronger than beer. After spending the rest of dinner brainstorming with Daniel on the best way to ask Jessica to homecoming, I craved a glass of wine, or twelve, like a cactus needing a monsoon.

As much as I wanted to sabotage Daniel's chance of snagging a teenage model for a homecoming date, I can't do it.

He's not mine to keep.

During the cross country meet the following morning, my mind chewed on a morsel of an idea that dinner gave me.

Driving home from the high school afterward, I swing by the nicest restaurant in town. With a seven p.m. table for the Berrys booked, I move to phase two of my diabolical plan.

As suspected, my father's late eighties sedan was parked outside their insurance office. If he were still in that nostalgia of the previous evening, where he watched the love of his life and his young daughter playing on the beach, then this might work. Maybe my parents can remember the deep love they have for each other.

"Hey, Dad," I say, flopping down in the guest chair in his office in the way that only teenagers can pull off.

"Hey, pumpkin." He looks up from the stack of papers on his desk, reading glasses hanging off the end of his nose. "How was the race?"

"It was great! I won." I didn't win, instead placed third. What's a little white lie when you're trying to keep your family together?

My dad drops his pen, awe brightening his already warm face. "Really? That's amazing Josie. We should celebrate."

I lean forward on the desk. "I'm glad you think so. I could totally use a burger from Fergie's. Think you and Mom want to take me tonight?"

The gaze that he held like a father gripping a child's hand on a busy street drops back to his desk. "Oh, I dunno honey, I'm going to be here for quite a while. So much paperwork to get caught up on. Why don't you and your mom go tonight, and maybe I can take you to Reba's for breakfast tomorrow."

I take a deep breath. I didn't expect resistance. I expected my parents to fake it for my sake, like Peter and I faked it for our kids until faking it became so painful it was better to admit the truth.

Were Mom and Dad already past this point? Have they been faking it for so long and, like every other self-absorbed teenager, I didn't realize it until I catapulted back and was a self-aware, can-fix-every-thing forty-something?

"It's almost one. Are you going to spend six more hours here? What's going on? Is there something you aren't telling me?"

Dad lifts his gaze back up. Emotions scurry across his face like a class dismissed to recess. Sadness. Love. Frustration. Hopelessness.

One emotion causes me to crash back against my chair. It's one I'd been feeling more and more with Aubrey.

The realization your kids no longer need to be protected. I'd done my job and it's time to start peeling back the parental protective layers.

Finally, my father takes a deep breath. "You know, you're right, Josie." He leans back in his chair, meeting my posture. "I don't have to be here that much longer. Sure, let's take you out tonight to celebrate."

I hop up from my chair and nearly knock over his stack of papers while leaning across the desk to plant a kiss on his cheek. I try not to linger, to re-catalog the warm smell that was decidedly my father. "Thank you, Daddy!"

He laughs and straightens his wayward work. "I don't think anyone on earth has been this excited about going to Fergie's."

My heart sings a happy little tune that's two decades away from being written when I see Mom's car in the driveway. I run into the house, dropping my duffle bag at the front door, something I would've chastised my kids for, before taking off through the house looking for Mom.

I find Patty, mom-jeans-covered butt in the air, leaning into the deep freezer in the garage.

Should I ask Mom to hold onto these for the next two or three decades for me?

I snap out of my future-past fashion reverie. This isn't the time for hoarding clothes out of Mom's closet for the future.

I have a marriage to save, dammit.

"Mom!"

Patty jumps, banging her head on the open lid of the freezer. "Josephine Elise! What in the world? The house had better be on fire, young lady."

"No, but I won my meet today!" My little white lie is getting more opaque each time I tell it. "And we're going to Fergie's tonight to celebrate!"

Mom pushes her hair back from her face with fingers winter white from digging in the depths of the deep freezer. "That's nice, you girls have fun." She turns to dive back in.

"No, I meant we, the Berrys, not Em, Sof, and me."

Patty looks between the freezer and me. "Oh honey, I need to defrost the freezer and check everything for freezer burn. This is one of those tasks that once you get started, you have to see it through. It'll take me well into the evening."

I narrow my eyes and push out my bottom lip so far that a four-year-old beauty queen on the verge of a tantrum would be proud. "Are you seriously brushing me off to clean the deep freezer?" My kids don't realize how lucky they have it to grow up in the time of 'making memories.' Being a Gen-Xer essentially meant my mom was responsible for getting me out of her womb, up and walking, and then school, friends, and MTV would take care of the rest. "Your only child is a senior. In just a few months, I'll graduate and go off to college. And you'll be sitting around with a clean deep freezer wishing you'd spent more time with me."

I know the barb will lodge in the soft, mushy center of Mom's heart, right between where unconditional love and tough love reside.

My mother leans against the side of the freezer, arms across her chest with a seen-better-days dishrag dangling from one hand. One eyebrow reaches for the stars and her eyes narrow to laser-focused slits.

I know this look. It's one I've given my kids time and time again. The look that says *don't you play that game, missy*. The look that says *I didn't fall off the turnip truck yesterday*.

The look that calls bullshit.

Seventeen-year-old me would have buckled under that look. However, forty-seven-year old me can go toe-to-toe with the woman who taught me how to parent fearlessly. I meet my mom's stance with my own obstinance.

Finally, she flinches. "You're getting too good at that. I already feel sorry for your future kids."

The mention of my kids, a throwaway comment Mom lobbed as innocently as a whiffle ball lands like a live grenade. Tears sting my eyes like they're under attack by angry bees instead of heartache.

I clear my throat, my voice a child burrowing deep under the covers, afraid of the monster of the truth.

"Something tells me you and my kids will be partners in crime." The words come out thick with love and longing. "Okay, dinner is at seven. Wear something pretty." I cross the distance and tug on a strand of her hair that'd gotten loose from the death grips of the banana clip. I should ask her to save this for Aubrey, too.

Her hazel eyes soften, the skeptical lines on her forehead loosen, and for a second something flashes across Mom's eyes.

Can she feel it? That her teenage daughter was hers, but also wasn't?

Surely, I'd notice if the roles were reversed and Aubrey woke up thirty years older. Right?

"What?" I whisper.

It's Mom's turn to clear her throat. "I swear you're growing up before my eyes. It's like you started your senior year as this new, more mature person. You're going to do great in life, Josephine, no matter what the future throws your way. You'll hit it head-on like you do everything else."

CHAPTER 19

There's something humbling about stepping into the nicest restaurant in town and seeing it with the maturity and worldliness of someone who'd dined at the chicest restaurants in Paris, New York, and London.

All the white linens, delicate China, and tiny portions mean nothing when the warm, affable owner of Fergie's, Seamus Ferguson, greets my parents and me with hugs.

"Alan! How is it that you look more and more debonair every day, you scoundrel? Patricia, I swear you must be aging backward." The Irishman turns his attention to me, and my heart melts a little for what the future holds for this kind restauranteur.

The tsunami of growth heading west of Austin will crash into his establishment, essentially sending him into early retirement.

Last I heard, Seamus was struggling to stay sober and keep up with the latest dining trends.

"Dear Josephine. It hurts me a little to see you almost an adult, because that just means I'm that much older myself. Come, Berrys, I have the best place for you."

We settle into a table near the window.

My gaze roves over the dining room, like seeing a long-lost family member for the first time again. The dark-wood tables are worn smooth, the tops glossy from years of drips, spills, overly harsh cleaners, and diners' elbows.

Wood paneling covers the walls, a look that would make lesser places feel claustrophobic, but at Fergie's, it feels like a tight hug from a beloved grandmother. The waitstaff isn't the typical high schoolers making gas money. Seamus pays well, so many of the servers have been there for as long as I can remember.

Stepping into Fergie's and sitting at my family's favorite table soothes me like a mother calming a child, reinforcing that while things will change, I'll graduate, this building will be demolished for a *chi-chi* West Coast grocery chain, and in three decades my marriage will suffer the very fate I'm trying to prevent for my parents. While all of this may come, for a few minutes I can slip into the past like stepping into my favorite pair of Uggs.

My hand itches for my phone. To text Emily that I'm back at Fergie's, Daniel wants to ask Jessica Dawson to homecoming, and I need a dial-and-dash, our code for one calling the other in the middle of a disastrous date to give a plausible excuse to bail.

Not just to bail me out of dinner with my parents so they can rekindle their relationship.

I need Emily to bail me out of the past. To bring me back into the future, present, to where the past is already set. Where there's no chance of driving my parents further apart or sending the love of my life into the arms of a teenage model.

Where I have no chance of making one small decision that could lead to my children never being born.

"Josie, are you okay?" Mom's voice cut across the desolation brewing in my heart. "You're looking a bit pale. Are you getting sick?"

I touch my forehead with the back of my hand and startle at the clamminess. "I don't know. I suddenly don't feel so hot."

My mother gathers her purse and pushes back from her chair. "Let's get you home."

"No!" My shout echoes off the walls, pausing the pleasant din of conversation. "I mean, I can get myself home. You guys stay."

"Pumpkin, this was to celebrate your win," Dad says. "It wouldn't be the same without you."

I've been looking for a way to gracefully bow out of dinner so my parents can have a romantic evening alone. Feigning sick is one way out, but despite how much of a latch-key kid I was— am—I'd definitely not be walking out of here alone if Mom thinks I'm sick. At least, not if she thought I have anything viral or bacterial.

"Oh, it's just that, well, I think I'm getting my period."

My mother leans back in her chair, dropping the grip on my arm. Like all the moms of the eighties and nineties, Patricia signed the waiver permitting the school to teach me about menstruation and bought me a package of pads and tampons with an instruction brochure when I got my first period.

"Oh, well, I see," my father stammers. "I'm going to wash my hands. This is your mother's territory anyway."

When Dad escapes, I turn in my chair. "Look, I'm okay. You know how bad my cramps can get." It's something Aubrey and I bond over, teenage cramps. "Why don't you and Dad stay and have dinner? How long has it been since the two of you had just a night out on your own?"

Mom's gaze darts to the hallway leading to the bathroom.

I watch, waiting for any flicker of tale-tell emotion that will betray what she's thinking. Instead, only sadness.

Is it sadness because her heart is broken, or she'll break her husband's heart?

Is it because they'll have to tell their daughter they're divorcing, or because she realizes I already know?

Sadness is an invasive emotion. It takes over, quickly drowning out everything else. It's possible to try to cut it back, pull it up, or even burn it, but in the end sometimes it's better to learn to live around it.

The corners of my mother's mouth quirks up and down as if they are trying to pinpoint how they should react. She smooths my hair. "You will always be the best thing your father and I ever did. Call the restaurant and let them know you made it home."

I wait until I'm out of view of the restaurant to do a little fist pump.

The night air is clean and crisp, the only sound is the whisper of the wind as it whisks leaves from the trees. I tug my letter jacket close, both for warmth and for the hug I desperately want to give my seventeen-year-old self.

Will I feel it if my parents rediscover their love? Will I suddenly wake up on my office floor, my worried assistant shoving a glass of water in my hand, Emily on her way to castrate Peter, and my kids happily unaware their mom lost her grip on reality?

I shuffle along another block, only getting closer to my childhood home, no light-headedness, no tightening of my chest, no tunnel vision to indicate I'm about to be hurtled back into my present.

"Oh, come on!" I shout into the night. "Give me some indication of what you want me to do."

The universe is silent, but some dogs down the street voice their displeasure.

My legs suddenly forget their duty. I squat down on the sidewalk, the click in my knee I acquired in my early thirties silent. I should be enjoying this vacation to my youth. I should be partying and buying stocks.

I should be *carpeing the diems*, laughing at fate for giving me the rare opportunity to live twice. Instead, I'm crying on a crumbling sidewalk in my hometown because instead of trying to fix the past all I want to do is make sure my kids are eating their vegetables and brushing their teeth.

"I just want to go home."

Headlights illuminate the ground in front of me.

I stand, wiping the tears and mascara mix from my face.

A truck slows as it approaches.

Even in the dark I recognize the head inside. I'd always recognize him, no matter where.

No matter when.

"Jo? What's wrong?" Concern coats Daniel's voice like melted butterscotch. "Did something happen?"

I peer into his truck to make sure he's alone before answering. "Have you ever been homesick while at home?"

The truck's transmission creaks as he puts it into park. Leaving his door open, Daniel crosses the street and wraps his arms around me.

I lean into him and let him ground me into the past, the present. I can't let him ground me into the future.

"All the time," he murmurs into my hair.

We don't speak the few blocks to my house. That's one of the things I missed most about Daniel. He knew when there were no words, when silence is the only thing that can soothe the soul.

Silence and companionship.

Peter, on the other hand, went into Mr. Fix-It mode. Worn out from a day with a newborn and toddler? Peter was there to take the kids off my hands. Felt like an unfulfilled shut-in? He took to organizing a girls' weekend with Emily for me.

When I was spending more to make my all-natural cleaners than what I sold them to mom friends for, Peter took to working on a cost-cutting business plan.

He fixed everything, except for our marriage.

Then again, it was me that was broken. He made the tough decision that it was irreparable.

"Flash the light if you want to talk," Daniel says when he parked in front of my house.

"Thanks, Daniel. I don't know what I'd do without you." I walk halfway up the driveway and turn.

He's still there, waiting until I got inside the house.

"Actually, I know what it's like without you. It sucks. I don't want to do that again. Okay?"

"You're stuck with me, Berry."

Chances are he thinks I'm talking about the summers he spends with his grandfather. Regardless, I hope those words land exactly where I need them to.

I sleep the unencumbered slumber of a teenager that night.

When I wake, the sun fills my window. I creep downstairs, hoping not to wake my parents. As gross as the thought is, I do hope they had a late night.

At the base of the stairs, rhythmic snoring pulls me into the den.

Wrapped in an Afghan with the recliner extended is Dad, only his socked feet and the top of his face uncovered. The TV paused on another home movie, this time of Mom and me dressed up at Halloween, a big witch and a little witch.

Even though in the video I'm the little witch, I can't help but feel like a huge witch for pushing my parents into what must've been an awful evening.

CHAPTER 20

The last place I want to be Monday morning is the halls of high school for my last homecoming week. *Again.*

The cheers breaking out in the halls, blue and white streamers strewn about in a way that only a teenager with unabridged enthusiasm can find beautiful, class shirts proudly proclaiming the year they're to be paroled from the prison of public education, it's a stark contrast to the crushing silence of my home.

I wait all day Sunday to hear anger-fueled whispers, a slamming door or even an all-out shouting match, but none of it happened. This must've been why I was so shocked and hurt by my parents' announcement the first time.

There was no crashing end to their marriage. More like leaves falling from a tree until the relationship was bare.

Maybe this is why my marriage failed in a similar manner.

I find Emily and Sofia at our spot in the cafeteria. The salad in my container looks about as appetizing as that time Aubrey gathered up all the grass clippings and made me a "salad."

I should be digging into the most unhealthy thing the lunch ladies are serving up, because, metabolism, but no amount of fattening food will soothe the disappointment churning in my stomach.

"Can you believe this is the last year we have to pretend to care about homecoming?" Emily punctuates her question with a snap of celery. "I might miss the banality of it," she pauses. "New SAT word."

I know for a fact Emily will miss much more. Despite her couldn't-care-less attitude she was nearly inconsolable the afternoon of graduation.

Before I can tease my best friend with that premonition, Emily's eyes light up.

I follow her gaze to see Jordan Chambers walk in, clad in his football jersey over faded jeans.

I snap my fingers in front of Em's lovestruck stare. "Earth to Em, need you back over here, dude." I should feel a little bad not being happier for my friend. Emily'll dump him after she meets her next soulmate. "I need to talk to you guys about something." I take a deep, fortifying breath. The kind that blows down stick houses. That blows truth into heartbreak.

"You're finally going to tell Daniel how you feel?" Emily chirps.

I roll my eyes with such ferocity that my daughter would be proud. "I think my parents are going to split up."

"Why?" Sof asks.

"Sweet!" Em squeals over her. "You should ask for a Mustang. Convertible. Red with leather."

"What the hell, Emily." Sofia's dark eyes are wide, her face furrows in a scowl. "She just said her parents might split and you're telling her which car she should ask for?"

Emily's face freezes like a cat caught in the middle of stealing tuna, but then bit by bit realization softens her features. "You're right, and to be honest, focusing on something like a new car is really just covering up how painful it is." A bit of the future therapist peeks out from behind the teenage facade.

The glimpse of my best friend as I know her now makes me even more homesick for the friendship we would grow into.

Emily was the first person I called when those two lines stared back at me when I was pregnant with Aubrey. She skipped happy hours to give me adult companionship when Peter was away on business trips, and I'd been trapped at home with two small children and the torture of brain-grating cartoons on repeat.

Em was the person I called when my husband of eighteen years turned to me one night while watching TV and said he thinks we should divorce as casually as asking me if I wanted another beer.

How I longed to open up to her now like I would in our future. To tell her that I'm forty-seven going on seventeen. That I love Daniel, and it feels as comfortable as the nightshirt I'd been sleeping in since 2002, but also as tight as putting a retainer in for the first time in decades. Even if things look the same, they've shifted while traveling through life.

Movement at the door catches my eye. Daniel walks in, with Jessica at his side. Not like they were together, but their shoulders bumping in a way that seemed less awkward and more intentional.

The teen model was luminous in a way that's completely unnatural. Hair that somehow manages to capture light brown, blond, and red, skin that's the perfect shade of tan without looking like she sits by the pool all summer, and, for giggles, a smattering of freckles across her nose to remind everyone she's still a minor.

I reach back into the recesses of my memory like I'm searching for an ingredient in the pantry to keep me from making yet another trip to the store, looking for any long-festering jealousy of Jessica, but I come up empty.

Was this new because I now see Daniel through the lens of someone with a failed marriage and a boatload of regret for rejecting what was lodged deep in my heart?

Or did something shift, ever so slightly in the universe that inched Jessica and Daniel closer together?

"Seriously, Josie, are you going to let Jessica move in on Daniel without a fight?" Emily's voice cuts across my memory excavation.

"He's like a brother," my standard response passes through my lips before I can catch it. "Anyway, he and Jessica are a better match."

"But he's not your brother. He's the guy who looks at you like you're the only person in the world," Emily said, softer this time. "But if you don't feel that, ask someone else to homecoming." She pauses, a smirk tugs at her mouth as a prelude to the three words that wreak havoc in every teenager's, and hell, forty-something's, life. "I dare you."

I try to fight it. Try to convince myself there's no reason to grant Emily the satisfaction of following through with it. Plus, is it even legal for me to ask a teenager out if my brain is forty-seven?

Going to the homecoming dance with someone meant nothing more than doing that awkward stiff-armed slow dance. I wasn't technically a cougar if I didn't have Botox, fake boobs, and hair extensions, right?

"Fine." I scan the crowded cafeteria. My laser sight settles on Ian Phillips. I could start working on a big item on my list. To save Ian from drowning in the spring. I could use those awkward slow dances to find out if he could swim, and if not, maybe casually recommend lessons.

Mind made as tight as a bed with hospital corners, I push myself up and stride across the cafeteria.

Ian was good-looking in a Vanilla Ice sort of way. Tall and still lanky, but with shoulders widening to welcome another twenty, thirty pounds of muscle weight. His face was shifting from the soft-rounding of adolescence into square-jaw manhood.

Nothing happens when I look at him. No feeling of my blood rushing through my veins. The sun doesn't seem to shine brighter when he's in it. No feeling that I can't turn away from looking at him.

"Hey, Josie," he says when I approach.

"Hey Ian, if you're not going to homecoming with anyone, wanna go with me?" I say with more confidence than a teenager should muster.

He pulls his head back slightly and shifts his eyes to where Daniel and Jessica stood in the lunch line.

Did other people think something was going on with Daniel and me? Was I the only one who missed the signs until I ran headfirst into the biggest one?

"Um, sure, Josie, that would be cool."

I smile, not as a girl who asked out a guy she likes, but as a mother who might save another mother a lifetime of grief. Who knows, maybe Ian has the cure to cancer locked away in that frosted-tips head of his.

As I walk back to my best friends with the strut of a hunter who easily nabbed her prey, I feel a warmth spread across my shoulder blades. Not from something physical striking me, but a sensation that takes my breath away, like being clobbered with a stray dodgeball.

I turn, almost expecting to see a portal back to my time behind me, but instead, my gaze collides with Daniel's as he stands next to Jessica, his tray piled high with food while hers holds an apple and Diet Coke.

I smile and toss a little wave in his direction, but it's met with a narrowing of his eyes.

Did he see me with Ian? It could've been as simple as asking if he had done his homework. Nothing was sealed with a kiss or even a lingering gaze.

I cross my arms over my chest and lift an eyebrow.

He laughs, glances down at his tray, and follows Jessica to a table.

After filling the girls in on my homecoming date, I spend the rest of lunch lost in thought. The first time around, I went to homecoming with Emily and Sofia. Daniel was there too, date-less, dancing through all the early nineties anthems with classmates.

Except for the final dance of the evening. A slow song. We'd just finished bouncing around, fists in the air, screaming the lyrics of a Red Hot Chili Peppers song at the top of our lungs.

The memory from three decades ago was as fresh as if it had happened just days before. My arms around his neck as natural as if I'd placed them there for years. His hands rested on my hips in casual intimacy. I don't remember if we said anything out loud, but through our gazes we were seeing each other in a new way.

As someone to love.

CHAPTER 21

The rest of the homecoming week flies by in a mix of fevered reverie by the seniors and wide-eyed wonder by the freshmen. Since my homecoming date was also playing football that evening, we planned to meet at the dance.

Emily and Sofia follow me home after school that day. It won't take three hours to get ready for the game, but I want to luxuriate in having my two best friends with me again. To truly enjoy this moment, even if I'm still not convinced this is real.

Sofia flips through my CDs, the plastic cases smacking against each other as she looks for just the album to set the mood for the evening.

Em curls up in my window seat, tucking her feet under her. "Have you ever seen Daniel naked?" she asks.

The soda I gulped nearly sprays on my bathroom mirror. "No! Why would you ask that?"

"Just figure you would sit here all day waiting to get a glimpse of his hot naked body." She turns back to the window. "If I had a gorgeous neighbor, I would."

"How are your parents doing?" God bless Sofia for saving me from Em's probing.

I sigh and sit on the edge of my bed. "With you guys here, they'll act like everything is hunky-dory, but when it's just us, it's as quiet as a library."

"But maybe that just means they're comfortable with each other. You know, when you don't have to say anything because you know someone so well. Oh, we should listen to this." Sofia pulls out a Tori Amos CD and pops it into my stereo.

We spend the rest of the afternoon primping in the unhurried way of teenagers with all the time in the world. It's funny looking at how we approached homecoming compared to Aubrey's first experience with it.

Where my daughter and her friends wore dresses just slightly less formal than prom dresses covered by human-sized homecoming mums, we dress up just a little bit more than a usual date night with more manageable mums.

Sofia pulls on a black leather skirt and tops it with a chunky peach-colored sweater. Em dresses next, stepping into a red plaid baby doll dress paired with black tights and her Doc Martens, perfecting the beauty-queen grunge look.

I reach for the denim skirt I wore thirty years ago to homecoming, but Emily knocks my hand out of the way.

"You have a date tonight and a chance to make Daniel want to see *you* naked. You're not wearing this drab thing." She reaches into the back of my closet where an impulse buy she forced me to make lives. The teal dress emerges, as skimpy as I remember it.

Spandex before spandex was blended with other fabrics to make it less hooker-wear and more stretchy-mom-wear, the tank dress brings out my eyes in a way that had taken away my breath when I tried it on during a time-wasting trip to the mall. That shade was made for strawberry blondes with blue eyes, and the cut of the dress made for zero body fat. I never found a reason, or the confidence, to wear it before, but maybe Emily was right. If I was going to try to change things, to keep from sending Daniel to wherever he is in the future, perhaps a dress can do it.

I reach for it and take a deep breath. Probably the last good deep breath before slipping into a contraption that would leave nothing to the imagination.

I anticipate the dress to put up a fight when pulling it over my hips, but then again, skinny, pre-pregnancy hips didn't clash with Lycra. I turn to the side, expecting the pooch of my stomach to poke out, but only flatness stares back.

"Wow!" Sofia says, punctuated by Emily's wolf-whistle.

"What do you think we should do for her hair?" Emily asks Sofia.

Sof narrows her eyes and taps her chin. "Hmm…maybe a high ponytail? Something to see her face."

Em nods. "How about a pretty French twist? Sit."

I watch as my best friend gets to work back combing and tugging my hair into submission. I tear up with a glimpse into my future, well, my past.

My wedding day, the overpriced hair and makeup artist was an absolute disaster. Instead of the gentle waves I wanted to go with my sunset beach wedding, the woman over-moussed and over-curled it, leaving it in a crunchy, crinkly mess only overshadowed by the Tammy Faye Bakker-esque makeup.

Emily found me alone in my room an hour before my wedding holding back tears. With a softness I didn't know she had in her, she'd wiped away the garish face paint and reapplied it with the deftness of someone who had known my face her entire life. After fixing my makeup, she gently brushed my hair into a low chignon. "This will be better for everyone to see your beautiful face anyway," she'd said.

"Am I pulling?" My friend's teenage voice tugs me from the memory of my wedding.

My eyes glisten in the mirror. "Oh no, sorry, just having a weepy moment. I want this to last forever."

We finish dressing and load into Emily's Jeep for the dance.

Em, Sof, and I follow the early nineties hip hop into the high school gym. Balloon arches line the doors, welcoming us into the din of hormones and teen angst. The overhead fluorescent lights were off, a large disco ball hung from the rafters with several spotlights throwing light beams.

"Girls, one day we'll look back and this moment and realize the insignificance of it," Emily says. "I'm going to see if someone's spiked the punch yet."

Sofia and I watch her sashay across the gym floor.

"She's going to miss this way more than she'll ever admit," I say in a break in the music.

"Oh, I know," Sof agrees. "Come on, let's dance before some weirdo asks us to."

I follow my friend onto the dance floor to hop around and dance to a song from the eighties that draws everyone. We shout the song, not caring if it is anywhere close to a key, shaking our young booties, living like we'll be young forever.

It's a moment I want to live in for the rest of my life. My two best friends in my life. My dad still alive. Daniel nearby.

Why did I want to go back to my time again?

Oh yeah, my kids.

A pain flares through my heart. When I first came back in time, all I thought about was getting home, but the more time I spend here, the more comfortable I become living in my past.

I hope Kirsten hasn't tried to become their mom. I can only imagine the holy hell Aubrey would give her. And Ben—he'd pull out all his algorithm talk just to see the woman's pretty head explode.

I try to take a deep breath, but only a nip of it enters my lungs. Sweat drips into my eyes, and my heart threatens to take off sprinting.

"I need water," I shout to Sof.

Away from the crush of bodies, I inhale a deep calming breath. At least as much as the dress allows. I will get back to my kids. I know I will. I have no other choice.

I grab a cup of punch, hoping it's spiked, and fade into the dark corners reserved for wallflowers and couples making out. Another rock anthem starts, keeping the mass of teenagers bumping and grinding.

"Hey, baby, where've you been hiding all night?" Ian appears in front of me as if he teleported from the land of the drunk teenage boys. "I've been looking for you." The words crash together like bumper cars. "Let's dance." He grabs my wrist and tugs me toward the dance floor.

The blasted deejay chose that moment to switch to a slow song.

Ian pulls me close, and the yeasty tang of beer assaults my nose. He wraps his hands around my waist.

I remember my initial reason for asking him to the dance. Ian would never make it to high school graduation. He'll drown at the lake in less than six months during one of the spring keg parties.

"So, Ian, are you a strong swimmer?"

He leans down over me, swaying too fast and off-beat for this song. "Guess so. You wanna go skinny dipping?"

As much as I want to abandon my mission, I have to stay the course. "Um, not tonight too cold. Have you taken swim lessons?"

He pulls his head back slightly. "Nah, my granddaddy taught me to swim. Don't worry, I know mouth-to-mouth."

"Oh-kay, got it. If I'm choking, you'll be the first I call."

We go back to dancing, if that's what you call Ian's sloppy side-to-side swaying with the occasional crushing of my toes. Maybe I should tell him I had a dream he dies in a drowning accident. Would it scare him enough to think twice about diving into the lake?

"Nice dress, Josie. I thought you were pretty uptight, but glad to know you're down to party." His hands travel down to my butt, pulling me even closer to him.

I move his hands back to my waist and step back. "Thank you, but yeah, you thought right." Was Ian this much of a creep? I didn't spend that much time with him to know.

His eyes narrow to puffy slits, and his nostrils flare before his face contorts to sneering anger. "What, you asked me out." Hands move back to my butt, this time squeezing so hard that I'll have finger-sized bruises. "Then you dress all slutty. Don't be a tease."

Ian tugs me closer. This time the dress did nothing to block his growing erection. The little creep is getting turned on. I'm trying to save his sorry butt.

With all the force of a mother separated from her children by some space-time continuum, I push Ian off me.

Shock freezes his face, but it only takes a second for realization to dawn like the rising sun. Ian reaches for my wrist and yanks me toward him.

"Like it rough then?" He snarls.

Like a chemical reaction, my anger mixes with the frustration of being away from my kids for more than two months, churning with the desire to fix at least a few things in hopes of catapulting me back to where I belong so a bendy, young-enough-to-be-my-daughter yoga teacher doesn't end up becoming their mom.

Before I can stop it, my hand collides with his face. The pop from the slap coincides with the space between two songs.

"Would you want someone treating your mom this way? Or, how about your daughter? Not that you're going to live long enough to have one, despite my best intentions. But seriously, why should I even bother? The Me Too movement was sparked by creeps like you. What would your mother think if she saw you right now?" The words tumble from my mouth fast. I can't stop them if I try. Like a roller coaster without brakes, they just keep coming until I crash and burn in front of the entire dance.

The anger in Ian's face melts away, and fear slides into place. "What are you high on?"

Even though another song had already started, no one around us moves.

I glance around and see Em and Sof just on the edge of the dance floor. Sofia's eyes are wide, and Emily's fists are balled tight. Daniel and Jessica stand a few couples away. Her face impassive, but his narrowed eyes are laser-focused on Ian.

"What are you talking about? You too what?" Ian asks, his voice louder as if the crowd of stunned teenagers fueled his faux-indignance.

Trying to slip into my past was about as comfortable as putting on skinny jeans from my twenties after two kids. There's too much life experience to try to pack into the confines of a younger life. It was bound to happen.

I bust a seam, and nonsense spilled out.

I push through the people of my past, out the opposite side from where my two best friends stand. There is no way I can answer their questions or explain myself. I slip out the gym doors and start running.

Not caring that I look like an idiot with short strides due to an impossibly tight dress. Not caring that I pass peers looking at me like I sprouted a horn from my forehead.

Not caring that I probably just pushed the boy I love deeper into someone else's arms.

All I care about is my kids and how I need to get back to them more than I need air.

CHAPTER 22

I keep running until I'm in the darkened halls of the high school. Did I think I could run forward thirty years?

It'd be nice if that were all it took.

I swipe at my face, the back of my hand comes back streaked with mascara. How stupid could I be to think I could play God and stop something from happening?

Maybe Ian dying is what's supposed to happen. What if this was just the start of a disturbing pattern of behavior, and by trying to prevent his death, I might have just caused someone else's pain?

If that's the case, maybe pushing Daniel away is also what's supposed to happen.

I open the library doors. The grand room is empty, lit only by light from Mrs. Patel's office and the greenish-yellow glow of computer screens.

There's something about being surrounded by shelf after shelf of books. Maybe it's the timelessness of words written in the past to be both used and ignored by generations of high schoolers.

A door slams shut behind me. I'm in no mood for my friends' probing or patronizing sympathy in Daniel's eyes. I hurry deeper into the library, sliding into a corner and sinking to the floor.

The tears fighting for release fall down my face like an angry rainstorm. If anyone had to get propelled into the past, why me? Why not Peter? He's the one wanting to rewind time by dating someone half his age. I'm totally fine with being middle-aged.

"Josie? You okay?" A soft voice at the end of the row of shelves calls out to me.

I look up, and there stands the three souls I hope will be able to figure out whatever voodoo I need to get me back to my present.

Jake, Stuart, and Matthew approach as if I'm a wounded animal and might be capable of ripping open their jugulars.

A fair assumption given how furious I am at myself and a young asshole who, despite my murderous inclinations, I still want to grow up to become an older asshole.

I tuck my legs under me and pat the floor. "Just a bad evening. It's hard to know things and want to change them for the better. Maybe things happen for a reason. And then there's the whole butterfly effect and is the fact that I'm here already screwing up the world." I throw my hands up. "Hell, I might be the catalyst for the zombie apocalypse, and when I do get back, it'll be like living in *The Walking Dead*."

Matthew nods, his face pinched in thought. "Want to talk about it?"

I pause, instinct says to hold back, but then I realize these guys already know way too much.

What's another helping of crazy-old-lady on top of it?

"What if you know someone is going to die, and you think you could prevent it? Would you do whatever you could?"

The boys ponder my question for several minutes.

Jake speaks up first. "I see what you mean. You save a life, but was that life worth saving? But is that our place to judge, Josie? Are some things so written in stone that they happen, no matter how you intervene?"

There is so much wisdom in this young man.

"But what if this is one of my tests? As you'd said, the ancient Greeks believed we had to pass a series of tests," I say, my shoulders slumping. "I failed at it miserably."

"Does this person die tonight?" Jake asks.

I shake my head. "It's Ian Phillips, and he dies in the spring. He drowns one night during a party at the lake. It was stupid. The water was still too cold, and on a dare, he stripped naked and dove in. He never came up, and the rest of the school year was just one awful mess of guilt and remorse." Another deep breath fills my lungs. "As a mother, I can't imagine what his mom went through. To see your child nearly reach adulthood only to have it taken away because of a dumb dare."

"Did you tell him he's going to die?" Stuart asks.

"Worse, I might have planted the idea in his head." I recap the conversation during the dance. "What if I gave him the idea to go skinny dipping?"

My tightening chest likely had nothing to do with the ridiculous dress I wore and everything to do with the fact that I might have caused the very thing I was trying to prevent.

"Doubt it," Matthew says. "Something tells me that guys like Ian always welcome an opportunity to disrobe in front of an audience." His warm brown eyes soften. "Anyway, you don't know for sure yet. You might've cast enough doubt in his mind that he thinks twice about jumping in."

"You're probably right, and if he makes it to graduation, it'll be worth me making a giant ass out of myself in front of the entire school."

We sit there for a few more minutes. The guys update me on the progress of their research, well, lack of it in many cases.

Matthew is convinced I'm having a medical episode.

"I don't feel like I'm a figment of a dying brain," Stuart argues.

"Would a figment of a dying brain know it's a figment of a dying brain?" Jake counters. "It's like when you dream about someone, does that person even know you're dreaming about them?"

Sitting on the floor of a partially dark library with thudding music in the background and three teenagers arguing over how to help me feels oddly familiar.

It's not that I've been here before. This is all new to me. Maybe it's the rapport of bickering teenagers that feels like home.

"Okay, guys, I think I'm ready to go home. Give me a ride?" I don't want to return to the dance and face curious glances. I'm sure Em and

Sof will be at my house before the sun is mid-way through the sky tomorrow. And, I could bet my right ovary that Daniel will hang a concerned picture in his window to check on me.

Stuart twirls the keys to his El Camino around his finger. "If someone had told me I'd be taking a pretty girl home on homecoming, I'd've thought they were on drugs."

"Let me be clear. You're taking me to my house, not yours." The corner of my mouth twitches into a smile. Of course, he knew he was taking me to my house, but it felt like something I need to say. I lift my arms. "Can y'all help me up? This dress is a bit tight."

Jake and Matthew grab a hand to heft me upright.

We cross the empty library. A cheer erupts from the other side of the building. Likely the homecoming king and queen have been crowned. I can't remember who came away with the designation. Shows you how much that means in the real world.

"I appreciate you guys following me in here to check on me." I bump my shoulders against Jake and Matthew's.

The boys freeze.

I walk past them several steps and turn. "What?"

"We didn't follow you in here," Jake says.

"Yeah, we heard you come in," Matthew added.

I look to Stuart.

"The dance wasn't our scene, so we came down here to play *Dungeons and Dragons.*"

It's my turn to come to a dead stop. The door opened and banged closed again moments after I came in. Not immediately to be confused as a bounce from when I burst in.

"Huh, maybe I imagined it." I didn't imagine it, but I just can't explain it.

The boys push through the library door ahead of me. I bite back the reprimand of 'ladies first.'

I shiver as if someone's gaze is piercing between my shoulder blades. A glance over my shoulder was supposed to reassure me that nothing is there.

Instead, a shadow moves behind a bookcase.

CHAPTER 23

I often tell Aubrey humanity is blessed with the memory of a goldfish when it comes to making an ass out of ourselves.

She got her first period toward the end of eighth grade. All the other girls in her class had already gotten theirs, so we knew it was coming. We didn't realize it would wait until the regionals track meet. One of the few events of hers I missed because Ben needed a ride to a robotic competition, and Peter was away on a business trip.

Instead of thinking that the cramp in her lower abdomen was the start of her menstrual cycle, she thought it was a side stitch and pushed through the discomfort. Also, instead of realizing her teammates were shouting at her that she was bleeding during her two-mile race, she thought they were cheering her on.

I can see now my advice was bullshit.

Emily and Sofia both leave concerned messages on my answering machine. While lying in my dark bedroom, I see movement in Daniel's room. He pulls open his window and leans out, even in the darkness and across our backyards, the worry etched on his face is as visible as the craters on the moon.

I think about opening my window, chatting with him. After all, I've spent the majority of my life missing him and our conversations.

However, I know what will happen. He'll ask how I'm doing. I'll pretend I'm fine. He'll probe a little deeper. I'll give up a little more information. Then, long story short, I'll end up spilling my heart out like I'm having a breakthrough on a therapist's couch.

I'm in no mood for breakthroughs. Not because of what happened with Ian. I've had plenty of experience with drunk, handsy idiots. I'm not in the mood, because my mind can't stop circling the drain around who else might have been in the library.

Could it have been Emily?

No, she would have come in figurative guns blazing.

Maybe Sofia?

If she overheard us talking about me from the future, that could've scared her away, meaning I might've manifested one of the very things I was trying to prevent, but that gets into a whole level of physics and philosophy my brain just can't handle.

And, if it were Daniel, he would've made his presence known.

Which gets me right back to the outer edges of the mental drain I keep circling. Who was there? More importantly, what did they hear?

Monday morning, I pull my trusty Subaru into my usual parking spot.

Emily parks next to me. The look on her face through her driver's side window told me I was in as much trouble as the time my mom caught us sneaking back into my house at four a.m.

"I wanted to kick his ass, and now I want to kick your ass for hiding from us," she says, hopping out of her Jeep. "I don't know whose ass I want to kick more right now."

"Sorry, Em, I just couldn't."

Her bright blue eyes went from murderous to sympathetic so fast her expressions could have broken the sound barrier. "I know, and I didn't see what all he did, but Stephanie told Chris, who told Jeff, who I overheard telling Jordan that he was all over you on the dance floor and had it coming. They're trying to figure out what you said about 'you too.' Do you know if he's done this to other girls?" She leans close and drops her voice. "Or worse stuff?"

Great.

I try to save a guy's life and accidentally turn him into a social pariah.

I shake my head. "No, I was just mad and saying a lot of stuff."

School passes in a mix of sympathetic glances, accusatory stares, and blank looks. In other words, just a typical day of high school life.

I get to Home Ec as the tardy bell rings. Midway through the semester and we're mastering baking and have started talking about planning a week's worth of dinners. I'm assuming that's without a meal delivery service or DoorDash.

I send a little prayer to the patron saints of divorced mothers, promising if I can keep custody of my kids, I'll make them nutritious, wholesome dinners every night.

I take my seat at the back of the room and instantly feel twenty freshman eyes on me.

"You punched out Ian Phillips, right?" asks the girl closest to me.

"He's such a creep," says a shy redhead who eerily reminds me of Aubrey. "You know he made a list of all the freshmen girls he wants to 'do'." She rolls her eyes. "He calls it his to-do list. Ugh!"

"Yeah, starting with the freshmen cheerleaders." This girl, I remember. Ashley, a naturally beautiful girl who grows up to be a T.V. meteorologist on one of the Austin stations. "He's a pig. I'm glad you stood up to him."

I think of Jake's words and straighten.

Ian's future is now in his hands or entirely up to fate. That's out of my control. However, there's the other effect of standing up for myself.

I also stood up for an entire class of young women who, unbeknownst to most of the school and faculty, were being harassed by an upperclassman. They are now fully empowered to stand their ground and fight back.

"Has he bothered all of you?"

All the heads nod back at me. Even the girls I would've assumed would not have been his type affirmed being targeted.

"That son of a bitch," I mutter, but then I instantly feel terrible at slurring his mother because, after all, wasn't I trying to save him for her.

Time to arm these girls for the twenty-first century. "Okay, first of all, if he comes near any of you again, let me know. Secondly, never apologize for what you wear. It is not your fault how men react, so don't you dare let them try to victim-shame you. Finally, you have the right to give and withdraw consent. That includes touching and kissing. All of it." The speech I'd given Aubrey throughout most of her life flows out of me. "It's your body, so don't let anyone try to pressure you into doing anything you don't want to."

The heads nod vigorously this time.

"And, while we're the ones in this class, we are not the only ones who can cook and clean." I push myself to standing and hitch my hands on my hips. "Marriages are partnerships, so the idea that only women can make meals and clean a house is completely archaic. So, if any of you find a guy or a woman, you think you might want to spend the rest of your life with, lay down the law right away. Because I can tell you from experience that when you have been home with two kids under five, and one of them has an ear infection, and the other wipes their boogers on your white walls, and then your husband comes home and asks what's for dinner, you're going to want to tell him to shove it so far up his a—"

"Josephine Berry, what in the good Lord's name are you doing?" Mrs. Wheeler stands in the doorway, her fingers reddening as they tighten around a stack of paper.

My words hit me like tequila shots on an empty stomach. "I, uh, was practicing a, um, piece that I'll be performing. Like an open mic night thing, you know, what I imagine it would be like to be an over-stressed mom because there's no way I'm over-stressed or even a mom." I suck my lips to keep the treacherous body parts from saying anything else.

From the look on Mrs. Wheeler's face, she wasn't buying it. She also didn't want to think too hard about what I might've been saying. Instead, she passes out the photocopied recipe and divides us into groups while directing us to the pre-measured and sorted ingredients so we can whip together peanut butter cookies. The good old days when peanut butter was simply a condiment and not a deadly weapon.

"You're right, you know. If we don't stand up to him, he'll just keep doing it," Ashley whispers to me while beating eggs.

"The world is full of Ians," says a rail-thin girl, freckles covering her skin like the Milky Way. "We have to start standing up now, or else we never will."

I stay quiet this time, letting the younger girls in class own this moment of empowerment. Power comes from within, helped along with a little spark of inspiration. Plus, if I say anything else, my spark might blow back in my face.

With a feminine revolution underway in the freshmen class, I scoot out of Home Ec and hurry into the main building and up the stairs to Physics. My intrepid scientists are seated in their usual spots in the back corner of the lab-slash-classroom. A few curious glances follow me to an empty seat next to them.

"Can you meet us after school?" Stuart whispers. "We've made some good progress. We think."

Even *we think* progress is something.

I nod. "But let's meet here, not in the library."

After the final bell rings, I rush back to the science lab. The library, long a haven, feels as unsafe as walking down a dark alley alone. Someone was there. Just in the shadows. Watching.

The shiver I'd tried to hold back rockets through my body. Luckily, I hide it in the fact that a cold front had blown through that afternoon. Despite all the times I'd begged my kids to think ahead, I didn't have a coat with me.

The boys are there waiting, each with a college-ruled notebook, sharing notes.

"Hey, before we begin, was someone else in the library with you guys the other night?"

Three heads shake.

Damn.

That would've been the easy answer. A freshman could have bullied into silence.

One shoulder lifts in partial capitulation. Not that it didn't believe the boys, but more like it didn't have any suitable explanation either.

Then again, it was a shoulder not necessarily known for solving complex problems.

"Okay, whatcha got?" I say before I start contemplating what other body parts might think.

"I-we would like to try an experiment," Matthew says. "You said you were stressed and you stared at something from high school, and that brought you here. What if next time you're stressed, you're looking at something from the future to pull you forward?"

I open my mouth, but the words that wanted to jump out first had second thoughts and climbed back down my throat.

This could work.

That same claustrophobia tunnel vision happened not long after I fell back in time during the Yearbook class. Instead of waking up in the future, I'd woken up in the nurse's office. Matthew might be on to something.

"Okay, this is good, but there's one wrinkle. I don't have anything from the future. My phone with the pictures of my kids won't be manufactured for thirty years."

Matthew's face broke into a smile like the sun climbing the horizon after a long, dark winter. "I know, and luckily my brother is training to be a police sketch artist. If you can describe them, he'll do it for practice."

Warmth radiates from my chest, flooding my limbs with something my body soaks up like a desert soaking up a long overdue rain.

Hope.

CHAPTER 24

I have to wait a few weeks for Matthew's brother to come home from art school for Christmas break to sketch my kids. The days pass in that languid boredom I'd forgotten about. Quiet Sunday afternoons that weren't filled with binging a million different shows on thousands of streaming services or stuck on social media.

Like a junkie coming off a drug, at first I'd find myself twitchy and anxious on Sundays. After two months in my past, I could spend an entire Sunday afternoon lounging around, guiltlessly reading a Sweet Valley High novel.

It's the Sunday before Christmas when Matthew finally calls. "He's home," he says, all Deep Throat conspiratorially, when I answer the phone. "Meet at my house in an hour?" Rather than wait for my affirmation, he hangs up the phone.

These guys are getting a little too cloak and dagger with my life.

Matthew meets me at the front door, nodding as he leads me past the brightly lit Christmas tree.

"Michael and the guys are back on the screened-in porch. I told him that you're doing this for a last-minute gift for a couple of cousins who live in Dallas."

I nod. My stomach lurches like a dozen caffeinated monkeys bouncing around on a trampoline.

Do I remember my children enough to describe them to someone to draw?

The screened porch is more like a sunroom. Southern facing with three sides made up of windows, even my non-artistic self knew well enough that this is the perfect space to paint and draw.

Michael stands and extends a hand. Recognition blasts through me like a solar flare. The dreads are shorter, but in a few decades, they'll be down his back and laced with gray. His face is thinner, beardless, but the man who'll become one of the most famous artists out of Austin, heck, maybe even modern artist in the U.S., is about to draw my future children.

This piece will be priceless in so many ways.

"Hi!" I say, a little too brightly. "I'm Josephine Berry. You can call me Josie. But it's not like you're going to remember me or anything." Good God words are slipping out of my mouth like they're covered in Vaseline. "Matthew, can I borrow you for a moment?"

We retrace our steps back to the kitchen.

"What is wrong with you?" His face was stayed-out-way-past-curfew serious.

"I swear I wasn't going to do this, and you have to promise me you won't say anything to anyone, but your brother is a famous artist in the future."

His face is unreadable. Something between pride and fear.

Did I cause some cataclysmic shift in the universe by even telling him?

After several seconds, he breaks out into a huge grin. "Badass! So, here's the deal, our parents have been on him to 'pick a real major.'" He lowers his voice to mimic his dad. "I swear I won't say anything to him more than just stay with it, that he'll be okay."

Air flees my lungs. Hopefully, when I return to my time, Michael Fraser will still be a renowned artist and not doing police sketches.

It's odd sitting there, telling a stranger every nuisance of faces I've known since they took their first breaths, but aren't alive in my now. Am I concocting them, when I tell Michael about the cupid's bow of

Aubrey's lips and how my 12-year-old son seemed to already have that line between his brow from being such a serious kid?

I try to keep my descriptions tangible. To not explain that the scar in Aubrey's right eyebrow was because this fearless kid took off skateboarding after watching a handful of YouTube videos—like they'd know what that even meant. Or, how Ben looks more like he's on the verge of a midlife crisis instead of in middle school because the kid exited my womb doing calculus, and despite our best efforts to teach him how to be a kid, it just isn't in his DNA.

Michael's hand moves with swift grace. With each stroke of his pencil, each smudge with the side of his pinky, each shading of shadows, my yet-to-be-born children come alive.

When he turns the sketchpad around to show off his work, the lump in the center of my chest threatens to detonate and spray tears all over a future famous artist and his drawing of my children. It takes the willpower of a dieter in a chocolate shop, but I manage to not break down into a snotty mess in front of him.

"Thank you," I whisper. "That's perfect." I clear the maternal emotion away and try to summon the usual detachment of adolescence. "My cousins will like it. And hey, when you're a super-famous artist they'll have a collector's item."

Michael blushes, his gaze falling to his sketchpad. The look crossing his face says it all. I'd shed light on his biggest dream, and in that light, it was exposed, vulnerable. I know how that feels. Sitting there holding the likeness of two amazing humans who are my whole world has a bright glaring spotlight on it.

It scares the shit out of me.

"Thank you both," I say, standing and pulling my backpack on one shoulder. I should tuck the drawing inside to keep it safe, but I can't bear to let go of my children. "Merry Christmas. Matthew, I'll see you after the break."

Back in my car, I unfold the drawing, gently caressing the side of my children's faces. Even if it nearly kills me, I'll figure out a way back to my time.

My kids.

I drive home with the drawing nestled in the passenger seat. If I thought the seatbelt wouldn't tear it, I'd belt it in. Guess mom-arming will have to do.

Even though the sky is smeared with thick gray clouds, I feel the weightlessness of a bright spring day. One of my favorite songs comes on the radio, a poppy tune that was the song of the previous summer. Like me, it's out of place.

I roll down the window and blast the heater. I might as well make the most of the moment and at least pretend it's still summer. Like my visit to my past, the song will end, another more seasonally appropriate tune will play next, or an annoying commercial block. Then I'll be thrust back into the reality of a failing business, a budding custody battle, and a world absent of both my dad and Daniel.

Maybe here in the past I can find the keys to my future. To saving my business and keeping my kids.

I pull up to my house just as the song ends. Cutting the engine before the next song kills my good mood.

My parents' cars are parked in the driveway. A rare occurrence these days. Thirty years ago, I would've been so wrapped up in my teenage drama to have even noticed, but Peter and I did the same dance of avoidance. Both of us knew the conversation needed to happen, but neither of us wanted to be the one to start it.

I carefully fold the edges of Michael's drawing and tuck it into my journal, then settle it into my bag.

Only the heavy tick of the grandfather clock echoes as I enter the living room. It's only when I go to the kitchen, because that's where every teenager heads, that I hear murmuring voices.

My parents are seated at the table. Mom with a cup of tea, filled to the brim and with a tea bag, but no steam clouds the air above it.

Dad across from her, his normally ruddy face ashen, hands clasped on the table.

Thirty years ago, I would've asked who died.

Now, I know it's their marriage.

My father sees me first. "Hey pumpkin, been there long?" He strains to sound light and normal, but, instead, sounds like he might drown in grief.

"Just got home."

Mom takes a deep breath and pats the spot at the head of the table. "Sweetie, why don't you have a seat."

It's several seconds before my feet obey. The lightness from earlier flees my body, leaving me with a lead weight in my stomach, threatening to pull me through the floor all the way to the Hell that I know is waiting for me.

"We need to talk to you about something, but first, we want you to know we love you very much," Mom says.

"And this is about your mom and me. It has nothing to do with you," Dad says. "Despite what happens, we will always be a family."

I shake my head, dislodging the tears that sat at the ready all day.

"No," I whisper. "It's all wrong. Christmas is next week."

My mom grips my hand. "I know, honey, and trust me, we will make Christmas completely normal. You're just so mature." She sighs. "Pretending everything is fine would have felt like a lie."

Dad grabs my other hand. "I'm getting an apartment in town in the new year. I'll be here throughout the holidays. It's just sometimes love fades, and it's better to be apart than together."

I should shout at them. Tell them they're ruining my life. Ruining their own lives. However, there are some wounds that words can't fix.

I pull my hand from theirs, get up from the table, sling my backpack over my shoulder and walk back out the front door, closing the door on their pleading voices calling my name.

I'm not mad at them. I'm furious at myself. They weren't supposed to tell me for another two weeks. Instead of slowing down or even stopping my parents' divorce, I sped it up.

The thick clouds from earlier had darkened and lowered. A beady mist hangs in the air as I wander aimlessly through my childhood neighborhood, the short day turning to night as quickly as a waning lightbulb.

My hope darkening like the night.

CHAPTER 25

I walk a circuitous path through the neighborhood. If it were modern times, my phone would be blowing up with concerned calls and text messages. Then again, my mom would have set up a tracking app on my phone like I have on Aubrey and Ben's. I can almost imagine my parents watching my little blue dot circle and cross and double back, basically down every street but the one I live on.

On my third pass by Daniel's house, I decide to stop. Despite living behind each other for years, I had never been inside his house.

The doorbell trills at the press of my finger. Blue-white light of the TV flickers through the heavy drapes to my right, a laugh track from a formulaic sitcom dies away with the groan of a chair of someone lifting off it.

The porch light flicks on.

I jump like a thief caught in the act.

Daniel's father pulls the door open. Glassy eyes study me.

I tilt my chin, meeting his surveying gaze with my own. Standing this close to his dad, I see how much Daniel favors him. The same strong brow, his father's jawline was a little less defined, most likely from a combination of age and a six-pack-a-day habit.

"Hi, I'm Josie. I live behind you," I say, realizing this is the first time I'm speaking to his dad.

"Yeah, I know, you're the Berry girl." His voice is low, with a rich timber that sounds out of sync with the disheveled man in front of me.

"Is Daniel home?" Before the words die away, a familiar head appears behind Mr. Palmer.

The door opens wider, as Daniel moves to take his father's place.

The elder Palmer moves wordlessly back to his recliner, clicking the remote to reactivate the volume mid-jingle.

I glance into the living room. The Christmas tree sits in a corner, sparsely decorated but lit with a handful of presents scattered beneath it.

I think of my tree. A statuesque live tree that my dad wrestled in the front door and my mom and I decorated to a backdrop of holiday music.

About a week until Christmas, yet the presents under my family's tree already spill over.

"Hey Josie, what's up?"

I open my mouth to answer Daniel, but a sob answers him instead of words.

"I'm going out," he shouts over his shoulder, pulling the front door shut. He cuts a determined path down his front walk and pulls open the passenger door to his truck.

"Where are we going?" My voice is rough, like day-drinking-to-closing-down-the-bars rough.

"The Point."

There was something incredibly wrong with going to the make-out spot in town with a sobbing snot nose, my hair a dripping mess, and my heart shattered in a million pieces over the fact that as much as I tried, I couldn't save my parents' marriage. There's a good chance one of us will get hurt with one of the shards of my heartbreak.

The drive out there is silent. Just the sound of the tires on the asphalt and the heater trying to warm us broken up by my occasional sniffle.

I glance over at Daniel.

Even in the orange glow of his dashboard I see his jaw working as if he's forming words, but his mouth won't open to set them free.

What if I make my move?

If I tell him now how I feel about him. Could that be all that it takes to send me back?

Just good old-fashioned honesty.

Maybe now that he's dating Jessica, he doesn't feel the same way about me, and this coulda-shoulda-woulda feeling that's been squeezing me will subside, like that time I was determined to squeeze back into my wedding dress after two kids.

That time Emily had to come over and cut me out of it.

Maybe only Daniel can cut me out of this vise and send me forward to my messed-up life.

If only I could peer into his head to see how my declaration would land.

"What are you thinking?" His voice was barely audible over the sound of the road. "Because whatever it is, I can feel it over here."

I take a shaky but deep breath. "Oh, you know, nothing much. Tolstoy. College. When wedding vows will change to 'when death do us part, or the divorce papers are signed'."

Daniel grunts.

I'm not sure if it was meant to be a laugh or a cringe.

The truck turns off the highway and follows a rutted-out dirt road, the headlights dancing over packed-dirt earth. After a jarring and jostling mile, we pull into a clearing.

Daniel pulls to the edge, where nothing but the undulating blackness of the lake glistens ahead of us. After thrusting the truck into park, he kills the engine. The only sound is the lapping of the lake and our shallow breaths.

"Why is it that your parents, who by all accounts seem to have a pretty stable marriage, throw in the towel, and even when I tell my mom she'd be better off leaving my dad's sorry ass, she digs her heels in on the *'in sickness and in health'* part?" His eyes stare straight ahead, as glassy as the water facing us.

"Because your dad is sick. They just don't have the name for it yet."

I feel him relax on the other side of the truck as if that little knowledge that his mom is stronger for staying with his dad, not weaker, lifts a weight. "As for my parents, a marriage is like a tree. Sometimes it can grow stronger and sturdier over time, but it needs nourishment. Love is a big part of that, but it can't keep a marriage alive all on its own. Because falling in love with someone is easy, the hard part is loving them on their worst days and still wanting to do life with the person."

Did I just have the breakthrough on my own marriage that my therapist had been waiting months for?

Daniel releases a low whistle. "Damn, Berry, that's seriously deep. You didn't tell me you were taking college-level courses already." His words are in jest with an undercurrent of curiosity.

How did a teenager suddenly wake up with an astute understanding of how to keep a marriage from failing?

I pat his arm and plaster on my sweetest smile. "You know they say girls mature faster than boys. You'll get there soon, young grasshopper."

The tension building in the cab dissipates like mist.

"If you didn't show up at my house looking like you'd lost your puppy…" his voice trails. "I'd ask if you want to talk about it, but it seems like you've got it all figured out." Daniel pauses and cocks an eyebrow. "Plus, I'm just a dumb boy."

I punch him in the arm. "I might understand a little better, but it doesn't make it hurt any less." I lift one shoulder in a lazy shrug. "I could be mad or blame one of them for not trying harder, but that won't make them get back together. This is their marriage, not mine. I need to be there for both of them, because they've always been there for me. And, there'll be a time when they won't be here, and I'll be left with nothing but regret." The break in my voice mirrors the one in my heart. Despite my tight grasp on my tear ducts, they burst anyway, unleashing a torrent down my face.

Strong, gentle hands pull me across the bench seat, tucking my face into his chest.

Daniel's heartbeat is steady, soothing, and reassuring. His scent washes over me like a rogue wave, earthy, clean with a hint of peppermint.

While I listen to his heart, I feel my own get pulled in two. One half desperately needed to see my children. The other half wished it could be here with him, in this moment, forever.

CHAPTER 26

One of the cuts that sawed away at my marriage was my proclivity to come to Peter for help with something. In the process of asking my question, I came up with the solution. Quite frankly, it was better than anything he would've suggested. Yet, each time I'd come to him, he'd offer advice. Each time, I wouldn't take it, the bitterness on his face lingered just a little bit longer.

Not Daniel.

He let me talk it out, cry it out, and when I was spent of both words and tears, just quiet it out.

"What's next, JoBear?" He asks while we drive back to our neighborhood.

"After world domination?"

He chuckles. "Yes, after world domination."

I watch the dashed yellow lines of the highway pass beneath his truck. I couldn't control-freak my way into keeping my parents together, but I am in control of what I do and how I respond.

"I let my parents know how I feel and make sure they're serious about staying a family, even through their divorce." I nibble on my lower lip. "What's next for you?"

Daniel finally answers when he clicks the truck into park in front of my house. "My dad and I used to go fishing a lot when I was younger. Really, it was more like we sat in a boat with lures in the water. We talked too much to catch anything." He gazes past my house as if he could see inside his own. "Dad would tell me about growing up on the ranch and everything he and his cousins got into, and I'd tell him every detail of my life. That was." He pauses, clears his throat. "That was before he went to the Gulf."

I reach across the truck and throw my arms around his neck, hugging him with the ferocity of someone who hadn't seen him in years. "I think you should do that," I whisper into his hair. "Even if you guys don't say a word and catch a lot of fish. Just be there."

Before I close the door behind me, I pop my head back in. The question had been burning a hole on my tongue the entire evening. I was about to demand my divorcing parents to still act like a family, so why the hell shouldn't I ask it. "So, what's up with you and Jessica?"

Surprise brightens his gold-green eyes before he steadies his face and shrugs. "Hadn't talked to her since homecoming. Turns out, she was only really interested in what I thought about her and not really much about what I thought beyond that."

I close the door before I do something stupid. Like kiss him. Or confess my three decades of yearning.

Inside, my parents are waiting.

I can't tell if they've been sitting in the living room, perched on the edges of the love seat—ironic—the whole time or just since Daniel's truck pulled up.

"Hey," I say, pulling the door close behind me. "Sorry, I needed some air. I was with Daniel."

"It's okay, pumpkin," Dad says. Worry etched deep lines across his face, like glass cut with a diamond from a mistress's hand. "Daniel's dad called us. Brad thought you looked upset."

I tilt my head, the realization that Daniel's broken, vacant father recognized another parent's need to know their child is safe fills my heart with hope that my friend could salvage his relationship with his father.

"Okay," I start, plopping down on the adjacent couch. "Here's my list of demands."

My father stifles a grin, and my mother leans forward. If she had a notebook in her hands, she would've taken notes.

"First, no hating each other. No making snide comments to me about the other."

"No, sweetie, of course," Mom says.

"Never," Dad says on the heel of her words.

Feeling empowered, I sit up straighter, thinking back to the conversation I wish Peter and I had had. "Second, holidays together, always. And, if either of you should meet someone else," I pause, knowing full well that apart from a few dates Mom went on after Dad died, neither of them have another serious relationship. "They are welcome to join us, but must adhere to rule number one."

Two heads that had been joined in matrimony for nearly twenty years nod in unison.

"And finally, I still want a family, not two divorced parents. I know this is your marriage, and the decision to end it was tough. I'd still like to have dinner together as a family once a week. It can be here, out, or even at Dad's new place. You're dissolving a marriage, not a family, right?"

My parents look at each other, a silent conversation passing between them.

"Of course, pumpkin," Dad says. His eyes shimmer like a still pond in the moonlight. "This was never meant to hurt you. If anything, your mom and I realized you could probably feel that things are off. It's better to be honest than to make you feel like you're part of a lie."

My mom nods and grabs Dad's hand. "I will always love your dad, and I hope he'll always love me in some way. Sometimes, the best decision is also the hardest one."

We hug it out like a family that underwent an intense therapy session. The shift in the air is almost like static electricity in an approaching thunderstorm.

I look around my childhood home. Could this be it?

Was this all I needed to do to catapult myself back to my future and dysfunctional family?

The clock remains ticking. The full periphery of my vision takes in the Home Interiors countryside pictures hanging on the wall. Nondescript green scenescapes meant to evoke quieter, more peaceful times.

The crushed velvet pink and burgundy and gray upholstered furniture filled the edges of the room. Of my vision.

There were no darkening edges. No thrumming of my blood deafening my ears.

Just the metronomic ticking of a clock, my middle-aged parents staring as expectantly at me as I'm sure they did the day I was born, and my mother's terrible taste in home design.

I give them each a hug laced with meaning. For my mom, it was a hug of strength. Assuming I didn't royally mess up the entirety of the universe, she would need it to get through the early days of being a divorcee and the incredible pain that would follow when learning that her ex-husband died.

For my dad, it was a hug filled with a lifetime of laughter and love, of scraped knees and broken hearts, of public cheers and inside jokes. It was the hug I wish I'd given him the first time he and Mom told me their marriage was ending.

The hug I wished I could've given him every day for nearly three decades.

CHAPTER 27

The rest of the holiday passes as normal holidays do. With an equal part of anticipation and boredom. Mom and Dad seem much more at ease with each other. My dad's apartment won't be ready until mid-January, and instead of moving into a hotel, he just moved into the guest room that'd become part craft den and part abandoned hobby graveyard.

Their comfort around each other is so palpable I let my seventeen-year-old brain take the driver's seat for a few minutes and feel hopeful that maybe they'll reconcile.

Then, the cynic reaches over and jerks the wheel back toward reality.

The first day back at school after the break feels like a mini version of the first day of the school year. Everyone is decked out in their new clothes from under the tree. Excitement hangs in the air like the list from ozone-killing hairspray. For seniors, the realization that graduation is just a little more than five months away hits us like a new fruit salad recipe our grandmothers might try on us: tangy, a little bit bitter, but with a sweet aftertaste.

Emily pulls up next to me in the high school parking lot. Beastie

Boys blares from her Jeep, the top and windows off like it's June instead of January.

Tanned from spending Christmas with her dad down at South Padre Island with her long dark hair swishing down her back, she looks more like an exotic islander than a small-town Texan.

"What did I miss?" She shouts over the music as a way of greeting. It's the same way we've greeted each other after a long absence for our entire friendship.

I wait until she kills her engine and joins me in the parking lot. "Lost my virginity to Brad Pitt, and he begged me to run away with him, but I told him I couldn't leave you and Sof behind." The typical response is always unbelievable, especially if there is something momentous to follow. "But before that, my parents told me they're divorcing, just like I suspected."

Emily's love language is snarky barbs and expensive wine. It's how she soothed me countless times through college and our twenties, through postpartum breakdowns, and when I told her my marriage was over.

Standing here in our high school parking lot, with teenagers flowing around us like salmon swimming upstream to spawn, she grabs me in a ferocious hug. "I'm sorry, Josie. I know this hurts, and if you need to talk, you know where to find me." The bell cuts through the air like a banshee. "Which, at this moment, is late to class. Love you!"

I hustle to World History like a suburban mom trying to eke out one more errand before picking up a carload of over-sugared, over-scheduled, and over-stressed offspring.

Sofia sits in her usual seat, hunched over her binder, drawing concentric flowers in blue ink.

"Hey," I say, slipping into the desk beside hers.

She startles, as if shaken out of a dream. "Hi." The word is as blunt as a dull knife, but applied with enough pressure, it can still break skin.

Was this how the fissure started?

A crack formed over a long holiday in which Em took a vacation with her dad while I dealt with my family breaking apart.

What was quiet, shy Sofia dealing with?

Like most self-absorbed teenagers, we never asked.

Until now…

"How was your Christmas?"

"Fine." Her face, shielded by a curtain of her dark, wavy hair, remains focused on the doodles.

"Did you get anything good?"

She lifts a shoulder. "Some books."

Geesh, this was about as fruitful as talking to Aubrey and twenty times more frustrating because Sofia is one of my best friends, not a human whose sole purpose during her teenage years is to make me feel like I'm speaking a foreign language.

I lay my hand on her arm, feeling the heat through her sweater. "You know I'm here for you, right? Whatever it is, I have your back. Always."

The pen stops and a giant inhale lifts my friend's body. Sofia turns toward me, whipping her hair behind her shoulders like a soldier preparing to stand her ground. Her brown eyes, normally as warm and welcoming as a grandmother's kitchen, take on the cold steel facade of a trendy restaurant that serves over-priced, tiny dishes. Sofia's mouth opens, closes, as if it rethought what it was going to say, and opens again. "I know that. I've always known that. But don't you think it's time for us to start standing on our own?"

My argument readies for lift-off, but Mr. Lancaster calls us to order with his monotonic recitation into the Ottoman Empire.

While the teacher drones on, my mind flits from thought to thought.

What would it take to pull Sofia back to Emily and me?

Maybe she can tell something is different. That I'm different. Mental gymnastics of the space-time continuum twist up my brain for the remainder of the class.

I'm so wrapped up in my thoughts that I don't realize the bell rang until Sofia was bolting from her seat.

"Shit," I mumble. I let defeat wash over me, but like a wave, I mentally will it to go back out to the ocean of emotion.

I spend the rest of the morning in a dual state of listening to teachers, pretending I'm an eager student, and battling a severe case of I'll-never-use-this-in-my-adult-life.

Emily meets me outside the cafeteria, her hands clenching her lunch. "Did you know Sof changed her schedule? She's in the next lunch block."

I take a deep breath. "Something's up. I don't know what, but I feel like she's mad."

Emily goes chillingly still. It took me years to realize this is a defense mechanism. Internally she's going through everything one should feel—annoyance, hurt, anger. So that when an emotion finally lands on her face, it's the one that will cause the least amount of pain.

At this age, she's still fine-tuning her response. So instead of moving back to neutral, her eyes harden and mouth presses tight into anger.

"Being mad at her for being mad at us isn't going to help things," I snap. "We need to figure out what's up with her."

This time, her face softens into aloof neutrality. The kind of bored look that cats and serial killers wear. "Shouldn't you be asking her that and not me?" She looks down at the lunch bag in her hands. "You know, I'm not hungry." With that, my best friend turns and flows into the stream of teenage humanity.

I look at the bag in my hand. Suddenly, the PB&J with full-calorie chips sounds about as appealing as a rice cake with a side of air. The knot in my stomach replaces any desire for food.

If I have to go through this a second time around, I'd think I'd be in more control. Instead, I feel about as in control as a runaway roller coaster.

I head to the library. A bit early for my library hour, but also to find a nook to hide in so I can bring out the picture of Aubrey and Ben. The paper has already softened in the weeks since Matthew's brother drew it for me.

My thumb has caressed the charcoal lines of their faces so many times that, like an addict, I keep telling myself one more look, and then I'll stop, worried that I might rub away their features. Rub them out of existence.

The library is mostly empty. Mrs. Patel waves through the window in her office. I return the greeting and hurry to the back corner where the reference books are shelved. The small desk in the back nook is empty, just as I'd hoped.

The desk shimmies when I drop my backpack on it. Riffling through the textbooks, tampons, scrunchies, and spiral notebooks, my hand finally closes on the crushed velvet of my journal.

The cardboard spine squeaks. The front half of the pages are stiff, pregnant with ink written in the heavy hand of a teenager who had to chronicle every mundane moment of her life.

Midway through, the handwriting becomes more frantic. With a list of halfway checked-off items and written ramblings of a mother desperate to get home to my kids. The demarcation between when I was Josie Berry, seventeen-year-old living her best life to when I woke up as Josie Berry Gardner, a forty-seven-year-old divorcee who was on the verge of losing my kids and bankrupting my business was there in blue and white.

I smooth the page of the drawing on the desk beside me. The faces of my children, my inspiration for whatever musing I can conjure to get me back to my present, hover in my mind, as real as the paper in front of me. Stream-of-consciousness words flow out of me. Part meditation. Part begging. Mostly questions and musings.

Three pages in, I shake out the cramp in my hand.

"If Einstein couldn't figure out time travel, why do I think a middle-aged mom-turned-teenager can," I say to the pages in the journal.

The journal doesn't answer me, but the sound of something shifting, a gasp and then the determined plunk of a book hitting the carpeted floor behind me do.

I turn in my seat. A massive encyclopedia lies splayed on the floor. It doesn't take a physicist to know damn well that encyclopedias don't randomly jump off shelves unless some outside force pushes it.

CHAPTER 28

There's something unnerving about knowing you were watched. Nothing physical was taken except your privacy. The thing stolen would be nearly impossible to retrieve. In my case, it's the words I'd spoken aloud. That I'm attempting to figure out time travel, and I'm from the future.

Depending on whose ears heard those words, I'm either totally fine or totally screwed.

Either way, I need to get home to my kids. To my life, as messy and heartbreaking as it is, I've fought long and hard for all those mistakes. I'm not too eager to repeat them or test the path not followed theory.

I'd buried the feeling of an interloper at homecoming, convincing myself that it was just another introvert hiding from the horde of adolescents. Now, I can't help but think it's not random. That someone might actually be watching me.

After school, I hurry home. Dad didn't take much with him when he moved out, but his absence carved a hole in the completeness of my life, even with my parents meeting my demand of still spending time together as a family. It feels as if the house is mourning the end of the relationship as well.

With my journal, I tuck into my window seat, folding myself into the impossible pretzel-like posture that only a lithe teenager could find comfortable. The weak winter sunlight slices across the page as I study my list.

Mrs. Patel breaks her ankle. So far, so good on keeping the librarian safe.

My parents' divorce. I couldn't stop this. It's silly to think I could, but just by reacting more maturely, like someone who had been through it herself, the universe tilted just enough to make me feel like something did change.

Problem with Sofia. I look at those words, trying to figure out how to stop them from becoming a reality. The extra thirty years of life experience gives me no insight. Sometimes, a rift is a rift; it doesn't matter if it happens when you're seventeen or forty-seven. Life just pulls people apart, for no reason other than we get swept away on different currents; job, family, hobbies. They shift like the ocean, carrying old relationships out to sea while bringing new ones in with the tide. It's no one's fault, just the same as it's not the ocean's fault for eroding a beach.

Ian Phillips dies. As annoying as he was at homecoming, the jerk deserves to grow up. Hopefully to grow up to respect women and understand the meaning of 'no.' The details of his death are murky, not because of age but because no one saw him go under. Just weeks before graduation, it was warm enough to sunbathe by the lake, but the water clung to the winter chill. Like Mrs. Patel's ankle, this is an easy one; I just have to keep an eye on Ian.

Unlike Mrs. Patel, that means hanging out with someone who gives me the serious creeps.

Tell Daniel the truth. If this is the thing to bring me back to my own time, I might as well settle in for a re-run of the next three decades.

Do I tell him I love him and risk the future I have? Can I even return to that future, or is my being here already changing things?

What good will it do if I tell him, but then in the next breath tell him I can't be with him because if I do, I'll never meet my future ex-husband and have my future kids?

If I'm lucky, one of these other tasks will be the key to getting back home, and I can continue the emotional avoidance dance a little longer.

While I was focused on my journal, dusk settled over the backyard like a fleece blanket. My backyard and Daniel's adjoining yard are dark, but his window is lit up, and a figure sits in it.

Across the yards, his head is bent down, his long hair flopping in front of his eyes. One hand clutches the top of a sketch pad while the other makes sure broad strokes across the page.

As I watch him, Robert Frost's poem comes to mind. I'd just spent my second turn studying the poem in Senior Lit, and quite frankly, it hits much closer to home as a middle-aged mother of two who seems to be back at the start of the path.

Daniel's hand moves rapidly across the page as if shading something. The concentration crease between his eyebrows pronounced, even in the shadowy distance. Did that crease deepen with age, or did he see the early warning signs of the wrinkle and break that habit?

I straighten as a thought strikes me like an errant foul ball. What if I'm not supposed to go back down my first path?

What if I'm supposed to take the path not taken?

Like a sudden strike to a nerve, nausea slams into me like a tsunami.

There could be other kids, with Daniel or some other man I haven't even contemplated. They could be wonderful. Maybe not as messy. With their eyes up rather than down at their screens. I could have a supportive husband. A successful business. I could even still have a six-pack and a jawline.

Or, I could be lonely. Working around the clock in a soulless job. Married to someone abusive.

That's the thing about life. It's the sum total of the choices, the mistakes, the right calls, that we make up until that moment. If you change one of those—turn left instead of right, go out with Mr. Football instead of the geeky guy in your class, or choose a different college —it completely changes who you are. Who you become.

Movement across the yards snags my attention.

Daniel holds up the drawing with a desk lamp behind it, back-lighting it. It's me in profile, with my head bent over my journal, hair tucked behind my ear, and my eyes are narrowed in concentration. I should've known he was watching me while I was watching him.

I lift one side of my mouth in a half-hearted smile and back away from my window, hoping Daniel will just think I'm heading downstairs to raid the fridge instead of running away.

Frost was both right and wrong.

We *are* faced with divergent paths all the time, and ultimately the path we choose is the one we're supposed to be on.

I would move earth to get back to that path.

CHAPTER 29

February tenth rolls around like it does every year. Unlike previous years, I don't wake early to wish my son a happy birthday, nor do I whip up chocolate chip pancakes that are more chocolate chips than batter. I don't sing an off-key *Happy Birthday* or hand over a badly wrapped gift. Instead, I ball up in my rumpled sheets and bawl like a newborn with a gas bubble.

I try to shoo away concern about if Peter was making his birthday pancakes right or that his rich, pitch-perfect baritone probably hit all the notes. Like flies to chardonnay, these thoughts refuse to stay away.

Then again, it was March in my time when I fell back, so maybe it's not actually his birthday and this melancholy is misplaced, like me.

The weather is kind enough to match my mood: dark, ugly, and prone to downpours.

Morning classes flow by without any words from teachers making their way to my brain. It's too busy flitting between whether my kids are worried about me to why the science guys are no closer to a way to send me home, and why I entrusted this mammoth task to a trio of pubescent boys instead of NASA or the Jet Propulsion Lab or even some secret branch of the government. Then again, going to any of those groups will just get me locked up.

My journal lays on my lap, my gaze raking over my list instead of following along as a classmate stumbles through a reading of *Grapes of Wrath*. Maybe it's time I kick this into high gear and quit relying on the boys.

In Physics, I sit behind my team of teenage experts, or the ones available to me at the moment I slid into the past.

I lean forward and tap Stuart on the shoulder. "We need to talk."

"Are you finally asking me to prom?" He whispers back, way louder than necessary.

A few heads whip in our direction.

"You couldn't handle being my prom date." Because really, he couldn't. He'd crumple under my list of demands. "For real, we need to talk. I need to see progress on our, um, project."

Mr. Davies clears his throat, a not-so-subtle sign that he registered a disturbance, but isn't motivated enough to do anything about it.

"We've got some strong theories we're testing…"

I cut him off. "How are you testing them? I'm still here!"

"Well, Ms. Berry, if you feel like your time will be better spent elsewhere, by all means, please go and stop disturbing my class," Mr. Davies says, looking up over the top of his glasses, tired eyes, clouded with cataracts and too-old-for-this-shit stare a hole through me.

I stare back, meeting his gaze and raising it momma-bear-kept-away-from-her-cubs crazy.

He arches an eyebrow. "Goodbye, Ms. Berry; why don't you try my class again tomorrow."

Heat floods my body like a hot flash. I've never been kicked out of…*anything*. Not a bar on Sixth Street when Emily dared me to challenge an Irishman to a drinking contest of tequila shots—I won, but a two-day hangover was my prize.

Not that high-priced fundraiser Peter and I accidentally attended when we meant to go to the medium-priced cocktail party next door. Not even that time I volunteered to be an aide in Aubrey's preschool class because I thought the teacher was too lazy to continue the potty training from home, and I not-so-subtly pointed out a few more of her shortcomings—that resulted in her quitting in a fit of tears, and me having to finish out the school year as the teacher.

I've always been welcomed.

Okay, well, *tolerated.*

I gather my stuff, focusing on the meticulous shoving of a book and binder into an already bursting backpack. There are only fifteen minutes left in the period, so rather than wait somewhere else for the guys, I slide down the wall of lockers outside the Physics room door.

Six months I've been stuck in my past.

Six months of trying to fix everything, well, the things that have happened so far, so that I could hit upon the magic lesson and catapult back to my time.

Six months of worrying about if Ben is drinking too much coffee and getting enough sun or if Peter has taken Aubrey to any of her orthodontist appointments.

The bell rings, and I pop up to avoid being trampled by a herd of self-obsessed teenagers.

Stuart is the first out of the room. "What the hell, Josie?"

"You're going to get us all in trouble," Jake says.

"My parents will kill me if I get detention," Matthew chimes in.

Nothing like a chorus of geeks to chastise me.

I pull them out of the flow of students trying to hustle to their next class before the five minutes is up.

"Why am I still here? I thought you would have it figured out by now." I try to keep my words at the same decibel as the din of voices and slamming lockers. "Have you just been watching TV this entire time?"

Stuart's jaw drops, and his eyes widen before narrowing again. He pushes past me, with Jake and Matthew following.

I hustle after them. "Young man, don't you walk away from me."

Stuart stops at his locker, the other two boys backing him. "Or what, Josie? You're going to ground me?" He shakes his head, his dark bangs swishing across his eyes. "If you're this controlling with your kids they're probably thrilled you're gone."

He slams his locker shut.

I stumble back a step as if he struck me with his fist instead of heated words.

It's true. If he were my kid, he'd be grounded. But he isn't my kid. He's my classmate. My peer. One of three people who know my truth.

He just twisted that truth and stabbed me in the heart with it.

"You know what, forget it." I whip my backpack around my shoulders and knock a passing freshman in the head. "I don't need your help, after all. So just keep watching your stupid SyFy Channel, and I'll figure out my own way back."

"Fine, because if we're being honest, Josie, we're not even sure you're telling the truth. How do we know this isn't just some pretty, popular girl prank you're playing on us? That at some point every kid in school is going to laugh at us? More than usual."

Stuart and I stare each other down. Bull versus matador. At this moment, I feel more like the bull, pierced by his words. Luckily, I have the thick hide of motherhood.

Unluckily, the more I spend time away from my kids, the more threadbare it becomes.

"Cool, there's a whole channel for science fiction in the future?" Jake's soft voice cuts across the anger ping-ponging between Stuart and me.

I turn from the boys and push through the thinning crowd. "Don't cry, don't cry," I murmur to myself, running to the sanctuary of something else lost in time.

The library.

"Oh, Josie, you're here too," Mrs. Patel greets me. I'm early for my library period, not caring if I get in trouble for skipping whatever class I'm supposed to be in. Past me can deal with that. I'm damn determined to get back to my time.

The musty, woodsy smell envelopes me like a grandmother's hug.

Too?

I was hoping that I'd get the library and Mrs. Patel all to myself. To have the woman's calm spirit warm me, her wisdom guide me like a lighthouse in a storm even if she doesn't realize that heartache and fear roils under my surface like a leviathan in the deep.

I drop my backpack on the carpet behind the library desk and grab a stack of books. "While I re-shelve these, I can straighten up the History section."

With the books back in their home, I set to work organizing the errant books in Texas History. Dewey decimal numbers in the proper place, spines as lined up like Rockettes.

I can't control Stuart, Jake, and Matthew, and their lack of progress. Or the fact that I'm stuck in 1994. Or that I miss seeing my dad at random moments instead of pre-ordained times. Or that every time I look at Daniel, my heart stumbles like a drunk girl in heels. Or that I need a glass of wine like a bee needs pollen.

My chest heaves and my neck flushes. I try to make sense of the shelving system, but have a hard time focusing through the unspent tears clouding my vision. Not being in control is like an allergic reaction. Except there's no EpiPen to cure me.

I round the corner to return to the desk and nearly collide with Ruby. "Oh, hey, Ruby, sorry about that." The cracks in my voice match the ones in my heart.

The girl hunches her shoulders forward, her arms wrapped protectively around a battered, faded backpack. "No worries." She sidesteps at the exact moment I sidestep her in the same direction.

"Sorry," we both say and step again in front of each other.

My gaze meets her brown eyes. Her face softens, and her thin lips pull back into a smile. For a split second, we're eight years old again, the only girls in a classroom of boys, sharing secrets like candy.

We're having sleepovers. Me in my Strawberry Shortcake pajamas, Ruby in her oversized faded t-shirt. We're eating sugary cereal and watching Saturday Morning Cartoons. For a split second, we're friends instead of frenemies.

The moment passes, and Ruby pushes past me, rushing out of the library.

"Hey, Mrs. Patel, I think I'm going to head to the cafeteria for the rest of my lunch period," I say, reaching for my backpack.

My hand freezes above it. When I dropped it earlier, the zippers met like young lovers. Now, they're as far apart as an arguing married couple.

My heart thumps against my chest as if trying to bang its way out of my ribcage.

I yank down the zippers, letting the contents spill on the floor. My wallet. Keys. Stretched-out scrunchie. Binder. Spiral notebook. Physics book.

Nothing else emerges.

"No, no, no."

I turn it upside down. Only a tampon falls onto the floor.

No blue, crushed-velvet journal. No sketched picture of my kids. No list of things I need to fix. No pages of me trying to work out why I woke up thirty years in the past.

"Shit, shit, shit."

My backpack becomes watery as if it, not me, is drowning in heartbreak.

I crawl around the floor, looking in the cubby where I usually stow my bag.

Nothing.

I run back to the History section, my finger undoing the tidying I had done earlier just in case I accidentally shelved my most precious possession.

Nothing.

I speed walk around the library, retracing my steps, gaze as stuck to the ground as a piece of used gum under a desk.

Nothing.

The edges of my vision darken. Like the world is closing in on me. I suck in a wheezy breath and grip the edge of the desk.

"Josie? Honey, are you okay?" Mrs. Patel puts a warm palm on my back, calming me and forcing my lungs to slow down. "Did you lose something?"

I nod, dislodging hot, angry tears down my face.

"What was it, honey?"

I gulp air like a dying fish. "Everything."

CHAPTER 30

My journal doesn't resurface. Mrs. Patel helps me pull the library nearly apart. She walks me down to the office, her hand on my shoulder steadying me.

Was it something of value? Yes. How do I describe it without going into details about what's inside it?

The Lost and Found, nothing more than a big, overused cardboard box, feels more like my frame of mind than a place where forgetful teens leave semi-valuable possessions.

Somehow, I know as I riffle through the orphaned earrings, misplaced jackets, and a pair of holey socks that my journal won't be there.

It wasn't lost.

It was taken.

Whoever took it most likely thought they were getting benign teenage gossip. Something they could use to spread rumors about the fact that I really did have a crush on Daniel. Or that maybe I was secretly jealous of Emily or Sofia.

Little did they realize they hit the motherlode.

Literally.

I don't feel like going home after school. Mom is at the office, and my usual latch-key kid routine includes time gazing at the sketch of Aubrey and Ben and trying to journal my way home. Without it, I'm more than empty.

I'm lost in my own life.

I mindlessly traverse the streets of my childhood. Driving by the middle school where the memories of Emily, Sofia, and I cemented our friendship squeezes me like a much-needed hug. I circle the elementary school where the three of us met in third grade and, at least for two of us, formed a lifelong friendship.

I park my car haphazardly in a spot by the park across from the school. I drove by this park just a couple of years ago during a moment of nostalgia.

In my time, it was full of plastic play equipment that wouldn't get to butt-blistering temperatures in the Texas sun. The ground was covered with mulch, softening the blow for falling children.

Now, it sat in all of its toughen-you-up glory of my childhood. A merry-go-round that could catapult a careless kid ten feet. A seesaw just waiting to break some poor kid's tailbone. A mound of cross bars that could chip a tooth and break an arm in one fell swoop.

Sitting in one of the swings of a snaggletoothed swing set is Sofia.

The muddy, packed earth sucks at my sneakers as I approach her.

She sits hunched over; her gaze stuck to whatever the toe of her shoe is digging up.

"Hey," I say, flicking off a puddle of water from the thick rubber swing beside her.

My best friend startles, as if oblivious to my approach. "Oh hey, Jo, what are you doing here?"

The damp cold seeps through my jeans, but I'm less concerned about whatever germs might be soaking into my derrière, instead relishing this precious time with Sof.

"Driving around. Trying to find my way back home."

Sofia doesn't question my guru-like response. She just nods as if that makes all the sense in the world.

"Remember when Chip Mason got stuck on the fireman's pole?" she asks, gesturing toward the slide with the pole running alongside it.

"Oh my gosh, yes! He was stuck midway down." I double over with laughter at a classmate's expense. The memory floods back like it was not decades deep in my brain. "Did he pee himself? Is that why he wouldn't go down?"

Sofia throws her head back and laughs. "Maybe?"

For the first time in months, years, my old best friend is there. Carefree, her dark hair cascading down her back in thick waves, brown eyes dancing with mischief.

"Oh, and that time Jason Anderson hid in the cedar trees during a game of hide and seek and didn't hear the teachers calling us in," Sofia says.

"And then the police came out, and he thought he was going to get arrested," I finish her sentence. "He was such a shit. They really should've arrested him."

When her laughter fades, an uneasy silence settles back between us.

"I miss you, Sof," I blurt before I can talk myself out of it. "I have for a while now, longer than I can explain, but I miss you."

She nods and looks out over the playground as if looking for the ghosts of our childhood.

"I have no clue what I'll be doing this time next year. I've always known what was ahead of me and that you and Em would be beside me. But you're both going off to college and," she sighs. "I just don't know what the future holds for me."

I chew my lower lip, hoping to find the words she needs to hear. The first time around, Emily and I enrolled in a four-year college, Sofia stayed behind for community college. We would hang out when we came home for the holidays, but those visits tapered off.

"Do you wish you could go back and do it all over again?" she asks.

I snort. "Would you believe me if I tell you I am?"

Sofia's head whips in my direction. "What?"

I twist my swing in her direction, hoping she'll see I'm not joking. "My mind is thirty years older than my body. Like, I've gone to college and gotten married, had kids, started a business and," my chest seizes, probably for the first time since the reality of my divorce sunk in. "I'm in the process of getting a divorce."

Her face is so still I wonder if I said the words aloud or not.

"Wait, so you're how old?"

"Forty-seven."

"What happened to seventeen-year-old Josie?"

"Maybe we switched places, and she's beating the crap out of my ex?" I shrug. "I guess I'm still her. I'm not sure how the whole thing works. There's not exactly a manual for this. Trust me, I've looked."

"You're kidding, right? This is some joke. Or maybe you hit your head?" She cranes her neck, as if looking for a hole in my skull. "You said you were trying to find your way home." Sof holds up a hand. "How many fingers am I holding up?"

"Four, and no, no joke. Although it could be the manifestation of a slow, agonizing death."

Sofia finally scrunches her nose. "How long have you been here?"

I take a deep breath. Emily would be the one who would be forever mad at me for not telling her the minute I woke up in this time. Sofia would be the one to understand. At least, I hope so.

"I woke up in this time the morning of our senior photos. Before that, I was at my office in Austin having a panic attack because I made a bad business decision, and my ex-husband wants full custody of the kids."

"Did you marry Daniel?" She asks, as soft as a secret. "Is he your ex?"

I shake my head and look at the mud beneath the swing. "A guy named Peter Gardner. I met him after college. But, he wasn't Daniel, and while I never said anything to him, I think he always knew there was someone else with my heart."

Sofia pauses her interrogation and blows out a long exhale. "I've noticed you've been different lately. I couldn't put my finger on it, like you always held something back from us. You know? You've felt older. Kinda like hanging out with my big sister. I still see us when we were kids, but that's not who she is anymore."

She's right. I am like their older sister in a way. I've walked down the road of life ahead of them, and once you do that, it's hard to go back and walk blindly with someone. I know too much. I know the potholes of heartbreak. The floaty feeling of love. I know the shortcuts and the scenic routes.

"Does Emily know anything is up?" I ask.

Sofia shakes her head, her dark hair falling over her shoulders. "If it's not about Em and her latest crush, it doesn't exist."

"But we still love her—"

"Dearly," Sofia says on the heels of my words.

We laugh at the gentle ribbing of our friend.

"Am I," Sofia speaks after a long silence, but her voice breaks. She clears her throat and starts again. "You said earlier you've missed me for a while. Am I dead?"

"Oh, honey, no, you're alive. I've done enough social media stalking to know that."

"Social, what?"

I shake my head—another conversation for another day. "As far as I know, you're alive and well. We grew apart for some reason, and I've really missed you, but I don't know how to bridge that gap. Or if you even want me to." A deep inhale of cool, damp air fills my lungs. "Whatever I did, or do, please know it was never to hurt you. I love you, Sof, you're a sister to me."

Her pretty face breaks into a wide smile. "I pre-forgive you," she giggles, but her face drops like she'd grabbed a hot pan. "Tell me about your kids," Sofia says, breaking me out of the prison of my musings. "I bet you're an amazing mom."

It was my turn to smile. At the mere mention of my kids, my eyes burn with emotion. "You will adore my daughter, Aubrey; she could have been one of our friends. And, Ben, he's the most serious kid I've ever met, and I'm probably the only parent on the planet who hopes her child has a wild phase in college."

We sit in the park, letting the drizzling rain quietly soak us to the bone while dusk drapes over us.

Sofia never asks me about what the world is like in the future, maybe because she wants to journey life with wide-eyed wonder.

Instead, we talk about my kids. As if she's trying to soak up every bit of information about two souls she might meet or might not.

I don't know if I repaired the chasm between us. Maybe I just cemented it. Permitted it to happen. It doesn't matter, sitting there, soaked to my underwear and shivering, I feel lighter than I've felt in years.

CHAPTER 31

Honesty has amazing healing powers. Screw being the best policy. It's medicinal. Not only does the person who shares their truth feel better, lighter, but the person it's shared with feels valued. Trusted.

In the days following our playground talk, Sofia is more present. Spending time with Em and me between classes instead of scurrying off to her next class.

Even with Sof firmly cemented back in our trio, guilt curdles in my stomach each time our gazes meet. The passing acknowledgment of the truth I shared with her broke my heart because I didn't, couldn't, share that with Emily.

For all of the qualities that I love in Em, her carefree spirit, the fact she'll always show up with an encouraging word and a bottle of wine, and that I can tell her the most embarrassing things and she won't bat an eye, I know that something this outrageous and fantastical won't land well.

Her first response would be complete disbelief. Then, she'd drill me about everything from the future. After that, she'd drop hints like a klutzy waitress with a tray full of glasses, loudly and in front of a large crowd.

Luckily, she's still in that self-absorbed period of adolescence to realize that something is different.

After losing my journal and my meltdown with Jake, Stuart, and Matthew, it's nice to be able to confide in Sofia. When I feel especially homesick for my kids, I pull Sof aside and talk. Talk about how Aubrey could swing from old soul to sassy teenager in a sentence. Or how Ben helped me with my business taxes when he was ten just because he wanted to challenge himself. I told her about Peter, hoping to impart the lesson of love and loss to her.

We only had a few of these conversations in the three weeks since that rainy afternoon in the playground, but they did so much to ground me in both my present, past, and my future.

I'm starting to feel more like seventeen-year-old Josie and less like my forty-seven-year-old self. More carefree. Less worried about what the future might hold. Then again, maybe it's because I know.

I know the path I'll walk down for the next thirty years. Like a favorite running route, does that make it less exciting?

Or, does it mean that because I know of the cracks in the pavement, the buckles in the road, I'll spend more time looking up, enjoying the scenery rather than just trying to get through life.

It's on a lazy Saturday afternoon at my house that I'm basking in the simplicity of life. Emily, Sofia, and I are watching MTV, and I'm trying to withhold declarations of how long it'd been since I'd seen a video for a new song.

There's no dishes to do. No baskets of laundry. Or emails chirping on my phone. We're hanging out watching the same thing, instead of hanging out with our heads bent over phones. It's a perfect vacation to a place that can never be revisited—my past.

During a commercial break, Emily pops up from her spot on the floor and wipes orange fake-cheese dust from her chips down the front of her T-shirt.

"What are we doing? Life is passing us by!" She jumps around like a half-crazed, fully caffeinated banshee. "Spring break is in two weeks, then prom, graduation, and then the end of our youth as we know it. We need an adventure we'll remember for the rest of our lives."

"There will come a day when spending an afternoon watching

music videos will seem like an adventure," I counter, mainly because it's true but also because apprehension crept in like a teenager sneaking home after a kegger. We didn't have a spring break adventure our senior year. Emily visited her grandparents, and Sophia worked and I helped out at my parents' insurance office. "Don't you have plans already anyway?"

"But we have to make life happen, not sit around and wait for it." Emily's whining would make Aubrey proud. I need to tell her that her Aunt Em was a master teenage whiner. "And Nana would understand. She's the one telling me life passes quickly, anyway."

My mom sticks her head in, likely as a result of that maternal radar for the planting of a very bad idea. "You girls staying for dinner? I can run out and pick up some movies and a pizza."

The benefit of hindsight and age tells me this is more about my mom wanting to keep my friends and me close to her for a little while longer.

"Sure, Mom, that'd be great. Thank you!"

"Mrs. Berry, what do you think about us girls taking a spring break trip?" Emily asks. "Thelma and Louise style, just without the driving off a cliff. Oh, and probably without doing it with Brad Pitt."

My mom quirks an eyebrow, the left side of her lip quivers as she attempts to hold in a laugh. "Probably?" Her voice tilts, a tone she'd used, will use, with my kids when they share some far-fetched tale. "You girls should aim higher," she teases.

"But really, Mrs. B, what do you think?" Emily presses while my mother straightens a pillow.

"It's okay, Mom, you can say no." I try to hide my desperation, but it's a feral creature snarling to be let loose. This didn't happen before. So, it can't happen now. I'm fine with minor detours in my trip back to the past, but something like an actual trip could change everything.

I try to read her mind, try to ascertain if she's going to shoot this wild hair of an idea down or if she's actually entertaining allowing three teenage girls to go on a trip.

"Why don't y'all come up with some options, and we'll talk about it." She pulls the classic *'we'll see'* Mom move. "I'll call for pizza and get my checkbook."

"I'll help with the order," Emily says. "I'm vegetarian now."

"When did she become vegetarian?" Sofia asks as soon as Emily is out of the room. "She ate a burger yesterday."

"It's short-lived. She'll be so hangry in a couple of weeks that we'll force her to eat chicken fried steak."

Sofia snorts. "Hangry, that's funny."

I laugh to myself. Wouldn't it be funny if I inadvertently coined this slang by simply dropping it into the past?

My mind starts whirling with what else I could do to quietly change the world when Sof pulls me out of my plotting.

"In your past, we don't take a trip, do we?" Her voice is low as her gaze darts to the door.

I shake my head. "Em visited her grandparents, we just stayed around here, worked, hung out." My gaze follows hers.

Mom is on the phone with the pizza place, and Em is giving very specific instructions for the pizza order.

"I've tried hard not to change things, and I don't know if this is because I'm here, or what," I add.

Sofia leans over. Her warm brown eyes bore into mine. "Well, then, it'll be an adventure for all of us."

I laugh. "And here, I thought I was the adult trapped in a teenager's body."

Before she can respond, Emily comes skipping back in. "Okay, we have a pineapple and Canadian bacon ordered," she says, plopping onto the couch between Sofia and me.

"Canadian bacon? Really? You already gave up on vegetarianism?" Sofia asks.

"No, why? What do you mean? I thought that was like veggie bacon or something."

I already can't wait to get back to my time and tease the hell out of Emily for thinking Canadian bacon was vegetarian. "Oh, honey."

We sit for a second and then burst into a chorus of teenage girl laughter. The kind of laughter that rings high with innocence but also has the undertone of restlessness. Of being eager to taste more of life. Because that's exactly where we sat.

The three of us singing various verses of the same song.

Emily, the wanderer ready to greet the rest of her life with open arms and defiance.

Sofia, already weary, slipping into the future like wading into cold water.

I've already swam in the deep, and now that I'm back at the shore, I find myself both eager to stay where it's safe but also to get back in and swim back to where I was in life even if I have to battle a few sharks along the way.

"All right, girls, where do we want to go for vacation?"

CHAPTER 32

It was my mom who ended up suggesting a vacation spot; Galveston. Which is ironic since just a few years from now, after I graduate high school and go to college, after my dad collapses at work and dies and she sells the business, and against my warnings of hurricanes, Mom buys a beach bungalow in the Gulf-side town.

While Aubrey and Ben love visiting my mom and spending hours playing on the beach and in the surf, I always wished she would've stayed nearby to see her grandchildren grow up daily rather than dramatic growth spurts or FaceTime calls.

Mom pops open the door of our hotel room. Musty, overly-air-conditioned air tinged with the chemically enriched smell of bleach greets us like an attention-starved pet. Her room has a single king, and an adjoining room has two queens.

"Now," Mom says, heaving a bag of hardback library books on her bed. "I know you girls are just months away from going off to college and staying out all hours, but humor me for these next few days and be in by eleven and let me know where you'll be and who you'll be with."

I nod my head in maternal solidarity.

"I know this goes without saying, but no beer and no boys in the room, and you don't go anywhere with anyone you don't know or just met. We don't know what kind of families they come from," she continues, her green eyes sparkling as she lays down the law. A memory of Mom telling me I'm too strict with my kids hovers like an annoying gnat.

When I was a teenager, we could see our predators face-to-face and look them in the eye. The predator we don't see is much more terrifying than a zit-faced, bone-skinny teenage boy with an overdose of hormones and hair gel.

"But, most importantly," her face softens, and with it, my mom looks young, younger than I remember.

The years rewind like a VHS running backward, reminding me of when I caught Dad watching old home videos of me as a baby. That's the Patty standing before us, her brown hair shiny without the dullness of gray settling in, face smooth and full, devoid of the lines that betrayed every worry, regret, and heartbreak she tried to keep hidden.

"You're young only once, life goes by too fast. Today you're teenagers, tomorrow you'll be in college, and after that getting married and having babies. Hold on to this moment. Hold on to each other." Mom's eyes fill with tears, and her voice wobbles like a toddler learning to walk.

I cross the dank hotel room in two steps and crush her in a hug. To hold tight to the woman she is now, who she will be in my present. Seconds later, two more sets of arms wrap around us.

In the huddle of the hug, my gaze meets Sofia's. Her mouth twitches into an apologetic smile.

Is she apologizing for what happened in my life, or what could still happen?

It doesn't matter. We might remain best friends, become bitter enemies, or fall somewhere in between.

At this moment, we are the past, the present, and the future.

The rest of spring break goes by with no drama, no skirting the rules, no arched eyebrows from Mom. Just the three of us, really four of us because after my mother's talk in the hotel room, Sofia and Emily wanted to invite her to sit with us on the beach and hang out at dinner every night.

The Type-A in me fidgets with wanting to do something, anything, to try to get back to my kids. But, what can I do?

I'd told the three guys who could help me I didn't need their help. The drawing I'd hoped would jumpstart a panic attack and my list of things to fix while I'm here vanished.

I'm stranded in my past. An alien who knows the language and social norms of the time, but also has seen what the future holds. I feel like I'm constantly on the verge of spilling a big secret, like trying to keep the magic of Santa Claus alive for just a bit longer, even though my kids were privy to all of our hiding spaces.

"Earth to Josie," Emily says, bringing me crashing back to sitting beachside with puny waves rolling in.

"Yeah? I'm here, just thinking. What's up?"

"I was just saying that your mom tells us no boys, but she's not following her own advice."

I follow her gaze further down the beach.

My mom stands there in her one-piece, an open button-up shirt blowing in the wind as her cover-up and a hot pink visor cuts into her thick bob. She's laughing, chatting with a lean older gentleman, his skin like oiled leather and his hair white as snow.

After Mom and Dad divorced, she focused on me and my tantrum in my original timeline, foregoing dating or even just having fun with her friends to coddle an overindulgent baby of a teenager. When my dad died, I think it crushed her more than she expected.

In the weeks after Peter moved out, Mom stayed a week with me. Maybe it was to back me up in case my kids had a similar reaction to my divorce—they didn't—or to welcome me to the club of middle-aged divorcees.

"Josie, don't do what I did," she'd said then, at the end of a bottle of wine. "Don't skip out on finding love again because the thought of losing him, a *him* you don't even know for God's sake, freezes your heart. I'm now at the point that anyone I do find will likely die before I have him fully trained." A sigh tumbling into a laugh attempted to make her words a jest, but the truth was in the center.

The truth, my truth, was that I already know my *him*. I just didn't know where to find him in my future. I know exactly where he is now.

Several hundred miles inland, sitting at his window staring into a dark house behind him while his parents argue downstairs.

I couldn't tell him then, but I can tell him now.

If only I can be brave enough to make the hardest decision of my life.

If only I can find the words.

If only he wouldn't think I'd lost my ever-loving mind.

CHAPTER 33

There's a delineation in time after Spring Break. The weather warms in Central Texas, bright green leaves peek out from winter-brown limbs and the smell of summer is in the air.

For seniors, it's a trail mix of emotions. There's the salty, senioritis-afflicted students who see their release from the prison of public education on the horizon. Then the sweet, emotional, I'll-never-see-you-guys-again kids who cry at the mere mention of the final time of doing anything. Then there's me, the crusty, dry Melba toast that will cut the roof of your mouth.

That's exactly how I feel every time I see Matthew, Jake, and Stuart. Like my presence could gash them.

Jake's eyes widen, and his already pale skin blanches to near translucence.

Stuart becomes even louder and more obnoxious whenever I'm near as if trying to make me jealous.

Dear, sweet Matthew, when his dark eyes turn in my direction, they're filled with the heartbreak of watching a beloved pet die.

I'm running late to Physics when our paths don't just cross but collide.

The boys and I each approach the door to the class from opposite sides. Them, lost in conversation, me, head down to read the final part of a chapter for a quiz.

"Oof," I say, bouncing off Jake's bony chest. "Sorry about that."

Stuart snorts. "At least you're sorry about something."

I open my mouth, a nasty response ready to leap from my lips like a high diver, but it gets shoved aside for something else.

The truth.

"I'm sorry for so many things. We'll be late to the *next* class if I try to list them all." I push past them to take my seat but pause midway into the room.

"You know what, I *am* sorry," my voice is louder than I planned. As if I weren't speaking to three teenagers in front of me, but to whoever I wronged, will wrong. "I'm sorry I got mad at you guys. I'm sorry I put incredible pressure on you to do something that literally no one on the planet has done—or will do for the foreseeable future." I soften under the wide-eyed gazes at the three guys who believed me first. "But mostly, I'm sorry I hurt your feelings. I miss you guys."

Within seconds, a wave of overly-cologned adolescent boys crashes into me, pulling me into the center of a very tight, very warm group hug.

Mr. Davies clears his throat. "Well, now that we got that out of the way, do you mind if I enlighten young minds?"

Whatever words leave his mouth after I make up with the guys doesn't penetrate my brain. It doesn't matter. I won't use the velocity of an object falling through Earth's gravity to find my way back home.

The way I'll fall forward won't involve dividing the time it took the object to travel a given distance by the distance—or something like that. I'm not sure what it will involve, or if the three guys seated in front of me even have it in them to figure it out. What I do know is that a good heartfelt apology is as clearing as a rainstorm on a hot day.

Ruby's already in the library when I make it there.

For some reason, I always feel like my journal is nearby when I'm in the library. It's probably because that's where it went missing.

Or, I assume that's where it went missing. Maybe the backpack was open because someone was thinking about lifting my wallet with my meager teenage money shoved inside. It's like a ghost. I can feel its presence, but I just can't see it.

"Hey, Ruby," I say, dropping into the chair beside her. "I'm going to dig through the 18th-century literature section today to see if my journal might be there." I steal a glance at the girl, her face hidden by stringy hair. "You still haven't come across it? Haven't seen anyone snooping around back here?"

Her head shakes, the curtain of hair moves in waves. "Maybe you just left it at home?" Ruby says, her voice as thin as crepe paper and sounds like it could be torn just as easily.

"Hmm, maybe. I'll take a look," I say with about as much commitment as a yo-yo dieter in a pie shop.

Ruby and I babysit the checkout desk, each of us focusing on something other than the other. Uneasiness settles between us like a large man in the middle seat of an airplane, annoyance bumping like elbows warring for armrest dominance.

"Hey, Jo." Daniel's voice pulls me out of my passive-aggressive vision quest. "Senior kegger down at the Point Saturday night. You coming?"

My heart tumbles into my stomach, causing the Coke to rise back up my throat. The spring senior kegger at the Point.

A rite of passage of teens generations before me, but that all ends this weekend when Ian Phillips takes off into the lake in water that was much too cold. He never comes back up, and a party full of minors in possession did nothing but watch the lake swallow him whole.

"Oh, this weekend?" I rummage around in my closet of excuses but come up with something about as substantial as a string bikini. "It'll still be cool this weekend. Why don't we wait until it warms up some?"

He narrows his green-gold eyes and cocks his head, possibly looking to see if I've grown another head.

"Well, we could, but I'd have to ask Mike, who'd then have to check with Stephen because he's in charge of the bonfire, and then Reid's older brother is coming in from Houston this weekend, and he's going to pick up the kegs for us. And then next weekend is a big tennis tournament in San Antonio, so the tennis team will be gone. And the weekend after that we have our regional track meet, so I'll be back late. Then we've got prom, and after that—"

"Okay, okay," I cut him off. "I get it, but can we lay down a few ground rules, like no one goes skinny dipping?"

"That's oddly specific, but sure, I promise not to go jumping into the lake."

"And you promise not to let anyone else jump in the lake? I mean, you know, skinny dipping is so not cool," I try to make my voice light and carefree, but it comes across as squeaky and needy.

"I guess it depends on who gets naked," he says, his green-gold eyes boring into mine.

Heat floods my body. Is it possible that menopause followed me into the past?

My heart that'd been swimming around in the Coke float of my stomach shoots up to my throat, strangling any words that threatened to spill out like the foam of a shaken soda: messy, sugary and something that will likely stick to the bottom of my shoe.

"See you at Yearbook, Jo." Daniel's added wink is like throwing gasoline on a hot flash.

Only when he's left the library do I realize we weren't alone.

Ruby snorts next to me. "You're acting like something is going to happen," she says.

I whip my head to study her, but the girl keeps her face hidden behind her hair, a dull pencil in her hand, sketching what looks like a dark hallway with a figure at the end.

"No," I say casually. "Why in the world would you say something like that."

I hope my voice pulls off the role of a lifetime because my brain keeps screaming, *that bitch stole my journal.*

CHAPTER 34

Leave it to Mother Nature to try to help a sister out.

When Saturday night rolls around, so does one last cold front. It's not enough to usher in spring thunderstorms but enough to force teenagers to wear pants and jackets. Meaning the temperatures at the lake that evening will drive the seniors to cluster around the bonfire and away from the Arctic air blowing in off the lake.

I hope.

Emily, Sofia, and I arrive as the last of the sun's orange glow fades off the horizon. Usually, we'd get there well after the party started, but I pleaded with Emily to speed up her pre-party primp routine so I could get a visual on Ian Phillips before dark.

"Great, people are going to see the zit on my forehead and stare at it all night," Em whines into her cup of cheap keg beer. "How am I going to get Jordan to want to get back together with me if there's a third eye staring at him?"

Jordan Chambers. The guy Emily threw herself at in the fall for the Homecoming dance, only to dump at Thanksgiving for a mysterious college guy she met at a bowling alley while visiting her grandparents in Houston. For what it's worth, I'm pretty sure he was just a fast-developing high schooler. At any rate—or age— he stopped returning her calls before Valentine's Day.

Thus, starting Emily's disastrous love life.

I should've added that to my list. To lay the groundwork for Emily to eventually mature into an adult who can have healthy relationships.

Then again, that would deprive myself and her a lifetime of hilariously disastrous dating stories.

Maybe it's best to leave that one alone. Future me will need the laughs.

"If a boy can't see past the monstrous zit to the beautiful girl beneath, he's just not worth having," I say. "Even if the zit is so large that it's practically overtaking her face."

Em's blue eyes widen and then crinkle in silent laughter. "Okay, okay, I'm being a bit dramatic." She takes a sip of beer. "I just don't want to go to my senior prom alone."

"You won't be alone. You've got us," Sofia says.

During our Spring Break trip, we made a one-for-all, all-for-one pact of either we all have dates to the prom, or we go together. Seeing that neither Sofia nor I had boyfriends, it'll be a girls' night.

Em's face twists into a pout. "I love you guys, but it could be *the night* with Jordan, you know?"

The memory of prom and the aftermath snuck into my brain like a teenager creeping in past curfew. Emily was damn determined to lose her virginity on prom night. Like anything willed into existence, it would end horribly. Naturally.

"You know, Em, there's no prize for being the first to lose your virginity," I start a conversation I had with Aubrey just a few months earlier; funny enough, after going to Emily for advice on how to talk to my daughter about sex without making it seem like I was talking to my daughter about sex. "It should be special, something you'll remember for the rest of your life *with* someone you'll remember for the rest of your life."

Her eyes widen. "Really, *Mom*? Oh my God," she laughs so hard she snorts. "That's the corniest thing I've ever heard. I'm going to get some more beer and find Jordan."

Once Em is out of earshot, I turn to Sofia, my own laugh working its way out of my throat. "In thirty years, that's line for line what she'll tell me to say to my daughter. If I get to live this all again, I'm making sure Aubrey knows her Aunt Em coached me on 'the talk'."

A sad smile touches her face, and I realize my mistake. Even though she's one of a few people I trust with my truth, she's still left out simply because of something that hasn't happened yet. And might not.

Damn, time travel is a mind fuck.

"Oh, I'm sorry, I'm sure—"

"It's fine." She shakes her head. "I'm going to go, see, um, someone over there. I'll be back."

With that, my other best friend abandons me like I'd passed gas in church.

I sip my beer and study the faces around me. Faces that a few months ago were vaguely familiar.

Except for one.

One I thought about during those sleepless nights filled with regret and nostalgia.

That face now watches me from across the fire, oranges and reds lighting up his golden skin, reflecting from his eyes. My breath catches, and a shiver radiates from my heart through my body.

Daniel makes his way around the blaze toward me, his eyes steady on mine as he dodges bodies.

My teenage feet want to flee, but the grown-ass woman in my brain orders them to stay put.

"Hey, you cold?" He asks, pulling off his denim jacket.

"Why do you ask?"

"I saw you shiver from over there. Plus, you didn't dress for being at the lake."

I look down at my outfit. Or lack thereof. He's right. I didn't dress for being at the lake. A black, chiffon baby-doll dress with the tiniest flowers. From a distance, it's all goth, but up close, it would appease even the most pearl-clutching church lady. Black tights cover my legs but do nothing to keep the wind away. Of course, no nineties grunge outfit would be complete without black Doc Martens. I really need to bring some of this fashion into the 2020s.

Anyway, I need to keep a fish from ending up in the lake, and you don't catch fish with frumpy clothes. You catch them with skin. Especially the super creepy fish with big eyes and obnoxious teeth.

For the sake of fixing the magical thing from my past that needs solving so I can end up back with my kids I'd happily be the sacrificial worm.

"Well, you know, YOLO." I shrug. In my case, it's YOLT, but that sounds like something birds do when they lose their feathers.

"YOLO? Is that like those annoying chewy candies?"

Damn, kids and their slang. I can't keep up with what my kids say now and what I said three decades ago.

"Never mind. Hey, have you seen Ian?"

Daniel drops his confused face and picks up his annoyed one. "Why would you ask about that asshole?"

"Oh, you know, just because I, um, need to tell him something." I hide my wince at my pathetic attempt at playing it cool. More like playing it tepid.

"Actually," I step closer to him and lower my voice. His pine tree and sunshine scent warms me. "I heard some freshmen girls are planning on coming tonight. I want to keep an eye on him to make sure he behaves. You know?" I hold my face steady, hoping no twitch or diversion of my gaze gives me away.

Daniel nods twice and looks over his right shoulder. "Last I saw he was smoking a joint over there."

Great. Trying to keep a sober person from jumping in the lake is bad enough. Now I have to contend with a hold-my-beer-watch-this scenario.

"Lovely," I murmur.

Daniel grips my shoulders and leans in close enough that I think he's going to kiss me.

Hope he's going to kiss me.

"This time around, will you let me handle the prick? I have no doubt you can take him, but I'd love to have a reason to kick his ass." His breath kisses my faces, causing my knees to forget their purpose in life.

I nod, unwilling to allow myself to lie to him for the second time in as many minutes.

Seemingly satisfied, he gives my shoulders a squeeze and wanders over to a group of cross country guys.

I nurse my beer as I stalk the edges of the party. Like a panther, I eye my prey's every move. Lucky for me, Ian seems pretty content to just hang out near the keg, so my stalking is more like loitering but with a point.

In addition to the most uneventful stakeout in the history of stakeouts, I flit between clusters of kids like a well-trained social butterfly, dropping in and out of conversations with the practiced grace of a trophy wife.

The moon climbs high in the sky, its light teaming up with the glow of the fire to help me keep everyone in check.

Emily found Jordan, his letter jacket draped over her shoulders, proving all is forgiven.

Sofia chats with another group of our classmates.

Daniel and Jessica stand three feet apart. From their body language alone, the conversation looks painful and uncomfortable.

I have to admit, it makes me smile a bit.

Music thumps from someone's car. The crowd of teenagers swells beyond the size of our senior class. No doubt underclassmen heard about the party. Despite all of the people, Ian's tall, thin figure stays in the shadows, his face illuminated by an occasional drag on a joint or cigarette.

Ugh, the idiot will need every bit of lung capacity and sober brain cells.

I make another circle around the party before stopping at the edge near the water, nibbling on a snagged cuticle. Future me will deal with breaking this habit with expensive nail appointments, but present me is indulging in it.

A twig snaps on my right, and I jump, dropping my hands to my side like I'd been caught by my manicurist, who probably hasn't even been born yet.

Daniel emerges two clear plastic cups of beer in his hands. "You're making me dizzy," he says, handing me one of the cups.

"You're watching me?"

"I'm always watching you." He winces. "Wow, that sounded way more romantic in my head, but out loud it just sounds…"

He said romantic? My insides buzz like I'd just chugged hot sauce with an energy drink chaser.

"Creepy," I say, keeping the hyperactive kittens in my stomach from showing in my voice. He'd never said "romantic" to me before.

He laughs and takes a long drink of his beer.

Did he develop the same habit as his dad? Was future Daniel sitting somewhere in a worn-out recliner with a receding hairline and beer belly, bitter because I turned him down?

Does one person have that much power over someone's entire life?

"Look, Josie…" His voice trails, and he wrings the back of his neck with his free hand.

For the second time that evening, a shiver runs through me. He hasn't called me Josie in years. It was mostly Berry, or Jo, or JoBear, or even CuppaJo.

Never Josie.

The last time I heard "Josie" on his lips was when he professed his love in the middle of a rainstorm the evening we graduated high school.

"Daniel?" I breathe it more than speak it.

He clears his throat and knits his brows so tightly my grammy would be proud of his knit and purl.

A shout goes up at the party, pulling my attention away.

Ian and two other guys are slamming beers.

"Josie, are you planning on going to the prom?"

I drag my focus back to him, ignoring the energy tingling in the air. "Yeah, but with Em and Sof. Well, at least Sof, last I saw Emily, she was flirting with Jordan like he was the last man on earth."

Another whoop and cheers as the beer drinking contest comes to a close. Teenage bodies cluster so tightly together that I can't tell what's happening.

"Well, if it's not going to hurt Sofia's feelings, would you, maybe, I dunno, consider…"

Daniel's nervous. Never in the years I'd known him did Daniel seem anything less than sure. Not cocky, but confident. Someone sure in his decisions. Someone who always assumed life would give him what he needs when he needs it.

Someone who had dated a freaking teenage model was nervous.

"Would you go to the prom with me?"

His question lands on me like a cartoon arrow to the heart.

He didn't ask me to prom the first time around.

I went with Emily and Sofia.

Daniel and I danced one fast dance together, but that was it.

This was new. This was unexpected.

This could change everything.

I open my mouth to answer him when feminine squeals and masculine shouts of encouragement cut me off. Out of the corner of my eye, Ian races past. He'd already lost his shoes and shirt, his pants were halfway down his thighs, and he either dragged his underwear with him or went commando because a group of unsuspecting seniors egged on his blinding white ass.

"Shit." I hand my beer to Daniel. "We have to stop him."

He scowls at me. "Let his dick shrivel. Josie, did you hear me?"

Ian curses as he hits the water, but it doesn't slow him from trudging forward at the urging of an audience.

"Yes."

"Yes, you heard me, or yes, you'll go to the prom?"

Before I could answer—which is really fortuitous because I'm not sure what I'm answering—Ian disappears from the surface.

My gaze scans the crowd, looking to see if any other faces wear alarm, but most everyone has the attention span of my son's betta fish and has gone back to whatever they were doing before a classmate went streaking into the water.

I look back to the water. It's still, just a few waves lapping at the shore.

"He's still under." I take off running. Freezing water fills my Doc Martens. Dammit, I should have worn lighter shoes. My muscles seize at the cold, refusing to move forward as if they know better than my brain. They aren't wrong. "He's still under," I yell, hoping my voice rises over the music and chatter of the crowd.

Daniel shouts my name behind me, but I trudge forward.

Which is dumb because I just ran into the dark water without actually paying attention to where I am in relation to the last place I saw Ian.

The water laps at my chest. I try to keep my teeth from chattering, but they've got their own agenda. At my next step, my foot doesn't find the bottom of the lake. Instead, I fall, the lake swallowing me in a catfish hole.

The last bit of my body not accosted by the freezing water is pulled under. My eyes pop open, burning in the sediment and cold. Unprepared for the hole, I yelp, losing the little precious oxygen my shocked lungs could pull in.

My feet kick, trying to propel me back to the surface, but I might as well have worn cement shoes. My frozen limbs refuse to move. Nothing wants to work. Not my lungs, not my legs or arms. Even my will calls it in.

Maybe this is it. Maybe I'm not meant to survive. Sending me back to my past could be the universe's way of righting some cosmic wrong.

What if something terrible awaits my future, or, God forbid, my kids' future, and the only way to stop it is for me to die?

Is that the thing I had to fix?

To not have a future.

Maybe *The Terminator* is a biopic for my life, not a futuristic sci-fi.

I have just started to accept this fate when the water churns around me.

Arms lift me. Cold air kisses my face as I surface. Words float past me, but none sink in.

"I got Josie."

"I think I see Ian."

"Take her to shore."

"Someone go to town and call an ambulance."

"Too bad cell phones are still years away," I mumble through frozen lips.

"You're going to be okay, Berry." Daniel's soothing voice warms me.

"Y-yes," I say, my head lolling against his chest as he hauls me to shore.

"What's that?"

"Yes, to prom. I-I'll g-go t-to p-prom with you."

He chuckles but doesn't say anything other than to shout orders to get blankets and jackets and clear a path to the fire.

The cool sandy shore clings to my skin before I'm back in his arms. The glow of the fire drawing us like frozen moths.

Even though he's soaking wet, Daniel holds me close to him and presses his lips to my head.

"Ian?" I whisper.

"They got him." He leans up, looking back toward the water. "Looks like he's throwing up half the lake, but aside from that and a bad hangover, he'll be okay."

I relax against him. "Okay, Em, I can wake up now."

"I'm right here, sweetie." My best friend says, but not my best friend's voice that has deepened with age and experience, but my teenage best friend's voice, light, unencumbered by life.

"You must be psychic or something," Daniel murmurs, his voice more in his chest than in my ears. "If you hadn't been paying attention, Ian would have died tonight."

CHAPTER 35

Monday afternoon, I sit between my parents on their velour sofa, staring at the gaudy pink and gray floral pattern, wishing the flower could turn into a Venus flytrap and swallow me whole.

Ian ended up being fine. He was under longer than me, so where I just had a free ride into town in the back of an ambulance to have a doctor who must've just downed a sandwich with extra onions check me out, he had to spend a couple of nights in the hospital to make sure his lungs are clear and there are no effects of the cold water. The biggest casualty of the night was my Doc Martens.

My heart cries for those shoes.

"Patricia, Alan, what went through your minds when you heard what Josie had done?" asks the reporter from our hometown paper. Based on his worn-brown blazer and seriously-set features, I imagine Roger Masters once thought he'd break Watergate-style scandals, not reporting on small town teen antics.

"Well," my mom starts, tightening her grip on my hand. Not the reassuring type of tightening, the what-were-you-thinking-young-lady kind. "As a mother, my first thought was if she's okay. It was probably my second, third, and fourth thought, too."

"But, once we knew she was fine and heard from her friends what she'd done, how she'd kept watch over her classmates," my dad says, cutting Mom off. "That's just like our Josie. She's extremely mature and responsible, more like an adult than a kid these days." Pride glows in his eyes.

Of course, I knew he was always proud of me; he said it many times for many milestones. This is different from getting good grades and winning a race. This kind of pride says they raised a good human, someone who will put others first. Did Mother Teresa or Gandhi's parents have that same look?

"And, Josie, what went through your mind when you saw Ian go under?" Roger asks.

I can't very well tell him the truth. That I thought saving the prick's life would right some karmic wrong in my life and send me back to thirty years in the future.

Then again, he might get his Watergate moment.

"Really, not much," I say to the flowers on the sofa. "I guess I thought about how heartbroken his mom would feel." It's lame, but not as lame as 'not much.' I'm pretty good at media interviews for my little business. Practicing everything my publicist preached, speaking in soundbites, restating questions, clear, concise. Somehow, that knowledge fell out of my brain in the tumble back in time.

Satisfied that he got enough for a short article and a photo of me with my parents, Roger leaves, probably to go find something more interesting to write about. Like a lost cat or a sale at the Swap-N-Go.

"We're proud of you, pumpkin," Dad says, wrapping me in a hug. "But don't you ever do that again. I know I'm being selfish in saying this, but you could have died."

I think about how I'd feel in their place. If Aubrey or Ben put themselves in harm's way for someone else. Pride and fear would battle it out like boxers in a ring, and quite frankly, I'm pretty sure fear would win with me like it did with my parents.

"I can honestly say I'll probably never have to jump in the lake to save someone ever again." Or for at least the next thirty years. The statute of limitations runs out after that.

"I talked to Daniel's mom, and when we order his boutonniere, we'll order your corsage so they can match," Mom says, gathering her purse.

It's no surprise to my parents that Daniel asked me to prom. The paramedics wouldn't let him ride with me to the hospital, but he was there waiting for me and wouldn't leave until my parents showed up.

"It's about time he asked you out," my dad says. "But it's too bad it's Daniel. I'd been practicing my scary-father talk and think I've got it down. But he's a good kid, so I guess I'll have to save it for another time."

We take advantage of me staying home from school to run a few pre-prom errands.

It's weird being a minor local celebrity. The florist, Mrs. Mayfield, hugged me tightly as we picked out the flowers and ribbons for our corsage and boutonniere. The freshman working at the corner sandwich shop eyed me with starstruck wonder.

And, walking the halls the next day at school is even more unnerving.

The sea of students parts in my path, like I'm either a messiah or pariah.

"This is so weird," I say to Em and Sof.

"This never even happened to Jessica Dawson," Em whispers to me.

We get upstairs to the senior hall.

Ian's tall form is visible waiting by my locker. At the hospital, we were next to each other in the ER, but he spent his time crying and retching. Even now, he looks pale, his lips dry and flakey.

"Hey, Ian. How're you doing?" I ask.

Instead of answering, he crashes into me, trapping my arms at my sides while wrapping me in a fierce hug. His body shakes with silent sobs. "Thank you," he whispers through tears. "I wouldn't be here if it weren't for you. Of all people to give a shit about me." His words break into another sob. "I'll make you proud, Josie, I promise."

I pull back and feel my own tears falling down my face. "You don't owe me that. Just be a good person, Ian. That's all I ask."

He nods and pushes past me.

With Ian out of the way, Daniel, leaning against my locker, comes into view, smiling that lopsided grin that excites the butterflies in my stomach.

I grip my stomach to quiet them; sure their wings would become audible if he got closer.

"Hi."

"Hi." The top of my head tingles as if remembering when he kissed it after pulling me out of the lake.

"Little did I know that I'd be going to prom with a local celebrity," he says, his green-gold eyes twinkling in the florescent overhead lights.

"Ah, yes, I should have my people call your people about my rider. I'll need a steady supply of M&Ms, but only the yellow ones, or is it red?" I roll my eyes at my pathetic attempt to be witty. "Just kidding. I'll take all the M&Ms."

We stand there as students float past. Most stopping to give me a 'hey' or a high five. A few walk by with their heads tilted close, their eyes betraying that they were definitely talking about me.

"Do I want to know what they're saying?" I ask.

Daniel shrugs. "Someone started a rumor that you're a time traveler and knew this was going to happen, and you were sent back into the past to stop it."

A freezing flare flashes from my heart and flows through my body.

The fakest laugh I've ever laughed escapes my mouth. It's the laughter of someone forced to pretend their spouse's boss is funny. The laughter of someone going to see a date's favorite comedian only to realize it's more offensive than funny.

The laughter of a time traveler who thinks she was sent back to do something.

"Wow, someone watches too much TV." The bell rings, sending us scurrying to our next class like naughty mice.

The morning passes much like the school day started. Some people staring, some are oblivious to my existence and some are trying to get my attention.

Daniel's revelation about a rumor sticks with me like a pint of ice cream on the hips. Was this Ruby's doing? I have nothing more than speculation that she stole my journal. People have gone to prison on flimsier proof.

By the time I make it to Physics, I've chewed my nails down to nubs and have ripped off the cuticles of one hand. My favorite advice to give Aubrey has always been that she's not responsible for someone else's opinion of her. Like other pearls of wisdom filtered through the lens of adulthood, that's a truckload of crap. Because of my carelessness of bringing something as personal as my journal with me to school and then leaving it unattended, I *am* responsible for all of these opinions of me.

Luckily, today's class will be held in the adjoining lab, conducting small group experiments on volume and displacement theory.

I quickly team up with the guys, eager for some time with people who knew and accepted my crazy.

"Are you still, you know, you?" Stuart asks, setting up everything we'd need for class.

"What? A middle-aged woman in a teenage body?" I lean in and murmur. "Yep, still me." My gaze flits around the lab.

Most of the class is focused on the instructions for the experiments, but I catch at least two sets of side eyes flung in my direction.

"Have you heard what they're saying?" I ask.

"I heard you're a witch, and you put a hex on Ian but then had second thoughts," Matthew says, his focus on an equation.

"Oh, I heard you'd drugged Ian, and that's what made him jump in the lake," Jake adds.

"What?"

"There's also the rumor that you'd tried to kill Ian because of homecoming, but then you nearly died yourself," Stuart says with a sigh. "What are you hearing?"

I scoff. "Funny enough, the truth. That I'm a time traveler trying to fix things."

"Like anyone would believe that," Jake says with a smirk.

"*You* believe that." My voice is a little louder than I expected, and more heads whip in our direction. "That…that dropping this golf ball in the beaker will displace eight milliliters of water," I add as a piss-poor recovery.

"That's not on the worksheet," Matthew pops his head up.

I take a deep breath, drawing in patience with oxygen. "This could be bad. I mean, someone has my journal, and they're spreading stuff. What happens if someone believes them? What if the government comes for me in black SUVs and lots of helicopters and takes me to some secret underground bunker and hooks me up to all these machines?"

If Peter were here, he'd tell me I'm spiraling.

It's more than spiraling. It's a freefall into despair.

Stuart puts his hand over mine and only then do I realize I've wadded up my worksheet. "Two things, Josie. One, you've watched too much sci-fi and I hope I can find a woman as cool as you when I'm old."

"Forty-seven is not old," I feebly interject.

"And two, we know, we heard about the time traveler rumor. We started the others."

I blink. That is surprisingly astute and tactical. "Wow, that's pretty, huh, smart."

"Yeah, it's chaos theory in rumor form."

"I love you guys," I say, hoping they'll realize it's in a purely plutonic way.

"Does that mean you'll go to prom with me?" Stuart sits up straighter.

"Ah, no, I'm going with Daniel."

Matthew lifts his gaze from his worksheet. "Did you go to the prom with Daniel before?"

"Um, no, I went with Emily and Sofia."

His dark eyes stay on me, as serious as a doctor about to give a terminal diagnosis. It's the look of loss.

"Josie, if you go and fall in love with Daniel, what happens to your kids?"

A thumb instinctively rises to my mouth, but I realize I've chewed off everything worth chewing. He's right. I can go to prom; I can have an amazing night with the boy I've loved for more than thirty years.

But, no matter how perfect it is and how much I fall in love, I will still have to walk away from Daniel if I want to see my kids again.

CHAPTER 36

Emily and Sofia show up at my house mid-afternoon to start the excessively long process of getting ready.

Even though our plans shifted, I'm still able to go to prom with Em and Sof, just alongside their dates.

Emily was successful in snagging Jordan as her date. While Daniel was working up the nerve to ask me at the lake, Sof had her own paramour drunkenly confess his four-year-long crush on her.

Maybe this is good for us. Maybe Emily going to prom with Jordan will prevent years of disastrous relationships. Maybe Sofia and Cody will fall madly in love, and she won't disappear to wherever she disappears.

A thought that sours my stomach like pizza-fueled heartburn, maybe I won't fall in love, well, *any more* in love, with Daniel. Maybe he'll smell like expired cottage cheese instead of sunshine and pine trees. Or, he'll make incredibly insensitive jokes about pretty much everyone. Icing on the cake would be if he left me there for Jessica Dawson.

It would be much easier to break Daniel's heart if he wasn't so wonderful.

Emily stares into my bathroom mirror, holding her long hair back from her face. "I should just cut it all off."

"You look super cute with a pixie cut," I say, my mind tumbling through what to do with Daniel.

Sofia pokes me in the side with a long fingernail.

"You *would* look super cute," I recover quickly. "Forgot a verb."

She doesn't seem to notice, instead dropping her hair and shrugging. "Maybe when I go off to college."

The rest of the afternoon passes in a haze of perfume, hairspray, and teenage innocence. We laugh and gossip. Listen to music and pick apart the true meaning of nineties classics. We talk about college, what it will be like to live on our own, the lives we expect to live.

I let myself play along. To not know that Emily will be a psych major and end up being a damn good therapist. I keep to myself that after breaking Daniel's heart and sending him somewhere out into the world, I'll gain the freshman fifteen before I even go to college.

It was only by joining a college running club to work through my regret and remorse that I could come to terms with the mistake I'd made and fit back into my high school jeans. I keep to myself that a decision only looks like a mistake in close proximity. When scar tissue grows around that mistake, one starts to realize something beautiful took root. Like wonderful children who come out of a failed marriage.

No, not a failed marriage. An ended marriage. How could I call what Peter and I created a failure?

"What are we going to do with your hair?" Em asks. "God, if you weren't my best friend, I'd hate you for this hair," she adds, running her fingers through my strawberry blonde waves.

My friend's words pull me back to my bathroom and away from my internal philosophizing.

I laugh. She said a variation of those words to Aubrey just before I slid back in time.

If you weren't my God daughter, I'd hate you for this hair.

This would be a great opportunity to go with a style that would be more contemporary to the twenty-first century so my daughter can look back at my pictures and think what a chic mother she had.

Nope, we're still a stone's throw from the big-hair glory of the eighties. It's time to go big.

With my hair curled, teased, sprayed, back-combed, sprayed again, and then scrunched with a liberal amount of mousse, it's Sofia's turn to do my makeup. Thankfully, my more subtle friend is in charge of that.

Where my usual high school makeup routine is just a few swipes of mascara, powder, and lip gloss, Sof adds expertly drawn navy eyeliner and dark taupe eyeshadow that manages to make my blue-green eyes look both sultry and sweet. A few flicks of her wrist bring out my cheekbones from the adolescent softness of my face. Last, with a swipe of soft pink lipstick, I'm ready for the dress.

One area I indulged myself to make a different decision intentionally was my prom dress. Initially, I went with an early nineties classic: heavy bell skirt, velvet, and taffeta.

This time around, I'm taking advantage of a teenage body with something more streamlined. Spaghetti straps hold up a sweetheart bodice with a starry-night inspired sequined pattern dancing in swirls of blues: light, dark, and teal with streams of silver. The sequins taper off on the straight floor-length skirt, interrupted by a slit that stops mid-thigh.

Oh yeah, Aubrey will love this dress. I can't wait for her to see the pictures.

The doorbell rings, and I swallow back the wince at the thought of my daughter. My lungs fill with air and resolve. I will not do anything tonight to jeopardize having a daughter in the future who'll think I'm badass. Hell, I'd even settle for a daughter who'll think I'm okay-ass.

I study my two best friends.

Sofia's hair is long, loose waves, a perfect complement to the light blue chiffon dress. She looks like calm, welcoming tropical waters.

Where Sofia's walking meditation, Emily is an espresso with a Red Bull chaser. Hair pulled into a tight bun that would make a ballerina proud. Her red, taffeta dress clung to her petite figure like dog hair on the good couch.

"All right, girls, here's to an amazing night." I squeeze their hands.

"We'll probably forget the details, but damn, we'll look good in the pictures," Emily says.

She's not wrong.

Voices float up from the living room as the three of us prepare for an entrance befitting a starlet.

My father is quizzing the guys on the after-prom plans, reminding them to just say no to drugs, booze, and getting into cars with strangers, and I think I even heard him threaten bodily harm if Em, Sof, and I aren't returned exactly as we left.

I grip their hands one more time, selfishly holding them back. I'm not ready to share them with the world. This time, no matter how brief, belongs to us.

It feels like a moment for poignant words, for acknowledging that we're standing at the threshold of our lives. Behind us a life of growing and learning, the first presses of the mold of the people we'll eventually become.

Ahead of us, the unwritten pages of a book. Except for me.

Are the words of my story fading? Is the great author of the universe furiously backspacing to rewrite my story?

Like a palimpsest, will I go through my life for a second time feeling the ghost of my first life?

My mouth opens, hoping something memorable emerges, but Em saves me from an embarrassingly philosophical moment. "Let's go get 'em."

The murmuring voices stop when our heels echo off the wooden stairs.

A throat clears, probably one of the guys.

A sniffle, mostly likely my mom. And, a gasp.

My dad.

This was the closest he'd come to seeing me on my wedding day. Unless I somehow changed the health of his heart.

I doubt it.

But I hope.

Hope is different from naiveté. Naiveté is blissfully ignorant of how something can unfold. Being hopeful is knowing full well but still holding a little spark in your heart that maybe, just maybe, it'll be different.

Dad steps to the bottom of the stairs. His eyes shining with tears and his chin wobbles.

"Hey, pumpkin," his voice is stretched thin with emotion. "Forgive me, I just feel like it was yesterday when you were slow dancing on my feet." He turns to Daniel and cups his shoulder. "If she dances on your feet all night, it's my fault." Dad moves to the side, a subtle gesture carrying enormous weight.

"Hi."

"Hey."

We speak at the same time and laugh.

I take as much of him in as possible without breaking eye contact. His hair is freshly trimmed but still long on top, and the bright gold highlights are a bit more muted. A warm, clean smell wafts off him, not that he never smelled clean before, but his scent is so pure, unhampered by heartache and life.

"You look…" Daniel takes a deep breath as if the word he's searching for floats in the air between us. "Wow."

My stomach cartwheels, sticking the landing. Even though I know what's to come and that beauty fades and what's inside lasts forever. I can't help but do an inner fist pump.

After photos of each couple, of the girls and of the guys, I insist on one more. Of my parents and me. No matter how much of a mess I make of my future, I hope this picture survives.

CHAPTER 37

A short limo ride later, and we're at the high school gym. Daniel offers his arm.

I try to ignore the zap of energy flooding me, but a shiver rocks through anyway.

"Cold?" Daniel asks, starting to pull off his jacket.

"No, I'm fine. I'll warm up once we start dancing."

The high school gym is transformed by an among-the-stars theme. Dark blue fabric covered in silver foil stars covers the pushed-back bleachers. White and blue balloons crowd the floor with a handful of dancers. The bass of a popular hip hop song, one that still plays at gyms today to motivate their middle-aged clientele, thuds through the soles of my heels.

"No matter what they do, it still smells like a gym," Daniel's voice tickles my ear. He grabs my hand. Another shock zaps my body.

Perhaps it's not me. Maybe he's the human equivalent of an electric eel. "Let's get you warmed up."

We join in the growing crowd on the floor.

First, for a few fast dances, but then the music slows, Daniel puts his hands lightly at my waist and, thankfully, pulls me close. I don't know that I'd be able to look at him without leaning up to kiss him.

"So, Berry, there's something I wanted to talk about."

I freeze, missing a beat and accidentally stepping on his foot.

"Oof, your dad did warn me," he chuckles.

"I need to pee," I blurt out, racing in my heels to the bathroom in the way that someone with decades of experience running in stilettos has mastered.

In the stall, I lean my head against the metal door, letting the cold seep into my brain. I can't let him say the words. Because if he says what I know he's going to say, I'll be forced to break his heart when all I want is to be in this moment.

For real.

Without worrying that I'm changing my future with each breath.

Life is full of uneven playing fields. One of the few levelers is that none of us know the future. Sure, we might know that tomorrow we'll wake up with a roof over our heads or that we'll have our family waiting for us. However, it's never a given.

Knowing is worse.

Knowing I could correct one of my life's greatest regrets, but in doing so, I'd rip open another greater regret. As a mother, I'm accustomed to putting my desires aside for my kids, but I'd give anything not to know what's at stake.

My face warms, and I rub the back of my hand under my eyes. Remnants of my eye makeup stare up at me. Dammit, waterproof mascara is stronger in the future.

In the mirror, the damage doesn't seem too terrible. I fan my eyes, the miracle cure for fending off tears. Armed with scratchy paper towels, I gently blot my under eyes.

The door to the bathroom opens, music and crowd chatter wafting in ahead of Ruby.

She pauses, her hair hangs in tight ringlets, and a boxy satin dress drapes her frame. "Josie?"

"Oh, just an allergy attack," my voice is thin and reedy.

My former friend closes the door behind her and crosses the bathroom but still stands a distance away. "I'm here if you want to talk, you know. I understand what you're going through."

The thing about being an adult is knowing the right thing to do. I should politely thank someone for the gesture of caring. I should excuse myself to return to Daniel, a boy I've longed for my entire life.

I should keep my mouth shut because once words are breathed into existence, they're forever there. I can't inhale them back.

I know all this, but months of living as a teenager threw this knowledge out the window.

"Why would I talk to you? You have no idea what I'm dealing with, and if you did, how in the world could you possibly help?" The rage inside of me pops like an angry zit. More and more pus-filled words line up. "We're not friends, Ruby. You're just a small girl in a small town you'll never leave. You're a nobody. Now and in the future."

Ruby winces, my insults slapping her across the face.

My eyes sting again like furious ants are attacking them instead of my rage. Not rage at Ruby, but at myself. Because standing there, I did exactly what I always preach to my kids never to do.

I should apologize. Tell her I'm mad at myself. At the universe for this cruel test that's laid out before me. One without an answer key.

Ruby stands there, face hardening at my verbal attack. She tilts her chin up. "What are you, Josie? Really?"

The bathroom suddenly closes in on me like a coffin. I push my way past Ruby, the girl's face growing redder than Emily's dress, making it as far as the foyer of the high school gym.

"What are you?" she says again from behind me. The words aren't so much as spoken but growled.

"What?"

"*What* are you, Josie?" She shuffles, widening her stance like a boxer in a ring. Her face is so red it's nearly purple.

"What?" My vocabulary seems to have shrunk to one single word.

A few fellow prom-goers pause their conversations, side-eying us to ascertain if this were ticking down to a blow-out or will fizzle into nothing-to-see-here.

I take a deep breath. This is my fault. I can fix this. "I'm sorry, Ruby. I snapped at you back there—"

"Mrs. Patel breaks her ankle," she spits the words like they're sour.

A spear of ice runs through my body, nicking my heart.

I shake my head. "But she doesn't." The voice that comes out of me is small. Like that of a well-meaning but naughty toddler caught with her hand in a cookie jar.

Ruby takes a step in my direction. "She has been nothing but sweet to you. Why would you break her ankle?"

"I didn't, I—"

"Your parents' divorce."

More bodies crowd my peripheral vision. The susurrus of teenagers crowds the bleating guitar of a heavy metal anthem.

"Most marriages end in divorce these days."

Ruby skulks closer. Her nostrils flaring. "You wrote about it two months before it happened."

It's one thing to suspect something because there's always a measure of doubt. It's entirely different to know it to be true and wish nothing more in the world that I was wrong.

"Listen, Ruby, let's go somewhere and talk." I lower my voice, hoping it'll deflate the anger seething through her veins. "I can explain everything."

Movement attempts to steal my attention. That feeling of more bodies crowding into a tightening circle. Eager to see if a girl fight will erupt at prom and contribute to high school lore.

"No, you don't have to explain anything to me. But you do to Sofia." She gestures to my right.

I follow her gaze to see my two best friends pushing through the crowd.

Emily's anger radiates as if she could pull a dagger from her eyes and throw it at Ruby's heart.

Sofia, on the other hand, purses her lips into thin lines.

"Does she know that she's on your list?"

Sofia runs to my side and squeezes my hand. "Ruby, you have no clue what you're talking about."

"Problem with Sofia," the girl quotes my written words to me. "It's amazing you've lasted this long. Your family always has been one step away from being poor, like me, and now that you're on food stamps, she's going to drop you like the shallow bitch she is."

Is that what's been going on?

I knew that money was always tight with Sofia's parents, and she didn't covet the latest teenage fashion like most girls.

"Sof?" I whisper.

She shakes her head in response, her hand going limp in mine.

"And, what about Ian? Did you hate him so much that you tried to kill him?" Ruby says, nodding toward him in the ever-growing crowd.

If someone had told me six months ago—or hell, thirty years ago—that Ian Phillips would find his chivalry bone and come to my rescue, I would've said I must've died and woken up in an alternate universe.

Which, still could be exactly what'd happened to me. Which is why it felt both odd and completely natural for Ian to step between us.

"Listen, Runny Ruby," Ian says, bringing up a forgotten mocking nickname from when we were kids, and she had snot perpetually running from her nose.

Central Texas allergies are just slightly more unkind than kids.

"You wouldn't know this because you weren't there that night because you are a total *loser*." His voice bellows at loser, echoing around the now crowded lobby.

Ruby jumps at his words, seeming to shrink from her earlier power-bloated strength.

Ian leans in and sniffs. "Gah Ruby, you could have at least showered before prom."

She wilts another few inches.

A few kids chuckle, remembering the time in junior high when the P.E. teacher had to talk to Ruby about deodorant.

If public embarrassment were a class, teenagers would ace it. Somehow, the same humans who can't remember to do their homework can reach back into their memories to dig up the most embarrassing thing we've ever done or a nickname everyone called us for a few months in third grade. There're no limits to the cruelty of adolescents.

Which is why I have to stop this. Because I know exactly what these words, this scene, can do to someone. Especially someone like Ruby, who lives with an alcoholic grandmother who didn't want to raise Ruby's mom, much less the surprise offspring she ended up stuck with. Someone who was never given a chance for a normal childhood because the Universe is cruel.

I know the cruelty of the Universe all too well, but I also know that an act of incredible kindness can tilt the wobble back toward the just.

"Leave her alone." I tug at Ian's arm, but he's about as movable as a statue. "Come on, Ian, she's not wrong."

"What?" He seems to have caught the *what* plague. "What the hell are you talking about?"

That's a very good question, and one I don't have an answer for. "That, that I was really pissed at you for the way you treated me at homecoming, and I wrote in my journal that I wanted you to die."

Ruby's muddy brown eyes fly to my face, her expression mostly unreadable, but I think I see a bit of appreciation floating in her irises.

"And my parents," I say a little louder. "I see how much stuff Emily gets from her dad because of the divorce, and I-I guess I'm a little jealous."

My hands start shaking like my body is fighting the words coming from my lips.

"And Sofia?" Someone calls out from the crowd.

I turn to my best friend. One of only a handful of people who knows my truth. Her beautiful face wavers behind the tears in my eyes. I hope she can read the apology in them. I hope she understands I'm doing this to save a girl who's never been helped once in her life.

"She's been cold," I say, my throat constricting on the words. "Aloof, all year. Like she just doesn't want us in her life anymore. Like she's better than us."

A muscle in her jaw twitches, and she swallows hard. Is it because I spared bringing up her family's money troubles, or because, for better part of the year, that was the truth and by breathing life into it, I gave it shape.

Sofia opens her mouth as if she's going to speak but instead pushes through the crowd and back into the dark gym, her thin body wrapped in blue swallowed by a tacky prom theme.

Emily watches our friend retreat and looks at me. "What the hell did you do?" She chases after her.

Ian shuffles beside me.

"Listen, Ian, I'm sorry—"

He shakes his head, cutting me off. "I've never hated someone so much to want them dead," he shrugs. "I know I was an ass at home-coming. But then you saved me, and I thought that if Josie Berry thinks I'm worth saving—" His voice breaks, and he looks over my head. "Maybe what you wrote was right." He joins the dispersing crowd, some heading into the gym, back to the dance, others out into the night, maybe for a cigarette or an afterparty.

Or to talk about their bat-shit crazy classmate without being drowned out by the music.

Finally, it's just Ruby and me, still squared off, but both of us looking like we're on the losing end of seven rounds in the ring.

Or, so I thought.

"Ruby, look, can I just have my journal back? I can explain every-thing, but later and not here."

"What about him?" She gestures with her chin, and her gaze shifts to the left. "Are you going to tell him the truth?" Ruby turns and hurries out the lobby doors into the night.

I turn, hoping that *him* is anyone but Daniel, but I know better.

His face is a kaleidoscope of emotion. Concern, confusion, a tinge of disgust, but I hope that's directed at Ruby and this situation and not me, then betrayal.

A nervous laugh escapes my throat. "Wow, that was awkward." I try to play it casual, but it's about as convincing as a vegetable disguised as chocolate.

"What was that all about?"

I shrug. "Ruby and I used to be friends when we were in second grade. But we had a falling out, or well, my mom didn't think it was good for me to hang out at Ruby's house, and in third grade, I met Emily and Sofia, so…" I can't find the words, so I shrug again. If I keep this up, I'm going to have shoulders bodybuilders would kill for. "Anyway, that's ten years of pent-up rage, but I couldn't just stand by and let Ian pick on her."

Another click of the kaleidoscope and disbelief settles on his face. "What she said about telling me the truth. What is that? What are you supposed to tell me?" One more click.

Hope.

My arms wrap around my stomach, the closest I can come to

hugging my kids. My gaze scrapes the floor, looking everywhere but at the boy standing before me, begging me to tell him I love him.

"I, uh, who knows, I think she just had to get one more parting shot in."

Daniel pulls me to him. My body presses into his. This isn't the first time we've touched. I've kissed his cheek. Rested my head on his shoulder. Danced with him all night.

However, this is the first time our bodies fit together like puzzle pieces. The first time he holds me and I know he loves me, and I know I love him.

His face is inches from mine. Mouth hovering dangerously close.

"What do you need to tell me, Josephine Berry?" He breathes into my heart.

I love you. I know I'm only a teenager, but I've lived a life without you, and I don't want to do that again.

Those words won't take flight.

"I'm exhausted. Mind if we call it a night?"

The final click of the kaleidoscope crosses Daniel's face.

Click.

Hurt.

CHAPTER 38

It's been three days since I've gotten out of bed. Mom could tell something was up when I came home from prom. Maybe it was the missing eye makeup. Or the fact that Daniel only walked me halfway to the door before I hurried inside, not looking back at him. Like any good parent of a Gen X-er, Mom eyed me suspiciously and bit her tongue.

The rest of the world seems to have gotten the memo to leave me alone. No calls from Em or Sof. The blinds on Daniel's window stay closed, but I watch his shadow move across the room.

The look on his face haunts me. He wanted to hear that I love him like it's the blood his heart needs to keep beating. When I denied him that, it was evident that his hope died.

Humans can live without a lot of things. We can survive three weeks without food. Or three days without water. We could even go three minutes without oxygen.

Without hope, we're only living half a life.

I should know. Lying here in my bed, I can't rouse myself to shower, to eat, or even barely drink because the hope had drained out of me. Hope that I can fix some things in my life. Hope that I can get back to my kids. Hope that I won't be a major fuck-up when, if, I wake up.

The doorbell rings, but I ignore it. *Remote Control* is on MTV in my room, and I'm wallowing in the nostalgia of a long-gone game show.

"Josephine?" Mom's perfectly curled-under bob peeks in my door. "Some friends of yours from Physics are here with your homework."

I sit up and glance down at what I'm wearing. A future vintage Nirvana T-shirt (if I wash it on the gentle cycle for the next thirty years), no bra and flannel plaid boxer shorts. I sniff my hair.

It smells like stale heartbreak and regret.

Great, the only thing that will make the last three days suck even more is witnesses. I might as well welcome a few additional guests to the pity party.

"Sure, that's sweet of them."

Once Mom steps aside, Stuart, Jake, and Matthew look into my room. Their wide eyes roam to my bookshelf with a mishmash of teenage love stories and trying-to-be-cultured Greek tomes. Their collective gaze roams over my CD collection, everything from classical to heavy metal, alternative to hip hop, with a side dish of Loretta Lynn because she is so badass. Finally, they look at me.

"Are you still you?" Stuart says.

"Unfortunately. Did you really bring homework?"

He shrugs. "Four weeks left in the year, and it's mostly a recap for finals."

Jake opens his backpack and pulls out an unopened bag of Oreos. "I brought these instead."

I lay out my open palm. "Hand 'em over." With three cookies' worth of sugar hitting my veins, I'm starting to feel more human.

Stuart sits at the foot of my bed and grabs a cookie. "I'd ask how you're doing, but I can smell the answer."

I give him a rude gesture I'd ground my kids for doing, but they're not here, and I'm the adult.

Sorta.

"How are things at school? Am I cancelled?"

Matthew sits next to me on the bed, grabbing a palmful of cookies and popping one in his mouth. His nose wrinkles at my use of a term that will make more sense in thirty years.

"Actually," Jake says, sitting in my desk chair. "Everyone has your back. They think Ruby has some weird crush on you and got jealous."

I shake my head. "Not everyone. Em and Sof won't talk to me," I glance out the window. Daniel's blinds are closed up tight. "I've repulsed Daniel so much he can't even look at my house." I take another cookie, pulling it apart like all decent human beings do with Oreos.

There's a metaphor in that cookie, but there's also a lot of sugar, and I need that more than I need to find the meaning of life in mass-produced sweets. Happiness might not be found in the bottom of a bottle, but it sure as hell rides shotgun with sugar.

"And," I continue. "I hate that Ruby is taking the brunt of it. She's a teenager. She can't help what she did. I know better, and it didn't help." I sink into my sheets and pull the comforter over my head.

God, I really need a shower.

"That's not even the worst of it," I say into my sheet cocoon. "All of those things I was supposed to fix? I made them a million times worse. I'm never going to get back to my time." The smell of stale taco meat and old shoes is really starting to get to me, so I wiggle out. "The only way I can be sure of getting my kids back is to do everything exactly the same." A thought hits me like a sugar rush. "I don't remember exactly when they were conceived. I mean, I can work out the math, but how do I know that I'm conceiving Aubrey and Ben and not some other kids who'll bully others and do drugs and, I don't know, maybe even end up in juvie for stabbing a classmate in the ear with a pencil?" My chest heaves, whether from the emotional spiral or the sugar. Maybe both.

Three sets of terrified eyes stare at me.

"Stabbing a kid in the ear with a pencil?" Jake says.

"That's just messed up, even for you, Josie," Matthew chimes in.

Stuart nods. "We've got to get you out of this house."

Once the emotion settles down, my mind clears. How is where I am now any different than where I was thirty years ago?

I mean, well, it's massively different, but I didn't know then what life held for me. Even if I retrace my steps exactly, there's sure to be a crack I step on or a hole I stumble in, one that I might've missed the first time I walked that path, but I find it this time.

"Look, I'm not sure if I've ever said this, but thank you guys for believing me and trying to help. Maybe this is how it's supposed to be. Maybe I'm this weird immortal time vampire, and I'm going to live forever, but only until I'm forty-seven, and then I pop back to seventeen. Rinse and repeat, rinse and repeat, rinse and…"

"Time vampire would be a sick name for a video game," Stuart says, sparks of inspiration popping off him almost visibly.

"That's what you got from all of that?" I push the covers off me, making a mental note that no amount of laundry detergent can unstink these sheets and that burning them would be a kindness. "Wait, you should make that video game. But wait, ten or so years because technology will get much better and gaming will really take off." I might have to follow my same path, but I could give these guys, my unlikely friends, a launching pad for their future. "It doesn't look like I'm getting back to my time, but I'll make good on my promise. On the condition that you don't speak a word of this to anyone, because if I am a time vampire and I end up here again in thirty years, I will make your lives hell. Understood?"

Three heads nod in unison.

"Okay, so yeah, video games will be huge. Also, invest in Apple. Yes, I know they are in a down period, but Steve Jobs will come back, and they'll be better than before." It feels good to speak freely about the future. Almost like reminiscing about the olden days, except they're future days. "Speaking of, in about fifteen years, mobile phones will be in everyone's pocket, not the car phones we have now, but super sleek and small. And we hardly use them for talking, more for texting and games, social media. So invest in apps."

Matthew's face screws into a question. "Appetizers?"

"Social what?" Jake asks.

"Moving on, you guys getting all this? All right, no flying cars, sorry, but we do have some self-driving cars, but enter at your own risk." There's so much I could tell them, about wars and famines, about stock market booms and busts, but I'd prefer to give them tools for success, not tools to make them want to crawl into their own sheet cocoon. Except… "One big thing and I need you guys listening to me on this one. Whatever you do, do not get on a plane on September 11, 2001. Actually, don't even travel in the days before it. If you live in New York or D.C., maybe come back to Texas."

I can't do anything to save the lives of thousands killed on that awful day without getting arrested, but maybe I can save my three friends should fate thrust a middle finger in my direction.

"Oh, why? Is there a global EMP that knocks all the planes to the ground?" Stuart says. The little shit actually has excitement in his eyes.

"Not saying more. Just trust me on this one." I study their faces as if seeing them for the last time. Maybe I am, but I'm also trying to see who they'll be.

Stuart, with his dark, lanky hair that always looks overdue for a haircut, his soft middle, and pudgy face. I imagine he'll discover vegetables and working out, trimming his weight and hair to turn into one of those nerdy-hot tech guys.

Jake will finally become comfortable with his body, maybe under an armor of tattoos instead of multiple long-sleeved t-shirts he'll finally be able to stand up straight.

Matthew, who could still pass for the under twelve price at a buffet, judging by his older brother, he'll be one of those guys who comes back for our first reunion completely transformed.

The first time around, I barely noticed these guys. How many times had I walked by them in the hall without a glance in their direction?

Or sat behind them in class and asked them nothing more than if I could borrow a pen or piece of paper?

Teenagers, especially those in the nineties, could only see life as illuminated by the headlights of our circumstances. We couldn't see what was hidden in the dark edges out of our view. Like a girl raised in a home without love. Or, a boy wondering if he was the cause of his dad's melancholy rather than the brutalities of war.

Or, a girl who loved her parents so much that when their relationship ended, she turned her hurt into hate toward her father.

If nothing else, slipping back to my past allowed me to see beyond the glow of the headlights of youth.

I scoot to the middle of my bed and pat the sheets on either side.

I need a group hug, dammit.

"Come here," I say. "Fully dressed, of course."

Stuart climbs in on one side, with Matthew and Jake on the other.

I put my arms around them, feeling less like their peer and more like a big sister, or hell, maybe even a mom.

"I'm sorry if I was ever a shit to you, you know, before this year or even the first time around."

Stuart nods. "You know you can make it up to us by letting us touch your—"

"Do you *want* to go through life missing a hand?"

"Hey Josie?" Jake says.

"Hmm?"

"Don't punch me, but you really do need a shower."

CHAPTER 39

One should never underestimate the rejuvenating powers of a long shower. Especially after avoiding one for several days.

After the guys left and I ate the last Oreo, I roused myself back into the land of the living.

I haven't wallowed in a long time. Not since the guy I dated through most of college abruptly dumped me without explanation—I later met his husband, and all was forgiven.

During that wallow, Em curled up in bed with me, bringing me cheap wine and expensive cookies. This wallow felt, well, hallow, without Emily next to me.

When I pull into the school parking lot the next day behind a red Jeep, following it to our usual parking spots, I want to jump out of my car before I put it in park and give her a hug. Assuming she doesn't punch me first.

I park next to Em.

She looks over. The eye roll so pronounced I can see it through her sunglasses and two panes of tinted windows.

It's a surprise then that she doesn't hurry into the school to avoid me but instead waits in front of her car.

I approach carefully, hands out to show I come in peace. Or to protect my face in case she pummels me. If I'm doomed to repeat this life, I'm not going to ruin my face.

"You know," she says, studying her nails. "I think one of the reasons I decided to be your best friend is because I love your parents. I love how goofy your dad is and how your mom tries really, really hard to be cool, but—"

"Bless her heart."

A smile plays with Em's mouth for a second before it remembers she's mad. "Yeah, bless her heart." She drops her hands to her sides. "What I'm trying to say is I was jealous of you. *Am* jealous because even now that they've split up, they don't hate each other so much that they couldn't be together to see us off to prom or to have a family dinner once a week. Those are gifts of love." She jerks a thumb to the car behind her. "This is a bribe, and I'd give it back, with the clothes, and vacations, and limitless credit card to have my mom and dad peacefully co-exist. We have a lifetime ahead of us, we'll be able to buy our own damn Jeeps, and our rich prince husbands will take us on trips. But we'll never be able to be kids again." Her words ring through me like a tuning fork.

There is my best friend, dishing out amazing advice, the exact words I need to hear at the exact moment I need to hear them.

"But if you could, go back, would you?" I ask in case this is still an elaborate hypnosis session she's guiding me through. "Would you do things differently?"

Emily studies me, tilting her head to one side as she does when puzzling through a situation and trying to find the right words. Finally, she shakes her head. "No, the past is like a museum, a place we can only look, like looking at paintings. Once a painting is done and hung on a wall, the artist can't go back in to change it. But if she does, it changes it for the people who've seen it before and those who'll see it after. There's no value in changing the museum of our lives, but we can use the mistakes we made in the past to paint our future."

Holy shit, is the old Em speaking to me from whatever comatose state I'm in?

Does this mean I've learned my lesson, and I'll be waking up soon?

I pull her in for a tight hug. "You're going to be a fabulous therapist."

"What do you mean? I'm going to be a lawyer, you know, to fight corporate greed and bullshit."

"Well, if that doesn't work out, you will be amazing at your plan B." I pull back from our hug and check under my eyes for leakage. "How's Sof?"

Em throws her backpack on her shoulders and starts walking toward the building. "Embarrassed. She tried to keep her family's money situation quiet."

I stop. "Wait, you knew?"

"What good is having Daddy's limitless credit card if I can't force a best friend to take my help." An evil smirk crosses her pixieish face. "I always needed to stop at the grocery store while giving Sofia a ride home from school, and oopsie, groceries for her family showed up in my cart. Trust me, she didn't want to accept it at first, but it's astonishing how people fold when threatened by physical violence."

I nudge my shoulder into hers. "You're a wonderful person, Emily Murray."

"For God's sake, don't tell anyone that. I kinda like my badass rep." The tardy bell rings. "Gotta jet, see you later."

Contrary to what the boys told me, there are a lot of people giving me side-eyes.

Maybe they believe one of the many rumors about me and my "hit list." Or, maybe they just don't want to be associated with someone who'd take the punishment for the school loser.

When I make it to Yearbook class, Daniel isn't in his usual spot at our table. I'd looked for him all over the halls throughout the day but never caught a glimpse of his sun-streaked hair or gold-green eyes.

Mrs. Mitchell had rolled in a TV and VCR, the universal teacher symbol of a classroom babysitter.

Midway through the viewing of *Tombstone*, which she deemed appropriate to show us because we've all seen it, I make my way to the front of the classroom.

"Mrs. Mitchell, do you know where Daniel is?"

"Hmm?" Her eyes remain glued to the TV as Val Kilmer delivers his signature line. "Oh, yes, he asked earlier if he could use this period to meet with the guidance counselor."

Shit.

One date and he's already in therapy because of me.

"Have you chosen a college yet, Josie?" The teacher continues. "It might be good to have that conversation with the counselor."

Ah, yes, one beautiful thing about the nineties is we didn't have to decide on a major and college before we learned to drive.

"Good idea, maybe I'll run down and see if she's available now?"

"Sounds good, dear," Mrs. Mitchell sighs to the screen.

If I hurry, I can catch Daniel as he's coming out of the counselor's office and force him to talk to me. Or, maybe at least see if I can brainwash him into thinking prom night didn't happen.

The guidance counselor's office door is open. I pause outside, listening for voices before storming in.

Instead, the shuffle of papers greets me.

I peek around the corner, hoping to see Daniel sitting at the table with Mrs. Booth, but instead, I find her cleaning up a stack of brochures.

A flash of one catches my eye. The military. Is that what happens to Daniel?

Does he follow in his father's footsteps into the military?

"Oh, hey, Josie," she says, looking up at me. "Do we have an appointment?"

"Oh, no, sorry, I was looking for Daniel Palmer."

"You just missed him. He left about fifteen minutes ago."

The bell rings, pulling me to my next class—library aide time. I look forward to it like a root canal without drugs.

Thankfully, the library is full when I get there. Students working on their term papers or doing that last bit of studying before finals.

Ruby sticks to straightening the shelves, leaving Mrs. Patel and me to answer questions and check out books.

The atmosphere between us is quiet, polite, not necessarily cold. Lukewarm perhaps. Did teachers get a dose of gossip, too?

I feel like I should say something, but what? *You haven't broken your ankle this year because I hopped on the ladder whenever I was here. But, in another timeline, the snap of your bones haunted me for months.*

Yeah, that'll explain everything.

With only a few minutes left in my library period, I finish checking in a few books and go to retrieve my backpack. The top isn't fully closed, reminding me of another time when something was amiss.

My breath hitches. I pull the zippers further apart. There, at the bottom, is a book smaller than the rest.

My journal.

I take it out and study it. I thumb through the pages, and a slip of paper falls out. I unfold it, and for the first time in two months, I see my kids' faces.

My eyes burn with emotion.

Relief. Loss. Love. Heartache.

All of them dancing together in the dumpster fire in my heart.

I get the tingly sensation of being watched and look up.

Ruby's at the door of the library. Apology is written in her dark brown eyes.

"Thank you," I mouth it more than say it.

She nods and escapes as the bell rings.

I sleepwalk through the rest of the day. Chasing Daniel and Sofia. I'd assume a school our size wouldn't allow two people to avoid me as much as they have, but there must be a portal to some other place where crazy friends don't reside.

It's only when I'm jogging down the stairs for my last class of the day that I see a wave of long dark hair turn a corner. Instead of going right toward my class, I follow one of my victims to the left.

"Sof, wait, please."

She freezes, her shoulders hitching up. I know I'm awful, but am I that bad that she has a visceral reaction to my voice?

"Look, I just want a few minutes. To apologize." Even though the hallway is empty, I keep my voice low. "You know more than anyone else. You have to believe me when I say that I didn't know until the other night. You didn't share that *before*." I glance into a dark classroom to ensure it's empty. I half-expect Sofia to bolt instead of following me in, but she does. "You don't have to say anything, just listen, please." I take a deep breath, hoping words will come to me in that span of seconds. "Maybe this is what caused the rift. Maybe I didn't pay attention to how you struggled, but Em did and you're mad at me for being an oblivious teenager. And, sadly, I'm not any better as an oblivious middle-aged adult." I study Sofia's face for any signs that I should shut up before I make it worse or encouragement that I'm on the right path to repair our fragile friendship.

She just stares at the beige linoleum floor.

"What I'm trying to say is, I'm sorry. For what I did at prom, for what I did the first time we were in high school together. Hell, I'm sorry for what I might do one day in the future. I wish I could say I get better with age, but I just become more of a control freak. Someone who thinks only I can fix whatever is broken, make sure my kids eat their vegetables or make it down a ski slope without breaking a leg trying to take a selfie."

Sofia's brow narrows in confusion.

"That's a thing in about twenty years. Kids will drive us nuts doing it. Anyway, that's the thing this has taught me. Life is to be lived, not managed. Friends are to be cherished, not controlled. Young love is meant to be scary and exciting, and heartbreaking when I have to let it go for something more precious to me. Sof, I know you have to pull away from us, and that's okay. I get it. Please know that whenever you're ready to come back, I'll be here, with a hug and a big glass of wine, and absolutely no judgment."

Sofia nods her head and chews on her lower lip. Her eyes are watery when they finally meet mine before pulling me into a tight hug.

"Thank you," she whispers before pulling away and leaving me alone in the dark classroom.

CHAPTER 40

The first time I graduated from high school, I was beside myself with excitement—and anger. Excitement that I was about to be paroled from a twelve-year sentence, but angry because, at that time, I still blamed my dad for the divorce, and I was pissed that Mom said she wouldn't be at my graduation if he wasn't.

Looking back, I totally agree with her ultimatum. I was a petulant little brat.

When I graduated college, I was heartbroken and terrified. Heartbroken because just a year earlier, my dad died of a sudden heart attack, and I'd wasted years of our lives holding on to anger that'd grown stale. Like that loaf of bread that lived in my pantry too long, I should've thrown it out, but I always told myself I would the next day. Then the next.

And, the next.

I was terrified because, for once in my life, I was standing on the horizon of a vast future, and I was paralyzed with which step to take. I ended up taking a marketing job at a small start-up, and several months later, at a company happy hour, I struck up a flirtatious conversation with one of the software engineers. Peter made me laugh, feel beautiful, and like I had my shit together. Peter made me feel in control.

That is, until he ripped my foundation out from under me.

Now, graduating from high school a second time, I'm weighed down with knowing what the road holds and yet still wanting to walk down that path.

This is why humans aren't entrusted with the knowledge of our futures. We're fickle creatures. We only want the happy times, the successes, the ups without the downs. However, a blue sky without an occasional rain cloud becomes less brilliant. The same as a win without the disappointment of defeat is just another day.

I wipe away the steam on the mirror from a record-long shower. Nearly nine months ago, I looked at this reflection of a girl I hadn't seen in so long.

I hadn't *been* in so long. I wanted nothing more than to wake up, to get back to my kids, to fix whatever was fucked up at my company, to throw a punch at my ex.

I still want nothing more than to see Aubrey and Ben, but I'm perhaps even more crippled with indecision now. Because even if I make every mistake, every wrong decision, or every right one, I'm a changed person, and just by the virtue of my knowledge, I'm not going to be the same young marketing exec who meets their dad at a bar. I know how it ends. Will I be able to say yes when he asks me out? When he asks me to marry him?

I dry and curl my hair in loose waves that will most likely be straight the minute I step out in the late May humidity. Hope for good hair springs eternal. As does the hope that Daniel will talk to me.

He's warmed slightly to me since prom, but a cloud still lingers between us, as embarrassing and odorous as a silent fart. The only difference is I can't blame this on faulty sewer lines or an unsuspecting kid. The stench is all my fault.

While I brush my teeth, I pace the room, studying teenage ephemera that feels more familiar than the expensive artwork Peter and I would collect. The CDs, books, ribbons and trophies, the silly cartoons cut out of the paper, the *Save the Whales* stickers alongside the

Stop Deforestation button, next to the *Save the Planet* postcard just to make sure I cover all my bases.

Well into my second minute of brushing and another loop through my room, I look out the window. Daniel's blinds are pulled up, but his room is dark except for a sheet of drawing paper taped to the pane.

The drawing is far more juvenile than Daniel's talent, but that seems to be the point. It's a stick drawing of two figures. One with longer hair, both clad in graduation robes and hats. Their circle hands with dashes for fingers overlap.

I smile around a mouthful of toothpaste.

I think I'm officially forgiven.

With a feeling like a prisoner granted clemency, I finish dressing and throw a light dusting of makeup on my face. I give my reflection a final glance, a long one, like seeing a friend for the last time, drape my gown over my arm and grab my cap.

"I'll see you both there," I shout from the bottom of the stairs.

Only a shuffling of feet and clearing of throats answers me. That sounds an awful lot like…

I cross into the kitchen. The only thing redder than Mom's cheeks is her lipstick on Dad's mouth.

My mom's normally coifed bob is mussed, and her cardigan is as crooked as a one of those deals to buy twelve CD's for a penny.

Dad isn't much better. The knot of his tie is tugged loose and one side of his shirt is untucked.

"Hmm," I say, trying to decide if I should tease them.

My parents jump apart like guilty teenagers.

Mom pulls open the dishwasher.

Dad reaches overhead for a coffee cup.

They aren't officially divorced, so maybe there's still some hope. Then again, Peter and I had a hot and heavy make-out session after we'd decided to end things. Falling out of love sometimes takes just a long, if not longer, than falling in love.

"I'd tell you to get a room, but my graduation starts in an hour. See you there."

Luckily, despite my inner gloom, the weather is perfect for an outside graduation ceremony. The blue Texas sky stretches overhead, crisp, and fresh with just a smattering of white puffy clouds. The sun drifts toward the western horizon, wiling the final hours of the day away, watching the world beneath it go about loving and losing.

Emily and Sofia are waiting for me in the parking lot.

"Holy shit, we made it!" Em grabs me around the waist, lifting me in the air. She might be small, but she's mighty.

I look to Sofia, mostly to see if she'll flinch if I touch her.

"Come here, *chica*," she pulls me close. "You're my sister, no matter what happens."

They float away to hug other classmates. The glint of sunlight off a passing windshield catches my attention.

An El Camino pulls in, taking up two parking spaces. The doors pop open for my team of teenage Einsteins.

The memory of the first time these guys met me in this parking lot hits me like standing up the first time after too many shots of tequila.

I'm drunk with appreciation for these three boys, young men, who didn't have to believe my crazy story.

Hell, I don't even believe it much anymore. I'm starting to wonder if Peter, Aubrey, and Ben are all a figment of my imagination.

Maybe I spent too much time at the pool. Can sun poisoning cause thirty-year hallucinations?

"Are you still you?" Stuart asks. It's become such a familiar greeting. Like 'Hey,' or 'What's up?' or even 'How's it hanging?'.

"Still me. Tell the truth," I say, adjusting his valedictorian sash. "Have you ever once thought I was crazy?"

"Oh, plenty of times," Jake says, his robes draped over his arm. "But we haven't had this much attention from a girl well, ever, so we weren't going to ask too many questions."

"But we also feel good with the knowledge that the world still exists, at least for the next few decades, and we're not all cyborgs," Matthew says, pulling his robe across his shoulders, his salutatorian sash nearly dropping to the ground before a hand reaches between us to catch it.

I follow the hand up its arm to the broad chest and then to the tanned face and gold-green eyes.

"Hey, man, you worked hard for this. You don't want it getting dirty," Daniel says, handing it to Matthew. "Hey, Cuppa Jo."

Suddenly, I'm having a hot flash, probably only an emotional one, unless this time around I experience a super early menopause.

"Hey, saw your drawing." I pull my mouth up to an evil grin. "Glad to see you're graduating kindergarten today."

He laughs.

How would it feel to hear his laugh with my head on his chest?

With his finger tracing lazy circles on my naked back?

My foot climbing up his calf?

"Jo, you okay? You look flushed," Daniel says. "Do you need to get in the shade? Some water?"

I shake my head, both to dislodge the highly inappropriate thoughts and answer him.

"Look, I owe you an apology about prom. And, an explanation." I'm still not sure how to explain it, to tell him the truth or some version of it that doesn't get me locked up.

A screech of microphone feedback cuts through the teenager chatter. "All right, seniors, let's talk through the flow and get you lined up before your families arrive," the principal says, too loudly, considering he has the assistance of an AV system.

"Let's talk later at the party. Okay?" Daniel raises his hand, and I slap his palm in a high five. "See you on the other side, Berry."

"Not unless I see you first." What in the world did that mean? Obviously, the inappropriate thoughts have robbed my brain cells of any bit of common sense and witty banter.

I barely remember my first high school graduation. The emotion, worry about what lay ahead and anger with my parents consumed my poor teenage brain then.

Now I notice how the sun's rays filter through clouds on the western horizon. The way the lights of the football field hum like a beehive. How the warm air of the approaching summer dances with the streams of cool springlike air. Even how the most cynical of my classmates hide their sobs in throat clearing.

It also allows me to listen to Stuart's commencement speech.

My friend approaches the podium but gets too close, and the stadium is hit with a wave of feedback.

"Sorry," he says over the groans and gasps from the graduating class and the audience. "So, my fellow Class of 94," he pauses, looks down at his notes and rubs his nose. "I had originally written a speech to motivate you all to be all you can be, but what do I know about that? What, instead, I want to ask all of you is to think ahead thirty years and what future-you would want to tell your teenage self. Is it to see the world? Or, major in something you love and trust that you can build a life doing it? Would you tell that boy or girl you love them?" Stuart glances up from his notes and scans the crowd until his gaze lands on me.

"Life isn't a video game. We can't get to the end of life and go back and try another gameplay. But if we can, if there is a glitch in the system that allows us to do it all over again, I think maybe that could be a gift instead of a curse. It's a chance to make friends with someone you wouldn't hang out with the first time around. A chance to tell your parents you love them one more time. Or, even a chance to invest wiser than you did the first time."

A few parents chuckle in the stands.

"We might lose some things in this other game of life. You might marry someone different or have different kids. I might still be a kid, but I can tell you that you can't live your life chasing what might have been. Until I start a company that builds time machines, we won't be able to see where those other paths lead us. And, does it matter? Because as long as we try our best to be good humans, to love those in our lives, and treat others with respect, no matter which path we choose, it'll be the right path for us. Congrats, seniors. May the path you choose be the right path. Thank you." Stuart steps away from the podium, only the buzzing of the stadium lights echoes in his wake.

As if waiting for a cue, my fellow seniors erupt into applause, many shooting up to standing.

I try to will my legs to move, but my body is frozen.

Stuart is right. While my path changes, at my core, I am still me. Aubrey and Ben are half me. Aubrey—a combination of my dad and me. Ben with Peter's mind but with my mom's dark-blond hair.

The life I had might be gone, but maybe when I look at my other kids, the ones I hope to hold in my arms in just a few years, I can see something of Aubrey and Ben in them.

Maybe there really is no going back. I can't put leaves back on the trees in the autumn. I have to accept the cycle is over, but a new one will begin. That doesn't mean the fresh leaves aren't as beautiful as the ones before.

I look at my entwined hands, almost imagining the kids' hands inside them. I open my hands, releasing the beautiful souls back into the universe. I might see them again. I might not. But I'm grateful for every moment I had with them.

An elbow nudges me. "Josie, they're calling your name."

"Josephine Elise Berry," the principal's tinny voice echoes around the football field.

My parents cheer in the stands.

My body remembers how to work, and I stand. Low heels sink into the turf as I walk to the stage. Toward a future that is both certain and undefined. Away from innocence of childhood and the fact that I could return to my life before.

I shouldn't feel that special. Another hundred kids will make this same trek this evening.

Only, I've skipped ahead.

I know how it all ends.

CHAPTER 41

After the last kid with a mediocre school ranking and the unfortunate luck of being born last in the alphabet, after the tears and melodramatic promises to keep in touch—from people who will hang out together all summer long.

After the photos with grandmothers and aunts and uncles—and people so far distantly related a murder board is needed to explain the relation.

After the teachers head out to hit a secret teacher bar, we are finally free to properly celebrate like minors with little more than freedom and a few fake IDs.

Ian's parents were kind enough to leave for vacation as soon as graduation ended, an unexpected but welcomed benefit of him being the youngest of five children. My classmates, many still in their graduation robes, file into his parents' home on the outskirts of town like ants to sugar.

Gin & Juice rattles the windows with the shout-singing of party-goers getting only half the words right. I grab a wine cooler, the closest I come to a glass of wine, and wander around the vast house, letting Stuart's graduation speech soak in.

If I'm going to walk a different path in this life, then I'll do everything in my power to walk alongside the man I'd spent many wine-soaked nights perusing the deep pages of a Google search for.

The man I turned away this same night thirty years ago.

The man I'm going to tell, finally, that I love him.

To do that, I need something stronger than a wine cooler but without the sloppy inhibition-droppingness of shots.

I weave through the kitchen. Boxes of pizzas tower on the island, and the smell of warm, cheesy dough almost overwhelms me to stop. If I eat now, the carnivorous butterflies in my stomach will have all the fun and probably cause me to have uncontrollable gas.

No, better to stick to liquid courage for now.

A wrought iron door under the back stairs catches my attention. In many modern homes, it's not uncommon to find a little wine cellar tucked away. Could I be so lucky that Ian's parents were pioneers in bougie home design?

I push open the door and flip on the lights. I can almost hear the angels singing under Beck and my classmates proudly claiming to be losers.

It's a modest wine cellar. Really more of a wine closet, but beggars and choosers and all that.

Unfortunately, having a wine closet doesn't mean one has good taste in wine. After pulling out nearly every bottle and realizing there are no hidden gems, I grab a bottle of Cabernet.

With a full glass in one hand and my treasured bottle in the other, I go back to wandering around the party, looking for Daniel.

My aimless wandering takes me to an upstairs game room where, instead of being filled with teenagers making out, it's filled with three people who know me best. Matthew and Jake are engrossed in a game of *Mario Brothers* while Stuart coaches from the sidelines.

"Hey guys," I say, falling into a beanbag and holding my wine glass up high to avoid spillage. "Stuart, your speech was…" There's not a strong enough adjective for it, so I hold up my glass. "Cheers, my friend."

He blushes and ducks his head. "It could be a message for all of us. You're a good person, Josie. As long as you hold on to that, you can't go down the wrong path."

Jake and Matthew finish another level of the game and hit pause.

"Do you think we can still be friends," Matthew asks, his voice soft and pleading. "This time you go through life, I mean. I'd still like to be friends with you."

Even though he's about to go off to college and embark on his life, I can't help but see Matthew as a preschool-aged Ben asking innocently for someone to be his friend. My stomach twists like a dishrag trying to wring out the guilt of my decision.

"I'd like that." My voice is thick with regret. "I have a feeling I'll need friends who know my story. Someone who can reassure me that I'm not making a bigger mess of things."

"Josie," Stuart says, shifting his attention from the game to me. "Remember that first weekend after you told us…you know?"

"That I'm a middle-aged divorcee time traveler?"

"Yeah, that. Anyway, you got mad because we watched a bunch of time travel movies. There's one thing they all have in common, and that's the universe will always right itself. Your children are meant to be born, so they'll be there for you. In your future. Just have faith."

His words warm my heart. Maybe I'm not the only time traveler here. Is it possible that Stuart also slipped back in time and that's why he's so wise?

"You're forgiven for that." I need to get out of that game room before I break down crying. "I'm going to find Daniel. I'll see you guys later?" I grab my bottle, which feels more like a security blanket than alcohol, and head back into the din of the party.

Most everyone has moved outside. Groups of grads cluster around the pool, with a handful of guys stripping down to their boxers and diving in.

My gaze scans the crowd, trying to find Daniel's light brown locks. Could it be that in this timeline he chooses not to come to the party?

I'm searching through the crowd when a pair of arms encircles my waist.

"Jo! This is the end of the beginning!" Em slurs. "Wait, that's not right." She frowns into her cup as if whatever is inside could lend her wisdom.

Pretty insightful for a recent high school grad.

"How much have you had to drink?"

"Just one cup," Em shouts. "But I've filled it up a few times." Her expression goes from elation to confusion faster than prices drop on last year's unfortunate fashion trend. "You're not you."

I freeze the smile on my face, even though it's at risk of melting like a forgotten chocolate bar in the bottom of my purse. "What do you mean? I'm me."

"You're you, but you're not *you-you*." Emily takes a long gulp of whatever is in her cup. Likely truth serum. "Ever since we started the school year, you've been different." She purses her lips.

A gesture I know as her trying to line up her thoughts into sentences. This was the look she gave me before telling me the twelve-layer tulle wedding dress I had my heart set on made me look like a cake topper.

Or, before she coached me on what to say to Peter when I wanted to make my hobby a career. It was the look she gave me when she told me maybe I shouldn't try to win Peter back, that perhaps us moving on with our lives was best for everyone.

"It's like…It's like you didn't have that same angst the rest of us had heading into senior year. Like you were stressed, for sure, but where we were worried about SATs and college and stuff, you were beyond that." Emily shakes her head. "I'm probably not making sense. My grandmother would say you're an old soul and that you've been here before. Maybe that's all, and I was too self-absorbed to realize it until now. Anyway, I'm drunk and rambling. I don't think you're from the future like Ruby said. But if you are, I hope we're still best friends where you came from. Or, is it *when* you came from?"

It's my turn to grapple with words. I should've known better than to think she wasn't paying attention. Emily saw things before I saw them. She just waited until I was ready to hear them before pointing them out.

"You seen Jordan?" she asks, the moment spanning my best friend now and in the future fades like a dissipating mist. "I need to break up with him. We're too young to settle down. And it's not like we'll meet our soul mates in high school. That's what college is for." She claps a hand over her mouth. "Sorry, I mean, you and Daniel are different. But you also haven't told each other how you feel, so I guess you don't count it until you do." Em laughs. "Unless it takes you guys years to finally talk about it."

It's my turn to laugh, but mine is more uncomfortable than joyous. "Actually, have you seen Daniel? I need to find him and tell him that I love him."

My best friend's eyes widen, and she pulls me into a tight hug. "You'll make such pretty babies," she whispers in my ears.

My stomach clinches again as if Aubrey and Ben's eggs are giving me a swift kick in the gut.

"I think I saw him inside earlier, maybe getting a drink. Oh, there's Jordan," she clinks her glass with mine. "Here's to endings and beginnings and everything in between."

With that, my friend of four decades scurries off to break a heart. That little glimpse of my Em soothes my homesickness like a letter from my parents—even if she's seventeen and drunk.

I circle back into the house, stopping by the kitchen where the kids gathered there said he was going to find a bathroom. After visiting all the bathroom lines, there was no Daniel, but someone thought he was going outside for a game of basketball.

Ten minutes into watching a drunken game with no discernible teams *or* Daniel, I start to give up and lose my nerve.

"Oh, Daniel?" The head cheerleader, Lori, says in response to my mumbled question. "I saw him and Jessica walk toward the barn."

The half bottle of wine in my stomach bubbles in a cauldron of jealousy.

"Oh?" Luckily, I have three decades of faking nonchalance on this girl. After watching a few more minutes of the game, the term used in the loosest definition, I head toward the barn.

Cool air greets me as I pull open the heavy doors. The barn is nicer than my first three apartments. Hay covers the floor and my footsteps.

Luckily, the barn is well-lit, so I can easily make my way toward the hushed voices in the back.

There's always a moment when you're drawn to something, and you know you won't like what you find. Like when kids are quiet, and you think, that's nice, they're playing quietly. Then you realize you can't find your scissors. Or the matches.

"It'll be perfect. We can stay in the dorms freshman year and then get an apartment off campus," Jessica purrs.

Which is quite cliché, but the girl is one walking cliché.

"I think you'll love the weather in Los Angeles."

"Jess…"

I can't tell if he sighs her name in longing or frustration.

I edge closer to peek around the stall.

They're in the corner of the same side I'm trying to peer around, so I'll have to lean in to see anything.

Jessica says something, but her words are too low to make them out.

With a deep breath and a prayer to whoever put me in this mess, I lean around.

Just in time to see Jessica's long, thin arm snake around the back of Daniel's head and pull him to her.

This is a mistake. This is the universe fucking with me.

Frustration, fury, longing for my children. Hell, even longing for my ex-husband slams into me like an emotional tsunami. Everything in my body lets go.

My legs, I fall against the rough planks of the wall. My hands, the precious bottle of bad wine crashes to the floor.

"Jo?" Daniel calls to me across the storm.

"Sorry," my voice breaks. I push my body away from the wall and manage to take wobbly steps like a newborn foal.

"Josie, wait up. I've been looking for you," his voice is urgent.

I refuse to look back. My gaze is laser-focused on the door. A path out of karma's middle finger at my expense.

After a few wobbly steps, I break into a run.

Sprinting from Daniel, still calling my name.

Once I'm back into the warm, humid night air, I keep jogging away from the party and toward a copse of trees.

When the heavy metal guitar solo is drowned out by the crickets, I stop, bending over to catch my breath.

With a deep inhale, I look up into the night sky. There are no stars;

clouds cover the sky like a thick blanket. Lightning flickers in the distance, illuminating the edges of an approaching thunderhead.

Perfect.

I count down, and at the first rumble of thunder, I scream, hoping that maybe I am still in some sort of hypnosis and my friend is there.

"Wake me the fuck up, Emily. I'm done."

CHAPTER 42

aniel calls my name, his voice drawing closer until his footsteps shuffle behind me. "Josie," he pants my name.

"You must not be running much these days," I say, more to convince myself that future Daniel is likely a lazy slob and that maybe Jessica Dawson is doing me a solid.

He takes another step. His expression is curious and cautious as if approaching a cornered animal.

Which he is.

One cornered in her past.

"I've been looking for you," he says.

"Oh? To tell me that you and Jessica are running away together?" I cross my arms. "A text would have sufficed." I let a future reference slip, but I was fresh out of fucks to give.

"A what?" Realization washes over him like a flash flood. "Oh, is that what you thought you heard?" Daniel takes another step. "That was Jess asking for another try and me shutting her down. For good."

"How is 'getting a place off campus together' breaking up? That sounds more like shacking up."

"She was trying to talk me into following her to L.A. to be an actor. What is up with you, Jo?" He shuffles and runs his hands through his hair. "Look, you've been off for a while now. I don't know if it's your parents splitting up or just the stress of graduating. I feel like you're hiding something from me. And," Daniel takes a step closer. "We've never had any secrets before. But there's a big one sitting right here between us."

He's right. Ever since we became friends, I've told Daniel things I couldn't tell Sofia and Emily. Little things. Mundane things. Even what at the time seemed like a big thing but were minnows in the sea of life. Also big things, like how everyone else was trying to decide on a career, nothing tugged at me.

Or, how I wish I had a sibling to go through life with and whom I could count on to be there, even if it meant fighting over sweaters and sharing a bathroom.

Loving Daniel is a big secret.

My plan is to tell him I love him and hold back on the fact that inside, I'm thirty years older. However, standing there with lightning flickering in the distance, I can't tell him that without telling him the monumental secret. The one that threatens to only grow between us, pushing us apart.

"You're right," I say, my voice quiet under the rustling of the leaves overhead. "There's something I need to tell you, but I don't know if you'll believe me or think I'm crazy. Probably the latter."

Hope flashes across his face. Bright, like a meteorite illuminating the sky.

Of course, meteorites burn out or crash into the ground.

"Jo," Daniel closes the distance between us and cups the side of my face. "It's not crazy. I feel it, too."

Only one side of my mouth tugs up into a smile. "I know, you told me."

His eyes narrow in confusion.

"Thirty years ago," I say, pushing the words out before my brain can stop them. "On this night, except I was an idiot and didn't think you could be in love with your best friend. I was stupid and turned you down then, and I spent so many years regretting it."

"I don't understand."

"I don't either, to be honest. One minute, I was in my office in downtown Austin, having a panic attack because my ex wants custody of our kids, and this big contract that I'd mortgaged everything mortgageable on was falling through, and…" I pause to take a breath, both for my head to stop spinning and to see if Daniel thinks I'm suffering from a stroke. "And, there's a drawing you had given me, of me, a portrait, framed and hanging on my wall. The last thing I remember was looking at it and wishing I could be that girl again and tell you that I love you and I made a big mistake not saying it back to you. Next thing I know, I wake up in my teenage bedroom with my mom telling me I'm late for senior pictures."

His face is blank, as if waiting for the punch line.

"Say something," I whisper.

Daniel's gaze roams over my face. His gold-green eyes soft yet concerned. "Did someone spike your drink?"

I push away from him, needing some air but also not wanting to see when he realizes I've lost it.

"I know how this sounds, but this is what has been between us all year. The fact that I'm reliving our senior year. That I'm a forty-seven-year-old woman with a failed marriage, a failing business, and amazing kids who are my life."

Daniel takes a deep breath and blows it out slowly. "You're not lying."

I shake my head. "I'm not lying."

I cross to a worn-down tree stump and lower myself to it.

The night sounds envelop me. Dull music from the party broken up by the occasional shout or burst of laughter. A low grumble of thunder in the distance, like the growling stomach of a sleeping beast.

Daniel sits next to me. The warmth from his shoulder soaks into me. "So, the future. I don't know where to start. Do we have flying cars?"

I laugh. "That's the first thing everyone asks."

He whips his head in my direction so fast he nearly knocks me out. "Who is everyone?" There's an edge to his voice.

I turn to face him, the wood snags the back of my dress. "Stuart Lohenstein, Matthew Fraser, and Jake Beebe. They're the smartest guys in school, and I needed their help getting back to my time." I shrug.

"Turns out, none of them know time travel." The locusts fill my pause. "I also told Sofia, but it's because we're not friends in the future. It's not like we had a big fight; she drifts away, so I thought it would make sense to tell her. That if I do anything to hurt her it's unintentional."

"What about Ruby? All that stuff she said at prom," Daniel says after several seconds pass.

I take a deep breath. "She wasn't wrong, but I didn't tell her. She stole my journal, where I wrote about it as I tried to figure out what was happening."

He nods slowly.

I have to hand it to him, considering he just learned the girl he's crushed on for years not only loves him back but is also secretly a time traveler who married someone else and had kids with this person only to spend her life regretting turning him down, he's handling it remarkably well.

"So, you think you'll have to live your life over again?"

"Appears that way. My mad scientists weren't successful."

We sit in silence for a while longer. The party noise quiets to a low hum, but the thunder grows closer.

"Do we keep in touch? In the future." He chuckles nervously. "You know, after you break my heart."

I push off the stump and pace several steps before answering.

A flash of lightning flickers across the sky, illuminating his raised eyebrows. The openness in his face, the honest curiosity void of judgment, encourages me to speak.

"I did break your heart, and I guess mine, too. You left the party, and I never saw you again. The next day, you were gone. I thought you'd gone to your granddad's for the summer, but then your parents moved away, and I went off to college." My voice catches as if it doesn't want the following words to leave my mouth. "After my junior year of college, my dad—" I clear my throat. Even if I don't change anything with my dad's health, I know this time around, I'll be able to live appreciating all the time I had with him rather than regret pushing him away. "My dad dies, and even though my parents are divorced, my mom just can't stay here, so she sells the house and moves."

I sit back next to him. "In the 2000s, there's this thing called social media. It's cool and annoying at the same time and allows people to find each other on the internet and keep in touch. Anyway, I've Google stalked you off and on for years but never found you."

Daniel laughs. "I'm sure in about thirty years what you just said will make sense, but what?"

I grab his hand and squeeze. "If you're humoring me, you're doing it well."

He squeezes back. "JoBear, you've never lied to me. You're the least dramatic person I know." Daniel turns and tilts my face toward his. "And, yeah, I do love you." He leans in but hesitates a hair's breadth from my mouth.

My lips tingle in anticipation. The wind kicks up, and goosebumps break out on my arm. Probably more from the fact that if I lean forward just a bit, I'll finally kiss the boy I've yearned for most of my adult life.

"Are you going to kiss me?" he asks.

A witty retort works up my throat, but I bury it in his mouth.

My heartbeat stumbles as if the electricity from the approaching storm combined with the anticipation of waiting to feel his lips on mine to create a whole new power source. Maybe kissing Daniel is the solution to clean energy. It's quite possible this kiss could save the world.

It starts soft. Chaste. As if we've both been eager for this moment and hope it lives up to the fantasy that's played in our heads as we drift off to sleep each night.

The kiss kicks into its stride like a runner seeing a long, flat stretch ahead. Our lips move in sync like they've done this for a lifetime.

I tilt my head to deepen the kiss, and Daniel opens his mouth for me. We stay there, hands cupping each other's heads, mouths dancing to our own music.

A thought crawls into my mind like a toddler with a nightmare climbing into bed at the most inconvenient moment.

If I at least try to repeat my life, there's a chance I could see Aubrey and Ben again. However, sitting here, kissing Daniel, opening my future to a life with him, the realization that this closes the door on their existence cuts into my heart like a dull, serrated knife.

Daniel breaks the kiss and tucks a strand of my hair behind my ear. "Hey, where'd you go?"

My God, if he's this attentive at eighteen, imagine how amazing a partner he'll be with a few years of life on him.

I pull my mouth into the most confident smile I can muster, but it falls short.

His gaze falls away from mine. The serene smile at finally kissing the girl he loves fades into a tight grimace.

He knows that no matter what I just said, despite wanting to walk down this path of life with him, I am going to break his heart.

Again.

CHAPTER 43

When Aubrey was three, I almost lost her at a crowded store. The panic and helplessness still floods my body anytime I think of it.

My first trimester with Ben was not kind to my stomach. Morning sickness lingered so long, it became afternoon sickness and then evening sickness and middle of the night sickness.

While shopping, a particularly violent bout hit me right when Aubrey was begging for an overpriced doll. I scooped her up and ran for the bathroom like a secret Lululemon sale was happening inside.

I've never been one of those mothers who was too proud to ask for help. If a woman gave me a sympathetic look that said, "Been there, sister, I feel ya," then I happily asked for help. Except this time, the bathroom was empty.

With Aubrey in tow, I headed into a stall and, courtesy of my unborn son, spill the meager contents of my stomach. While retching, I caught sight of my darling daughter crawling under the bathroom stall.

Somewhere in the midst of my puking, I'd told her to stay where she was, but the distinct sound of voices and the tinny pop music playing over the store PA of the opening door invaded my vomit vault.

Then, nothing.

No little voice asking about the doll, or when we were going home, or that she was hungry, or had to poop. Just the sound of my traitorous, rebelling stomach and my heart pounding in my ears.

I swallowed back the next rising tide, ran back into the busy store, but no sign of my wayward redhead. The lead weight of dread took over the nausea in the pit of my stomach. My heart wasn't broken; it was shredded.

Luckily, a big bear of a man turned the corner carrying my tiny runaway in his arms, but that feeling of sheer panic stayed with me while I buckled her into her car seat with shaky hands and drove home, inhaling deep breaths of air.

It's a feeling I never wanted to feel again, yet sitting on a tree stump in the woods after kissing the boy I've longed to kiss, that same weight settles in my stomach, sloshing the wine I'd consumed earlier in the night.

"Josie, what's wrong?" Daniel's voice is soft, pleading.

I stand and stare into the darkness. Tears burn behind my eyes.

Is it possible to want two lives? To want this life with Daniel, but to also want the life I had with Peter, Aubrey, and Ben?

"What I know now, what I'd wished I had known thirty years ago, is that the best kind of love is built on a foundation of friendship," I speak to the darkness. "I also know that there is nothing like holding your child for the first time, watching them take their first steps, or call you momma."

"I'd love to have kids one day," Daniel says with an edge of defense in his words.

"And I'm sure you'll be an amazing father, but I've spent these last months desperately trying to get back to *my* kids." I glance up at the night sky. The storm moves closer, blotting out part of the canopy of stars while the other half shines brightly. "I'm not even sure if the path I took the first time can be retraced. I mean, maybe this time around Peter was never born, or he moves to California instead of Texas. But I have to try at least."

Daniel stands behind me, so close that I lean back against him as if drawn by a magnet. He snakes an arm across my chest, holding me close.

Protected. Safe.

I close my eyes. A life not lived flashes behind my lids.

College years spent together, studying in a cavernous library, Daniel probably a pioneer in environmental studies, and me in business school.

Graduation and living together in a cookie-cutter apartment with walls so thin we tell our neighbor 'bless you' when he sneezes. We'll have a low-key wedding, maybe something in a garden. A few years later, Daniel's face will light up when I show him two pink lines on a stick.

He'll hold my hair back during morning sickness, he'll tell me I'm beautiful when everything is swollen, and he'll happily get up in the middle of the night for feedings or diaper changes.

We'll be lovers, friends, partners. Everything all at once.

Like the thunderstorm, it's there on the horizon, a life with the boy who'd stolen my heart with his golden-green eyes and playful smile. Like the thunderstorm, the winds of my life shift, pushing it away, leaving only flickers of what could have been.

Not every cloud is meant for rain. Just like not every path laid out before me is meant for traveling. What if addiction reaches out and sinks its talons into him like it did his father?

Or what if he develops a wandering eye?

What if I do?

It's easy to assume the life you didn't choose is better than the one you did. We romanticize the coulda-been, glorify the almost-was, mourn the near-misses.

"We could've had a great life," I say on the tail of a sigh. "Maybe in some parallel universe we do, but in this life, I have to find Peter. Even though he'll break my heart, he'll give me two amazing kids. They are worth the pain of a broken marriage." I turn around and look up.

His beautiful eyes shimmer in the darkness. Daniel sniffs and looks away.

"For what it's worth, I'm breaking both of our hearts." I cup the side of his face. "I wish I could tell you that you'll have an amazing life and be successful, but your future is a mystery to me."

"Are you sure this isn't us getting a second chance?" His voice is quiet, pleading.

"No, I'm not, and I might be royally screwing up, but that's what life is about. Just fumbling along, doing the best we can, hoping we don't hurt the people we love and that we leave the world in a better place."

He looks down at the ground, toeing the dirt with his Doc Martens. "I don't know that I'll ever meet anyone like you."

A wry laugh escapes my lips. "I should hope not. I don't think the world can handle more than one Josie Berry. But I do hope you meet someone you love so much that you don't think about me every day. Because I didn't, and I thought about you for nearly thirty years. It's not healthy to go forward looking in the rearview mirror. My therapist taught me that."

We stay silent, looking at each other. The frogs and locusts playing the power ballad that will forever be the soundtrack of this moment.

"I should probably go," I say. If I don't, I'll change my mind. I can't do to him what I did to Peter, live a life wishing I'd taken another path; not for another man but for two little humans who are part of my heart and soul.

"I have something for you, so I'll walk you to your car."

It's only a few hundred feet back to the party, but we walk slowly.

Neither of us speaks.

What is there to say?

Daniel just learned I'm either a time traveler or delusional, or both. He also learned that as much as I love him and want to be with him, I've chosen someone I haven't met yet so I can have my children. With that kind of rejection, he's probably going to move to Nepal to become a Buddhist Monk.

"Hey, Daniel," I say as we approach his truck. "In thirty years, when you get an invitation to the high school reunion, will you just RSVP yes? It'll stop me from driving Em nuts by asking her constantly if you're coming."

He laughs. "Okay, anything for Em's sanity."

Anticipation floods my body like a kid staring down a large box on Christmas morning. I have a pretty good guess what he'll give me, but it wasn't given to me on graduation night the first time around. Instead, it was left inside my car as a goodbye before Daniel took off for wherever life took him the morning after I broke his heart.

He reaches in and pulls out a sheet of drawing paper. I know what it looks like before I even study it in the faded yellow glow of the dome light of his truck.

"I worked on this all year," he says shyly, handing me the drawing that will eventually end up on the wall of my office.

Even though the drawing is in graphite, he caught the shades of my strawberry-blonde hair. My eyes twinkle as if caught in the aftermath of a laugh. My lips pursed into a smile.

This was the girl I wanted to be again, but am I?

Did I spend the last nine months being her or trying desperately to be who I grew up to be?

Maybe that's what life is. A series of choices, both good and bad, mistakes, minor and massive, and moments, forgotten and memorable, that refines us.

We're who we are not just because of the paths we take, but also because of the paths we didn't take. The choices not made mold us as much as those we do.

"If you think it's crap, you can throw it away. It won't hurt my feelings." Daniel's voice cuts into my thoughts.

"It's perfect, and I can promise you that it's something I will treasure for the rest of my life."

I lean on my toes and kiss him, passionately at first, but then it turns into the most heartbreaking kiss ever.

A goodbye kiss.

When we break, he rests his forehead against mine.

"I love you, Daniel. Have an amazing life." My eyes stay shut, afraid the tears will break through the dam if I open them.

He nods against me. "I love you, Josie. Guess I'll see you in thirty years." He steps away.

His absence is like a warm blanket being ripped off.

I keep my eyes closed as he shuts his car door. The engine grumbles, the transmission clicks when he reverses and then again when he puts it into drive. Gravel crackles under his tires. When he turns onto the highway, the engine revs, slowly fading away as Daniel Palmer leaves my life again.

With a big gulp of air, I open my eyes. In the outside floodlight, I study who he saw. The girl he loves.

The girl who broke his heart twice.

Even though I know I made the right decision, the heavy weight of regret settles on my shoulders and wraps around my chest. The air I hold in my lungs becomes nearly suffocating as I try to push it out, but it refuses to budge. Is it possible to drown on oxygen?

The sounds of the party move away, as if I'm on a rushing train, being taken to some far-off land where I won't be able to hurt the people I love. Even the bright moon has abandoned me, the world growing darker and dark.

My only companion is a beeping. Steady. Strong.

Maddening.

The ground rushes up. It doesn't catch me.

I keep falling.

And, falling.

Falling.

CHAPTER 44

The hold on my lungs finally releases when I hit something solid. Air expels in a violent coughing fit. My eyes blink open, but only briefly. Blinding white light sears my pupils, unleashing a fresh set of tears.

"Josie!" My mom leaps into maternal mode, helping me sit up. "Hang on, honey, let me get you some water."

A plastic cup is thrust into my hand, and I take a sip, calming the burn squeezing my lungs. After a few more sips, I try my eyes again.

The walls are faded white, just on the verge of being gray. Machines stand sentry on one side of me. I glance down.

I'm cocooned in a hospital bed.

My head whips toward my mother. Her signature bob is still there, but so are the wisps of gray that I'd grown accustomed to.

"Mom! You're old!" I cringe as the words slip from my mouth. Apparently, my filter broke in whatever caused me to be in the hospital.

"Well, you're no spring chicken yourself, Josephine." Luckily, her words ride out on a wave of humor, and her face is awash in relief.

"Eeek!" A squeal pierces my ears. "You're awake!" Em flies across the room and tackles me in a hug.

An IV tugs at my arm as I wrap my best friend in a hug. "Your hair is so short." I touch the edges of her pixie cut, a look she'd been rocking since our twenties, but after seeing her hair long for months, it's as jarring as the time she'd shown up at my apartment with her head shaved after a bad breakup.

Emily self-consciously tousles it. "Funny you say that. I'm thinking of growing it back out. Not as long as it was in high school, but maybe a little longer than this." She waves it off. "But forget that, you're back!"

"I can skip the 'where am I,' clearly, it's a hospital, but why? Where's Aubrey and Ben? How long have I been here?"

Mom and Emily exchange glances so heavy with meaning that they'd be charged extra if they were checked bags.

"So, yes, you had some sort of incident at your office," Mom says. "You passed out and hit your head. They couldn't wake you, so you were brought here, and they ran tests on your heart and brain. All seemed fine, but you didn't wake up."

"Oh-kay." My mind races back to the beginning, to what I thought was a panic attack. Was it more than that? "How long ago was that?"

"Three weeks, honey." Mom brushes the hair out of my eyes.

Was this all just a three-week-long dream?

"Where're the kids?"

"At school," Em chimes in. She glances at her phone. Oh, how I had missed that stupid device forever stuck in my hand or back pocket. "But Peter should be bringing them up here any minute."

I straighten at his name. Do I have enough strength after lying here for three weeks to punch him?

God, I hope so.

"Don't worry," my best friend says, lowering her voice. "These last few weeks have cured him of his need for full custody. Your mom and I made sure they didn't just live on DoorDash and screen time."

Ben and Aubrey are alive.

I don't even try to stop the tsunami of sobs.

"Oh honey," Mom pulls me against her chest, holding me while I bawl.

Even if there was never a risk of losing my kids, just knowing they exist is a balm to the fissure of my heart.

"It's okay, you're going to be just fine. The doctors said they didn't see anything medically keeping you unconscious. Maybe you just needed a break."

Em rubs my back, soothing the hiccuping that always comes with a good cry.

"Sorry, I just had the weirdest dream while I was out. I'm glad to know it wasn't real, that's all."

"Welcome back, Josie." A tall, handsome-enough-for-TV doctor stands in the doorway.

It's only in the presence of this gorgeous man that I ask myself the most important question of all time.

Am I wearing a diaper?

"I'm Dr. Harrison. It's nice to meet you finally. You've given us quite a scare. How are you feeling?"

That's the second most important question. I flex my feet, happy to find that while the joints in my ankles cracked, they still moved. More needles and wires protrude from my body than a disastrous knitting project.

"I think I'm okay." I swallow, the bit of saliva in my mouth burns on my parched throat. "Dehydrated. Could probably use a glass of wine. Or twelve." I punctuate that with a laugh, just in case this hospital doesn't serve wine.

The good doctor perches on the side of my bed, one side of his mouth tugging into an amused smile.

How many patients hit on him daily? All of them, probably.

"Well, medically speaking, you should wait a bit before a glass of wine, or twelve. But I'll order some tests to do another check on every-thing. If things look good, you can probably go home as early as tomorrow." He pats my leg and rushes out of my room, likely to visit the next patient who'll swoon over him.

I open my mouth to say something about the hot doctor when he pops back into my room.

"Emily, we still good for tomorrow night?"

Her face flushes pink, and her big blue eyes widen.

It's a look I hadn't seen since, well, a couple of months ago when she decided she was in love with Jordan Chambers.

"I'm looking forward to it, Craig."

He meets her blush and knocks on the doorframe before leaving.

"Promise me you didn't make out with my doctor while I was passed out here in this bed."

"Of course not! We're not horny teenagers. We went to a supply closet." Her phone buzzes in her hand. "Oh, I gotta jet. Sof just landed."

I sputter on the water I just sipped. "She's talking to us?"

Emily knits her brows together. "Maybe I should ask Craig to check your head pretty closely. We don't hear from her as much as we'd like, mostly because the internet in Senegal is iffy at best."

"Senegal? Is that where she went?"

Her eyes flash to my mom.

No doubt *Craig* is going to hear about all this.

"Well, that's where she's been for the past year. Before that she spent some time in Indonesia, and then Venezuela. Wherever there's poverty and kids who need someone to keep them healthy, our Sof is there to save the day."

I lean back and smile. Maybe that's where Sofia's been for all these years, and I was in a self-centered spiral of raising kids, launching a business, and ending a marriage.

"Oh, and guess what," Em says, pulling her purse strap on her shoulder. "Three weeks of a feeding tube got you reunion-skinny!"

A thought presses into my mind. A theory to test, but I'm almost afraid to speak. "Hey, did Daniel ever RSVP?"

My best friend smiles at me and presses a kiss to my temple. "No, sweetie, not yet. But have faith."

She leaves, and my mom chatters endlessly about how she reorganized my pantry, cleaned out my fridge, screamed at my lawn crew for their God-awful early starts, and how TVs these days are just too hard to operate. Her words flow past me, barely sinking in as I scan my body.

I shift, awakening that hitch in my right hip. When Mom turns her back, I peek down my hospital gown, my boobs were back to their southern progression.

Em was right, that little layer of fat at my waist was gone.

The most beautiful voices in the world fill the hallways outside my room.

"You really should focus on your finals more," Ben says. "You'll never get into a good college if you don't start taking school more seriously."

Well, it's good to know Ben stepped into my role while I was out.

"Yeah? Well, you need actual sunshine, not the glow of a screen," Aubrey retorts.

Likewise for Aubrey.

They stop just inside my room, both frozen with their jaws dropped.

My beautiful children. Aubrey looks a little thinner. She's always had a nervous stomach. Ben, his blond hair shaggy and grazing his eyes. It must be driving him crazy.

"Mommy," Aubrey's voice cracks, and she flies into my arms.

A second later, Ben's little arms encircle the other side of me.

"I'm back," I cry, inhaling their scents I know so well and missed so much. "I'm back. All I wanted was to be back here with you two." I hold my children like my life depends on it. Because it does.

A throat clearing pulls my attention away from the loves of my life.

Peter leans against the sink. Like Aubrey, he's gaunter, his hair a bit grayer. His cheeks are wet, and his face loosens in relief. "Hey guys, be careful, your mom is still hooked up to a lot of wires and tubes," Peter says.

My heart stumbles at the sight of him. Not with love, even though I did love him, just not as much as he loved me. With gratitude. Without him, I wouldn't have these two pieces of my heart.

"Thank you," I mouth to him.

He nods, likely thinking I was thanking him for taking care of them. In reality, I'm thanking him for so much more.

For giving me my entire world.

CHAPTER 45

Turns out *Craig* is a pretty damn good doctor. As promised, as soon as I got caught up with three weeks of teen and pre-teen drama, I was whisked away for a boatload of tests. By the next morning, he was back in my room, making me swear on a stack of self-help books that I'd take it easy.

Walking back into my house overlooking Lake Travis, a pang of homesickness for my childhood home stabs me under the ribs. Will my kids feel as nostalgic for this house as I do for the one I grew up in?

"I'm going to get to work," Ben says, trudging up the stairs like a little old man.

Aubrey turns to me, her gaze drifting briefly down to her phone. "What can I help you with?"

I smooth a long strand of hair behind her ear. "I'm going to take a long shower and rest. Go do Tik-Snap-Gram or whatever became an overnight sensation while I was out. Anyway, we gotta ease Grammy out of her caregiver role."

My beautiful daughter smiles. "Yeah, we can't cut her off cold turkey."

"It's for her own good."

Aubrey hugs me again. "I love you, Mom."

My room is exactly the retreat I'd left. After a marathon-length shower, I wrap myself in my plush bathrobe, carefully maneuvering around bandages where I was poked and prodded.

Breaking one of Craig's rules, I tug an ottoman to the corner of my closet and stand on my tiptoes to pull a banker's box from the high shelf. I grimace through the pull in my groin from the catheter—better than a diaper, I guess—and drop the box on the floor next to me while I sit cross-legged on the ottoman.

I haven't been able to ask Mom about Dad. She hasn't brought him up. That he wasn't sitting in the hospital room with her told me everything I needed to know.

"Josie?"

"In the closet." I pull my senior yearbook from the box and hold it in my lap. My breath is shallow, but I try to slow it. The last thing I need is another panic attack sending me to another point in my life.

Mom looks up at the empty spot on the shelf. "Don't make me call Dr. Harrison."

"I'll just sic Em on him."

My mother laughs and sits next to me as I study it. Class of 94 embossed on the cover, blue and silver ribbons weave across each other. A design I advocated for its timelessness just a few months ago.

"I felt nostalgic too before my big reunion," Mom says.

The spine cracks when I open it. With Mom looking over my shoulder, she comments on how that's exactly how she remembers us.

A few pages in, we get to the senior pictures. Most of the yearbook is in black and white, but the graduating class is honored with color layouts.

My gaze lands on my picture. Mischievous squint to my eyes. Youthful face. And…I rub my eyes.

Pink hair.

"Oh, I guess I really did it."

Mom snatches the book from my hand and sighs. "I always told myself if that's the most rebellious thing you did, I'd gotten off light. But still, Josephine Elise, what were you thinking?"

That it wasn't real.

"I guess it's my fault," Mom continues. "That weekend of your senior pictures, your dad and I realized our marriage was over, so I wasn't quite as attentive."

I shake my head. "I just wanted my kids to think I'm cool."

We flip through more pages. Sofia's sweet face stares up. I haven't seen her yet. Emily was dropping her off at her parents' house to spend time with them, but some late-night Google stalking told me she'd done several tours with Doctors Without Borders, always signing up for the most precarious regions to care for the most precious souls. It's so very Sofia.

I pause at Daniel's page and study his face. Just two days ago, I was kissing those full lips and breaking our hearts.

"Your dad and I always thought you two would end up together," Mom says. "Don't get me wrong, I do love Peter, and I wouldn't trade Aubrey and Ben for anything in the world, but you never looked at Peter like you did at Daniel. I guess it just wasn't meant to be."

I swallow a sob and put the yearbook back, fishing for my college photo album.

The first page is both familiar and foreign. I'm in denim shorts and an oversized Beastie Boys T-shirt, posed in front of the open hatchback of my ancient Subaru, the inside packed to the gills with the worldly possessions of an eighteen-year-old about to head off to college.

Next to that is Dad with his arm around my shoulders, his ruddy face beaming. I can almost feel that moment, the hot late summer Texas sun, Dad telling me over and over again how proud he was.

I flip through the album. Pictures of faces I remember but whose names were lost in time. Emily, Sofia, and me at Christmas in matching sweaters. Mom, Dad, and me in front of the tree. More pictures of my spring semester, "studying" by the river near campus. Back home for the summer.

This time, just Em and me, and wait, is that Ian Phillips in the picture?

Like a victim in a horror film, as I turn the pages closer to my father's death, my heart flutters like a scared bird.

There we are; Dad's shirt drenched in sweat and his face even redder as we move a mattress up the stairs to my first apartment. More party pictures of my junior year.

Halloween, I'm sitting in some guy's lap wearing something I'd never let Aubrey leave the house in. Christmas, I'm holding up a set of car keys from an opened box and Dad beaming proudly beside me, and the following picture is a nineties model Ford Bronco I have no memory of driving.

Some memories are more tangible than others. The school pictures feel real. The ones of Dad helping me move are translucent. When I look at them, I remember that moment happening, but when I look away, it fades back to Mom and me trying to heave that mattress upstairs.

Is it possible to have two sets of memories?

If I lived two lives it would be. How can I remember both rejecting my dad and not seeing him again until his funeral and our final Christmas when he bought me a newer-used car because my trusty Subaru was become about as reliable as a boyfriend with a roving eye?

I turn the page. Only blankness stares up at me. Dad died toward the end of my junior year the first time. I couldn't extend his life, but I could give us both the gift of a few more years together.

I only wish I'd done that the first time around. So, I could remember the moments much more saliently.

Tears fall on the blank album pages, and my mom squeezes my hand.

"Even though we divorced, Alan was my best friend, my first love. I'm glad you made us still do everything as a family. Knowing that he left us too young, I don't think I could've survived his death without these memories to hold on to."

"Is this one of those talks about how I need to play nice with Peter?"

"You need to stand up for yourself and your kids, but divorcing Peter doesn't instantly make him the enemy. Speaking of, I came here to tell you he dropped by to check on you." Mom squeezes my hand once more and leaves me to dress.

With a final glance into the box, a dusty blue velvet book stares up at me. I'm almost afraid to crack open the spine. To read words I'd written both thirty years ago and just a few months ago. I flip through the pages, looking for the one thing that kept me going through the last few months of my senior year. Finally, I find it; a quickly drafted sketch of Aubrey and Ben.

My thumb caresses it as it did for those months when I fell back into my past. This piece of pulp and charcoal got me through some of my darkest hours. A lone tear slides off my chin and drips onto the page, splashing just between my children.

I don't stare at it too long. I have the real thing back.

After putting the memorabilia back in the top of my closet, I study myself in the bathroom mirror. The tiny lines from too much sun grace my forehead, reminding me of summer vacations where laughter far outweighed the need for sunscreen. As Em said, the feeding tube diet did help me drop that bit of belly fat, but my six-pack is as forgotten as some of the people I partied with in college. In its place are the faded stretch marks from carrying two amazing, challenging, healthy babies.

With yoga pants that hadn't actually been to yoga and a tank top, I pull my damp hair into a bun.

Laughter pulls me into the family room. Ben and Peter are side by side on the couch, a game controller in each hand.

"No, you don't," my ex says, his face lit up like a kid.

"Ha, gotcha, Dad."

"What're you guys playing?" I ask, my heart smiling at this father-son moment.

"Time Vampires 4: Senior Year," Ben says.

"Wh-what?"

Holy shit, it can't be real.

Can it?

"Yeah, it's this cool game where you're a time traveler, and you go back to high school, but you've got this list of things you have to fix from the first time you were in high school, and if you achieve them all without being found out you get to go back to your time," Ben explains. Quite frankly, it's the most excited I've ever heard him.

My knees give out like a table with an elephant dancing on it, and I fall into the chair next to me.

Peter springs up, dropping the controller, and kneels beside me. "Josie, are you okay?" He puts two fingers on the inside of my wrist, as if he knew what he was doing. "You look white as a ghost."

"I'm fine," I say, surprised my voice is steady when the rest of me wants to grab my computer and Google this game. "Hey, Ben, can you give us a second, please?"

"Oh sure, I've got work to do anyway."

Peter waits until our son's footsteps echo up the stairs. "You know, any other kid, I'd think he's on the computer looking at porn."

"But he's actually working."

He laughs. "At least we'll be taken care of in our old age." His gray-blue eyes study me, reminding me of when I saw him across a crowded bar in the late nineties and fell in love.

Even if it was love with a little L.

"I'm serious. Are you doing okay? You gave us all quite a scare."

I nod. "Remembering to take it slow is the hardest part. Leave it to my best friend to start dating my doctor so I have to follow his orders."

"The things Em will do for you." One side of his mouth quirks up into his wry smile.

The same smirk I see on our daughter right before she dishes out some well-earned snarky comment.

We laugh, and for a minute, I wonder if perhaps we're not in the midst of a divorce. Maybe this time around I loved him with my whole heart instead of the tiny shard left behind in Daniel's wake.

I poke around my memory, looking for anything other than the conversation about our marriage being over, Peter moving out, and telling me he wants custody of the kids. No, that's the only thing there.

"I'm glad you're here," I say. "Thank you for taking care of the kids while I was..." *Reliving my senior year.* "Out. I want you to know that while I'm sorry our marriage ended, I don't regret us. Our divorce doesn't have to mean that we're not a family, and that includes Kirsten. Even if someone might think she's our oldest daughter, she's family."

Peter laughs. "Well, I came to drop this off." He hands me another manila envelope.

Anger curdles in my stomach at the memory of what the last envelope like this held.

"My attorney updated the custody arrangement. You have primary custody. I won't lie; these last few weeks were hard, even with your mom and Em helping out."

"Kirsten doesn't want to be a mom, does she?"

"No, but that's fine. She's fun to be around, but she's barely someone I'd share a dog with, much less kids. Josie, I didn't mean for that to be an indictment of your capability as a mother. Hell, you were both parents most of the time. I guess I was afraid they wouldn't want to be around me unless they had to."

"They're teenagers. They don't want to be around anyone unless they have to."

"Yeah, I realize that now." Peter glances down at the envelope, a sad smile crawls across his face.

I rest my head on his shoulder, and he grabs my hand.

"I believe there's a universe where the two of us grow old together," I whisper.

"Just because we're divorcing doesn't mean we can't still grow old together as friends. Family. You said so yourself."

I lean up and chastely kiss his lips, pulling back before either of us gets the wrong idea. "If I had to do it all over again, I would a million times, even if I know we'll both end up hurt," I say, staring out the picture windows looking over the lake. "Life is as much about the hard times as the good."

CHAPTER 46

The office looks both completely familiar and foreign. The ivy still clung to the white brick wall. Black window frames boldly state that the business inside has its shit together and is doing things.

I park and lean my forehead on my steering wheel. The self-help podcast host's soothing voice echoes throughout my car.

"Breathe out the self-doubt; breathe in self-confidence. Cleanse your aura. Take a moment to find peace and balance. Open your space and mind. Breathe out negativity; breathe in your intentions for the day."

"My intention is to make it through the day without curling up in the fetal position," I say to her annoyingly soothing voice while shutting off my car.

Mom and Peter told me Mamacita should be the last thing I worry about, but I have twelve people inside whose lives depend on me steering the ship straight through the storm. Even if I'm not sure if I'll find a gentle rainstorm or a category five hurricane.

"Josie, you're back!" Corey, the receptionist, hops up from behind the desk and pulls my bag from my shoulder. "We heard you were discharged but didn't expect to see you for a bit longer."

"Don't tell my mom, but I snuck out of the house. Even rolled my car down the street before starting it so she wouldn't hear it."

He blinks twice. Of course, he's too young to remember when cars were loud enough to snitch on us.

"So," I say when the silence became cringey. "I'll be in my office catching up if anyone needs me."

It'll be just a few minutes before the rumor mill spits out word that I'm not only back to the land of the living, but also hopping back into the saddle. Even if I'm riding backward.

My office is as I remember. Family photos fill the wall behind my desk. Baby Aubrey. Baby Ben. The two of them as they grew up. Even a family shot of Peter, me, and the kids.

I go to the adjacent wall. The one made up of more random bits of my life. Travel photos I'd taken and had framed. Art bought from local artists in far-flung locales. Pictures of me in the kitchen mixing up cleaning products while a toddler sits on the counter beside me.

Finally, right in the middle of all that, the drawing I'd seen a few days ago. That sketch sent me back thirty years and then propelled me forward again to my kids. What is it about this picture that became a portal in time?

Maybe Stuart figured out the answer, and it's in the video game.

I haven't been able to bring myself to Google Daniel. What-ifs play through my head like a litter of rowdy puppies.

What if he has more of an online presence? What if I do find an obituary? What if he married Jessica Dawson, and they are ridiculously rich with supermodel children?

"I heard you were here," Marla says from my door. My national accounts director glares, but a teasing smile plays on her lips. "Shouldn't you be home resting?"

"Trust me, when your best friend hooks up with your doctor, going to work is resting." I fall into the chair in front of my desk. "All right, give me all the gory details."

Marla sits in the chair next to me. "Spoiler alert: Bixby's didn't go out of business, and they honored their order. An investor came in and bought the store and gave it an infusion of cash. Bixby's called just last week to place another order."

"Wait, so we're not all going to be homeless?"

She laughs. "Nope, but we are going to be busy as hell. I drafted a plan to meet their new order. Want to take a look this afternoon after you get settled in?"

"That would be great. Thank you so much for keeping everything going."

We stand, and I hug Marla.

"Let's talk about expanding your role here as well."

The world didn't stop while I was out. The kids stayed alive and even did fine. My company didn't implode. It actually might have taken a giant leap forward. I'm not solely responsible for keeping the world on its axis.

"Oh hey, Marla," I say when she gets to my door. "Do you know who bought Bixby's? Was it a rival grocery chain?"

"That's what's interesting. A venture capitalist with no grocery stores in his portfolio. He's mostly a tech guy, so this came out of left field."

I grip the back of the chair, almost *knowing* the answer to the question I'm about to ask. "Do you know his name?"

"Yeah, Jake Beebe. He's a local guy, so we think this must be a sentimental acquisition." Marla laughs. "God, wouldn't you love to be so rich that you buy grocery stores just because your mom used to shop there?"

My laugh is hollow, but she doesn't seem to notice. "Yeah, right?"

Or, so rich that you buy a grocery chain because a crazy classmate claimed to have come from the future because her business was about to go under due to said retailer filing bankruptcy.

A coincidence is a one-off situation. When grouped together, they become something bigger. Some might call it a pattern. In this case, it's becoming a cluster.

What else has changed that I don't know yet? I thought I knew my life pretty well, but do I now have to learn a new script?

Shit, what if I flub a line?

I spend the rest of the morning staring at my email. Words I should register look like a foreign language. Emails that need a response get deleted, or half responses that make no sense.

Shortly before lunch, Corey sends me an instant message.

Sofia Diaz is here to see you. Says you're expecting her, but she's not on your schedule?

I stare at the words, the cursor blinking expectantly, waiting for my response.

Why am I so scared to see her?

Is it because she'll be the first person I confided in during whatever time warp I fell through that I'm encountering in the present?

My hands shake as I type a response.

Sure, bring her back.

I straighten my top and adjust my jeans as I stand. Should I throw my blazer on, or is that too formal?

Her voice greets me before I see her. A little deeper but still clear and soft as she laughs at something Corey says.

Then she's there, standing in the doorway.

Sofia looks the same as I last saw her. Just without the cap and gown. With a bit of sag in her cheeks and gray streaks in her dark hair.

She glances out the door, waiting until Corey's footsteps recede. "I hear you're a time traveler back from a trip to high school."

I don't even attempt to hold back my surprise. "Have you been waiting thirty years to say that?"

Sof laughs and wraps me in a tight hug. "Truthfully, I always thought you were nuts, but you never said anything else about it. The day after graduation, you had a killer hangover and seemed a bit spacey… then three weeks ago Em calls me freaking out that you had a panic attack and was in a mysterious coma. Two and two equaled five."

"So we've been friends this entire time? Like we never made you mad?"

She sighs and sits at the edge of the couch in my office. "Every time the stress got to be too much, and I wanted to hide from the world, I forced myself to call you or Em. You guys never did anything *to* me, but if I had to guess, the me you knew before must've felt inadequate. It's easy to get so wrapped up in your own shit. When it was time to dig out, I might have been too embarrassed to show up, covered in, well, shit, begging to be your friend again."

I shake my head, dislodging a stray tear. "No, you could've come any time, and we would've welcomed you back. Plus, I was probably literally covered in shit, so we could have been twins." I sit next to her and study her.

In addition to the streaks of gray, her hair was shorter, grazing her shoulders rather than cascading down her back. She was thinner, wiry, as if she spent her days saving lives rather than living on processed food and booze. I clasp her hand in mine. "Tell me everything, Dr. Diaz."

That's how we spent the rest of my first day back in the office. Sofia telling me about working her way through college and medical school. Of being drawn to help those in places with little infrastructure. How she is not just fluent in Spanish but can also hold her own in French, Arabic, Hindi, and even some lesser-known tongues spoken in remote African villages.

How she's had a few affairs with fellow doctors, but the true love of her life is seeing a child on the brink of death recover and lead a happy life.

"Do you know if Daniel's coming to the reunion?" She asks as we get to the end of her story.

I shrug. "The last time I asked Em, he hadn't RSVPed. I did tell him at the graduation party that he has to be here." I nod toward the drawing on the opposite wall. "I almost chose him, but couldn't let go of my kids." My gaze shifts to the other wall and the family pictures. "Even if it meant going through a less-than-perfect marriage and divorce, Aubrey and Ben are worth it."

Sof studies me, narrowing her warm eyes. "Have you ever thought that this doesn't have to be an either-or situation?"

"I can't exactly live two lives, trust me, been there, done that. I have a hard enough time keeping one life humming along."

She chuckles. "Think linearly, Jo. You and Peter are divorcing, yes?"

"Yes." Her words are so heavy with meaning that if they were my purse, I'd hurt my back. I sit up straight. "What do you know? Have you talked to Daniel? Did he not marry Jessica Dawson and have a ton of supermodel babies?"

Sofia hugs me one more time and stands. "I gotta go. I'm meeting Em, Craig, and one of his doctor friends for happy hour."

"Wait, where's my invitation?" It came out exactly as whiney as I intended it.

"One, I believe Dr. Harrison has told you to take it easy, so you're lucky I won't tell him and Em I just saw you at your office. Two, booze, and therefore happy hour, is definitely against doctor's orders." She makes it to the doorway and turns back. "And three, we gotta keep you single for Daniel."

And with a wink, my best friend leaves me with hope taking root in my heart.

CHAPTER 47

"Hold still, you're going to make me mess up your eyeshadow," Aubrey says over the Taylor Swift playlist she insisted would get me in the mood for my thirtieth high school reunion.

I wanted to argue that Sonic Youth and Beastie Boys would've been more of a mood setter, but the music doesn't matter. I just love being with her, soaking in her teenage confidence.

"Okay, open, but not too wide."

I pop my eyes open and gasp at her handiwork. My hair hangs down in loose, beachy waves. An expert hand layered the right amount of shadow around my blue-green eyes to give them the perfect smoky look. My face is flawless. Wrinkles magically erased, cheekbones found, and pout demur, yet sexy. All that time on social media paid off after all.

"I think you should wear the blue dress," she says.

The two options hung behind us. One was black, with ruching in all the places middle-aged women want camouflaged and a respectable midi length.

The other was teal-blue satin with a sweetheart neckline and cap sleeves that flowed into a fitted bodice with a fit and flare skirt that hit a few inches above my knees.

Clearly, one was picked out by me and the other by my daughter.

"Mom, you're totally hot," Aubrey says as if she became a mind reader while I was reliving my senior year. "Daniel will think so if you wear the blue one."

My head jerks in her direction. "How do you know about Daniel?"

She shrugs. "Em told me about him in one of her *carpe the diem* talks."

Ah yes, there've been more than a few times I've walked in on Emily giving advice that only a non-maternal figure could say.

"Okay, but if he's not there, don't blame me if you end up with a total creep as a stepfather."

Aubrey gives me a bless-your-heart smirk, kisses my cheek, and leaves me to dress.

I have to admit, my daughter's right. The dress is perfect and feels more at home on my body than something more age-appropriate. Maybe that's because I'd just spent nine months in a teenage body.

After ensuring the kids would survive the evening, I hop in my ride share for the reunion.

It's hard to tell if the rabid butterflies in my stomach would've been there normally or if they resulted from going solo to my reunion in hopes of seeing the love of my life is not married to a supermodel.

Totally normal stuff.

The car pulls up to the hotel along a red carpet with a scrum of photographers. It doesn't surprise me that Em would've gone for a Hollywood red carpet theme.

"Yay! You picked the blue," she says, wrapping me in a hug. "I knew Aubrey would talk you into it."

"I'm starting to think that you and my daughter are conspiring against me."

"You're just starting to figure this out?" Em turns to her date, the doctor who knew me better in a vegetative state. "Craig, doesn't our girl clean up well?"

He leans in to kiss my cheek. "Yes, the dress is a step up from a hospital gown. You do look great, Josie. I think tonight I'll release you from my orders and allow you a couple of drinks. In moderation, of course."

"Well, if I have any sort of episode, I'll be well taken care of," I nod to Sofia standing just to the side, chatting with a tuxedo-clad man I don't recognize. Maybe this is the colleague she had happy hour with. "So, any last-minute RSVPs come in?"

Em lowers her full lashes. "No, honey, I'm sorry, nothing in the last few days. I told them to add a few walk-ups to the count just in case." She gnaws on her lower lip. "I don't think you should worry though. Call it a hunch."

A waiter walks by, and I grab a champagne flute off the tray. "No, it's fine, that's perfect. He and Jessica are probably off on their private island being fabulous."

Her eyes narrow, and she purses her lips. "Jessica Dawson? Oh, she's already here." Em nods past me.

I turn, and there's the teenage supermodel. Still tall and model thin. Her honey-colored hair is piled high on her head in a messy bun. The man next to her was at least a foot shorter and two feet wider.

"Did she bring her dad?" I whisper to Em.

"Husband, apparently, he's some exec at a movie studio. Think she's wife number five." Something catches Em's attention. "Oh, the deejay needs me. See you in a bit."

With Emily off and Craig, Sofia, and her date talking medical talk, I study the crowd filing in.

Faces I'd seen just weeks ago carry a little extra weight, wrinkles heavy with life, and gray or receding hair.

"Josie Posie!" A male voice shouts behind me.

I turn just in time to be swept up in a bear hug. It's only when he puts me down that I merge the man with a paunch and thinning hair with the guy who got too handsy at homecoming and whose drunk ass I saved from drowning.

"Honey, this is Josie," Ian says, addressing the woman beside him.

She's pretty with sharp eyes. Something in her aura tells me she also has a matching sharp tongue.

"She's the one who saved my life and helped me get my shit together. Josie, this is Michelle."

"It's so nice to meet you," she says. "I love your Mamacita line, by the way, it's the only thing I'll use in our house." The woman leans in. "I should also thank you, for not just saving Ian's life, but knocking some sense into him. I can't imagine life without him."

I open my mouth but no words take flight. What was her life like before? Did she live feeling like part of her soul was missing?

Someone else catches Ian's eye, and he drags his wife away.

I move over to the side, among the couples who obviously need more date nights. Just a couple of weeks ago, I saw most of these people thirty years younger.

The air shifts in the ballroom. The kind of thing that happens when royalty walks in.

I make my way back into the fray of the party.

My classmates gather in a crowd around the entrance. Thankfully, the platform stilettos Aubrey shoved on my feet give me an edge.

Stuart Lohenstein, Matthew Fraser, and Jake Beebe walk in, shoulder to shoulder, my sweet geeks who put up with my mood swings, pathetic attempts at bullying, and wild stories.

Like the rest of us, they've aged, but where many of our classmates got older, they got hotter.

Stuart is a good six inches taller with broad shoulders that funnel down to a tapered waist. Finding a gym, and probably a good trainer, completely transformed him. His dark hair is long, curling around his chin.

Matthew looks like his brother, with long dreads pulled back in a ponytail with just a hint of silver woven throughout.

Jake, still tall and wiry, but head up high rather than studying some spot on the floor.

I push through the crowd and stop in front of them, my chest heaving. I missed the hell out of these guys.

Three pairs of eyes settle on me. Study me.

"Are you still you?" Stuart asks.

"If you guys don't hug me, I will kick your ass," I say. "And you better believe that I can still do it."

On cue, they wrap me in a tight group hug.

"We weren't really sure if you would remember," Jake says.

"Or if it was an elaborate joke," Matthew adds.

"But then things started happening, like you said," Stuart says, shifting his gaze to the group that began dispersing around us.

"My son loves your video game," I say to Stuart. "I haven't played it yet, but something tells me I'll beat it on the first try." I turn to Jake. "And you. I can't decide if I should punch you or kiss you."

"Both?" Jake says a wry smile on his face, now incredibly handsome with stubble covering his cheeks instead of pimples.

I turn to Matthew. "And was it my imagination, or is your name on the building of the hospital wing where I woke up?"

He shrugs. "Well, when you invent a device for minimally invasive brain surgeries while you're on the medical staff, they'll name buildings after you."

"Well, you should know I was well taken care of in the Matthew Fraser Neurological Center, even if I felt a bit called out."

"We heard you were in a coma," Stuart says.

"And then I heard that Bixby's was filing bankruptcy, and I realized this was what sent you back," Jake adds. "Honestly, even if the chain goes under, I am happy to pay whatever it takes to keep you from losing your house. But, something tells me it was a worthy investment."

"Josie?" A voice that sounds like it's been raked over rocks cuts through the reunion with my boys.

I turn and find a boxy woman with a sharp chin-length gray-brown bob standing behind me.

"It's Ruby, Ruby Bell," she says.

My fists clench, not to hit the woman but to protect myself in case she comes after me.

She takes three determined steps toward me, her brown eyes boring into mine. "I want you to know that—" she spits the words out but stops and nibbles on her lower lip. "I want to say thank you, you were kind to me when you didn't have to be."

I shake my head. "No, Ruby, I owe you an apology. I should've realized you weren't living in the best environment. We weren't equipped to handle that back then. You look good. You doing okay?"

Ruby's face brightens, and she's transformed. "Yeah, I run a shelter for kids with parents battling addiction. Josie, these kids are so amazing. The hope they have in the face of so much pain. It's truly life-affirming."

I lean in to hug her. "I'm so proud of you, Ruby. You were given a shit childhood, but it looks like you're more than making up for it."

She wanders off to catch up with another classmate, and my geeks have their entourage to attend to.

I grab a fresh drink from a passing waiter and return to my spot in the shadows. I feel like I've been here for eons, but it's probably been an hour at most. My eyes grow heavy. I hate to admit that Craig might be right.

Is it getting used to being back in a forty-seven-year-old body, or still recovering from whatever medical mystery befell me?

The flow of alums into the reunion dwindles to a trickle. My gaze skirts the party, looking for golden-brown hair or a lean runner's frame, but nothing stands out.

Just more former classmates awkwardly catching up, dancing as far as their stiff knees and wonky hips would allow, or drunkenly hitting on the cheerleader they'd finally worked up the courage to talk to.

The last of the champagne flows down my throat, and, with a sigh, I discard the glass on a cocktail table.

I rejoin Emily and Sofia with their dates. Their sympathetic glances answer the question on my face.

"I'm wiped out," I shout over the bass track of a Snoop Dogg song. "I'd hate to overdo it and have my doctor on my ass."

Em shakes her head while dancing with my doctor. "Not possible, he's on my ass."

It's been a long time since she's been this obviously smitten with someone. Maybe thirty years.

"You okay?" Sof asks.

A rogue tear escapes. This is why hope is a bitch. It's uplifting, whispers to reach for the sun, promising all is possible without getting burned. Then there's the tumble back to earth, stomach dropping to toes, heart splatting on the ground.

Hope shattering all around.

Nothing hurts as bad as when a shard of hope pierces the heart.

"I'm just tired. Swear, that's all."

She wasn't buying it, but I wasn't selling it that hard.

I squeeze my tear ducts tight as I escape the next song, a cheesy power ballad from an early nineties summer blockbuster, and dig my phone out of my purse to hail a car.

The bright lobby assaults my eyes as my shaky fingers struggle to pull up the app.

A familiar scent wafts into my nostrils. Piney, like sunshine on a hayfield.

I look up and gasp.

A rumpled dark suit covers his tall frame. He's still lean but broader across the shoulders. A golden tan alights his face with a fan of wrinkles at his eyes. His hair was still long on top, tousled, with a hint of gray mixed in with the blond and brown streaks.

It's been both a lifetime and a heartbeat since his lips were on mine. Both a lifetime and a heartbeat since I broke his heart, but told him I'd be ready in three decades.

My heart takes off sprinting; lungs forget how to work. Feet frozen in place; my knees turn to mush. Brain disbelieving the man standing in front of me, yet I can't tear my eyes away from him.

"You're here," I breathe the words.

"I'm sorry I'm late." Daniel's chest heaves, like he ran.

"I didn't think you were coming. I—"

He takes two steps to close the gap. "You told me to come here, but I've been a bit off the grid, so I couldn't RSVP."

"Are you a Buddhist monk in Nepal or a super-secret spy?"

Daniel laughs and looks down. "Somewhere in between." He reaches for my left hand, rubbing his thumb over my naked knuckles. "Did you do it? Walk the same path?"

"I guess. I passed out after you left and woke back up here. Thank God, I didn't want to go through two long labors again," I laugh, nervously. "Daniel, I'm sorry—"

"JoBear, don't." He cups the side of my face with a warm palm, just calloused enough to send tingles down my spine. "Life isn't a straight highway. The people you have in it are there when you need them to be, and when they leave you, it's only so you can travel your path. I always knew we'd find each other when it's right for both of us."

"Does this mean you're single?" My voice is heavy with emotion.

He kisses my knuckles. "Does this mean you're divorced?"

I open my mouth, but words seemed so inadequate. Instead, I grab the back of his head and kiss him like he's my past, my present, my future.

The End

A NOTE TO MY READERS

Dear Reader,

Thank you so much for spending time in Josie's world!

As a kid, I loved the Choose Your Own Adventure books. There's probably a lot a good therapist could unpack there for why, but mainly I think because it allowed me to explore other choices. And, while the path we forged, no matter how hard, might be the best for us, it's kinda fun to see what else could have been.

If you enjoyed This Time Around, please tell a friend, or, even better, tell the whole world via a review on Amazon, Goodreads, BookBub or wherever else you share great books you've read.

What's next for me? Well, I didn't plan for this, but looks like Josie's BFF Emily has a story to tell. I'm super excited about that one! Sign up for my newsletter or follow me on Instagram to learn more.

xoxo,

Kim

ACKNOWLEDGMENTS

I started writing This Time Around in the summer of 2020. While the world was shut down, I was in the midst of editing Dire's Club, a book about a group of people facing terminal illnesses. As you can imagine, it was hard to work on that book then. It was during this summer that my bestest writing friends and I would meet every so often in the evenings in a parking lot (maybe with wine in our tumblers) and we would write while socially distancing. This Time Around became lovingly known among us as "The Parking Lot Book." These ladies were also with me at a post-pandemic retreat where I wrote, "The End." Sarah Gamez, Susan Sheehey and Chrissy Szarek, thank you for always cheering me on and kicking my butt.

Thank you to my parents for fostering a love of books in me from an early age. To the most awesome sister and brother in law, Angie and Mike Madrid thank you for always supporting me.

To Carol Barreyre and Mia London for diving into Josie's world and helping to make it better.

To Colby, I can't imaging doing life with anyone else. Thank you for putting up with my crankiness when the words won't come, and my absence when they do.

And, finally, thank you, dear reader. Without you, I'd just be a girl telling myself stories. Thank you for opening your heart and your mind to my tales.

BOOK CLUB DISCUSSION GUIDE

If you're reading This Time Around for your book club, feel free to use these questions as a reader guide.

1. This Time Around looks at themes of being middle aged and looking back on your life. Do you think this is something unique to Josie, or do most people wonder about the path not taken?
2. Initially Josie had trouble living without many of the modern conveniences, but then she found herself enjoying life from three decades ago. If you could slip back into time for a bit, when would you go and why?
3. If you were given a do-over in life, is there one choice you would have made differently? And, how do you think that would have impacted your life? Would it change it dramatically, or would you still be right where you are?
4. What do you think would be more difficult, going back thirty years in time and knowing too much, or going forward thirty years and knowing nothing?
5. By going back to her senior year, Josie had the benefit of maturity to look at some aspects of her teenage life. Is there a

moment that you would approach differently with the life experience you have now?

6. Would you want to go back and re-live your senior year? If not, is there another year of your life you would want to go back to? Why?

ALSO BY KIMBERLY PACKARD

The Phoenix Series

Phoenix

Pardon Falls (Phoenix Book 2)

Prospera Pass (Phoenix Book 3)

Standalone Titles

Vortex

The Crazy Yates

Dire's Club

ABOUT THE AUTHOR

Kimberly Packard is an award-winning author of women's fiction.

When she isn't writing, she can be found planning her next trip, asking her dog what's in his mouth or curled up with a book. She resides in Texas with her husband Colby, a clever cat named Oliver and a precocious black lab named Tully.

Her debut novel, *Phoenix*, was awarded as Best General Fiction of 2013 by the Texas Association of Authors. She is also the author of a Christmas novella, *The Crazy Yates*, and the sequels to *Phoenix*, *Pardon Falls* and *Prospera Pass*, and her stand-alone titles *Vortex*, *Dire's Club* and *This Time Around*. She was honored as one of the Top 10 Haute Young Authors by Southern Methodist University in 2019. Her most recent novel, Dire's Club, was awarded the 2021 General Fiction of the Year by the North Texas Book Festival.